INSTINCT

Book 2 of The Evolutioneers Series

Anna Alexander

AnnaAlexander.net
Newsletter
http://eepurl.com/Q0tsz

House of Rosenorn
Instinct
ISBN: 9780998520346
Print Edition

Ripley Jorgensen had believed the biggest shock in his life was developing shape-shifting powers, but that was nothing compared to learning that one of his teammates, the woman he loved, was a complete fraud. Not only did she steal someone's identity, she may have committed murder.

Alisia had figured there was no better place to hide out than in a hidden mountain fortress surrounded by superheroes. Surely no one from her past would think to look for her there—that is, until her murderous father hired the Evolutioneers to find his missing daughter and blew her cover. Now she's on the run with not only her former friends right on her tail, but also the man who has her scent embedded in his soul.

Ripley doesn't just want answers. The beast within has determined that Alisia is its mate. Until he claims her as his own, the fight between man and animal grows stronger every day. And if she should refuse him? The man would be lost to the beast. Forever.

Dedication

Para mi familia. Siempre.

And to my own Therian (Therrien). Love you more.

*mic drop

Find Anna Online

Website

annaalexander.net

Facebook

facebook.com/pages/Anna-Alexander/282170065189471

Twitter

twitter.com/AnnaWriter

Newsletter

http://eepurl.com/Q0tsz

CHAPTER ONE

T HE MUSCLES UNDER Ripley's skin rippled with the blistering need to shift into an animal form. Didn't matter which animal. Hell, even something as low-key as a sloth would do. At least that might slow the incessant urge to tackle and mate, he hoped. The farther away he traveled from the woman his animal claimed as his, the harder it was to ignore the call of his beastly instincts.

He cracked each knuckle in his fingers and resisted the urge to jump out of the moving vehicle and race back to headquarters. With the Rover cruising at a steady eighty-five miles an hour he was more likely to end up as a human road stain instead of an escapee.

He turned to Max who was sitting comfortably in the driver's seat and asked, "Tell me again why we're heading out to BFE in the dead of the night to meet with the good Reverend Lowell?"

The leader of the Evolutioneers maneuvered the SUV down the dark and twisty road with nary a twitch of difficulty. "Same old, same old. Prominent member of society needs to have a delicate situation taken care of, blah, blah, blah."

"Delicate situation? That sounds dirty. He didn't knock up some underage parishioner or something equally distasteful, did he? I thought we didn't work those kinds of jobs."

"I had the same thought when I got the call, but Crystal said she saw you and me at this meeting, so we're going."

Ripley grunted and shifted in his seat. Max's wife, Crystal, was an exceptional clairvoyant whose visions always came true. If she saw them at the meeting, then they were at the meeting.

"Why didn't she tell us what happens and save us the trip?"

Max chuckled and turned off the highway and onto a narrow dirt road. "You know it doesn't work that way. Believe me, I'd much rather be home, making love to my wife, than out in the middle of nowhere."

That's it, Ripley glared at his boss, *just rub it in that you have a woman back home who actually wants to have sex with you.*

And that little tidbit right there was what made his predicament with the beautiful Alisia Caldwell so damn frustrating. She did want to have sex with him. Craved it with all her senses. Well, at least her body did.

The scent of her arousal was as decadent as cinnamon-dusted dulce de leche. The hitch in her breathing whenever he came near struck an answering chord within him that made the little hairs on his arms stand on end. At times her longing for his touch reached across the air with a force so great it slapped him in the face.

But whenever he asked her out she always said no, just no.

With her prickly attitude toward him softening once they had all moved into Max's mountain headquarters, he thought her more recent refusals were because they worked for the same underground crime-fighting agency and she didn't want to mix business with pleasure. And of course, it was possible that when she discovered her teammates possessed supernatural powers, including his ability to shift into any mammal, that might have also given her pause. Yet that wasn't the reason either. At least that he could discern.

When he was able to catch her for a moment alone, her body would tremble and she'd sway toward him, gazing at his lips as if she already tasted him on her tongue. Just as their lips were about to brush, she would jerk away, and say no, just no.

Damn. He stuck his head out the window and sucked in a breath as lust raced through his blood like it did every time he thought of the pretty blonde. Spasms ripped through his muscles, causing the Velcro along the seams of his pants to crackle under the pressure. His skin burned, sensitive to the abrasion of soft cotton against his thighs.

Max glanced at him out of the corner of his eye and frowned. "Are you all right? You got fleas, or mange, or something?"

Ripley flipped him off and closed his eyes in an effort to relax. "If you want the truth, I'm horny. Watch yourself, or you might start to look appealing."

"Sorry I asked." Max laughed. "Lucky for me, we're here."

Thank the lord.

"Here" was a little farmhouse in the countryside south of Tacoma, Washington. The Rover's headlights cut a swath in the dark night and illuminated the house's siding and porch. The unvarnished wood was weathered after years of facing the relentless Pacific Northwest rains, but the property appeared well kept, clean. And silent. Absolutely silent.

Ripley scanned the surrounding trees with a suspicious

eye as his ears twitched. "I know we're meeting a man of God, but this just feels skeevy."

Max hummed in agreement. Picking up his cell, he pushed two buttons and waited for a response. "Network? Yeah, we're here. Start recording."

A sharp sneeze answered his command. "Sorry about that, Maestro," Addison, code name Network, sniffled. "I've got you both up now."

"Are you getting sick?"

Ripley's acute hearing picked up the blare of her blowing her nose away from the microphone. "The mountain is blooming and the stupid pollen is messing with my sinuses," she grumbled. "You would think that living in a cave would keep out the little buggers."

"Are you going to be able to monitor us? We can wait for you to get someone else."

"Nah." She blew her nose again. "I'll be fine. I got a decongestant from Doc. Just get on with it."

"We'll be quick. As soon as we're done, go get some sleep. That's an order."

"Yeah, yeah." She laughed into the phone.

Max placed the phone into the inside pocket of his leather duster and settled his sunglasses on his nose. Hidden in the frame was a high-definition camera, and the lenses doubled as monitors that projected images Addison sent to them from headquarters.

"Therian, why don't you do a perimeter sweep? My spidey sense is tingling too."

"Great." Ripley unfastened the five-point harness seatbelt required in any vehicle Max drove. "Remind me why I'm stepping into potential danger based on a vision your wife had?"

"We're saving the world, protecting the innocent, help-ing those who can't help themselves, and it makes her happy. I like making her happy." His voice turned husky in the way it did whenever he spoke of his wife. Max would do anything for Crystal, even lay down his life. The sentiment was mutual since she had once done the same for him.

"You are so whipped," Ripley groused, despite the bite of jealousy that nipped at him. It was times like these that he was grateful to have his inner animal take control.

When he was in the body of the beast, his emotions boiled down to the basics: eating, sleeping, and pissing. He was able to focus on the task at hand, which controlled the battle between the man and the animal. If only he could maintain that balance as well in human form.

He didn't want to spend his life on four legs, didn't want to lose his humanity, yet each day the fight for who dominated grew stronger. Giving in to the pull to live as an animal full-time was not an option. That was not his life.

He tugged his T-shirt over his head and settled his necklace in place. The pendant held a camera, and a GPS monitor tracked his movements. Handy gadget when he was unable to verbally communicate his location.

His pants ripped neatly along the Velcro seams, obscur-ing the sound of popping of bones and cartilage as his skin gave way to thick fur. Max used his telekinetic powers to open his door for him, and the great wolf slipped to the ground, sliding along the pine needles on his belly until he reached the cover of the woods.

As his sensitive nose sorted through the scents of the forest, his mind wondered what business Reverend Lowell would want with the Evolutioneers. The team of superhe-roes Ripley worked with had become public knowledge six months earlier when they defeated a madman attempting to take over the country by crippling its financial structure. Public opinion was split between those who were in awe of this band of humans with extraordinary capabilities and those who feared the power they commanded.

Reverend Lowell preached the word of the Lord both on television and to his congregation in his mammoth church in the northern part of the state. The little information Ripley knew of the man from the media was that the reverend was a private man, a father of two grown children, and had kept his family away from the more public aspects of the church after the death of his second wife seven years earlier. His message of compassion and tolerance made him a much-loved figure on both sides of the political aisle. Often, he was asked to lend a calming, objective hand to many social debates.

Which again begged the question, what was the reason for this super-secret meeting in the middle of nowhere?

Ripley followed his nose to the back of the farmhouse. A black SUV hybrid was parked in the rear. One man stood guard near the door. Under the aroma of the man's natural musk was gun oil mixed with the scent of trees and damp earth. Hmmm. Curiouser and curiouser.

He trotted back to the front of the property after finishing his search and met Max, who was waiting behind the Rover.

"There are three men on site. One in the back, two inside. At least one is armed," he relayed after he shifted.

"Fan-fucking-tastic," Max sighed. "Just what we need, a man of God who has at least one man packing heat with him."

Ripley let a bit of fang show in his smile. "How about I

go in as a panther?"

Max laughed and shook his head. "Maybe next time. The shepherd will do."

"Can't a guy have a little fun?"

"If it's you, no."

"Where have I heard that before," he muttered, then dropped back to the dirt on four paws.

The pair made not a sound as they blended into the shadows and climbed up the darkened porch stairs to ring the doorbell. Two seconds passed before the reverend himself opened the door.

"I saw you arrive a while ago. I was wondering if I needed to go out and fetch you." He held out his hand. "Welcome, I'm Reverend Creed Lowell."

"Reverend." Max's mouth was set in a firm line. With his square jaw he looked as friendly as a rock. "I was just preparing myself to meet you. I'm a safety-first kind of guy with trust issues."

Lowell chuckled with a nod. "Ah, yes. Please, come in."

The reverend ushered them into a cozy living room, where another man waited. The four of them made an interesting quartet standing amongst the worn furnishings and lace curtains. With Max in his head-to-toe black leather with his trusty dog by his side and the two men in their Sunday best, they were *Blade Runner* and *Glengarry Glen Ross* standing in Ma Kent's living room.

Smoothing his hand over his silver-blond hair, Lowell then gestured to the man to his right. "This is Deacon Winston. He's in charge of daily church business so I can concentrate on the congregation and our civic responsibilities."

Ripley's nostrils flared as he separated the scent of dust

and cold plaster walls from the pine and soil clinging to the men's clothing.

Both men were dressed similarly in modest, single-breasted suits, one in brown and one in gray. There was not a thing ostentatious or flashy about them. So bland were they in their appearance, they almost blended into the soft cream wallpaper and tan and rose-colored couches. While the reverend looked like your favorite grandfather with his kind smile and lines of compassion etched on his face, his right-hand man stood stiff and was about as welcoming as a gargoyle. His black eyes were in constant motion, searching, observing in a way that made Ripley's hackles rise.

"Gentlemen." Max nodded in greeting. "I'm Maestro. How may we be of assistance?"

"Please, have a seat." Lowell released the button on his coat before sitting in a beige velvet armchair, then gestured to the matching one before the cold, empty fireplace. "My, that is a handsome canine you have with you. Is he a purebred?"

"He likes to think so," Max said with a chuckle. "Mostly he's a purebred pain in my ass. Sorry, I mean backside."

"I see, I see." The reverend smiled. "You must forgive me for not offering refreshments. This home is used as a summer retreat for families and Bible camp and hasn't been reopened for the season yet."

"No apologies necessary." Max settled in the offered chair, leaning far back in the seat with his palms resting on each arm. He might have looked relaxed and easy, but Ripley sensed the tension in Max's body while he stood at attention at his side. Everyone wanted a piece of the Evolutioneers, for reasons good and for ill. It would be stupid to let their guard down for one second, even if they were with a man of God. "I didn't get the impression that this was to be a social visit."

For the first time, the reverend lost his jovial expression. His smile quivered and he smoothed his tie flat over his belly. "You are correct. I called because I am hoping you can assist me with a rather…delicate situation."

There was that phrase again. "Delicate situation." The words went right into Ripley's brain and sent a frisson of warning across his fur.

The reverend paused to take a deep breath through his nose. "I need you to find my daughter."

"Daughter?" Max asked, stealing the thought from Ripley's mind.

"Yes. My daughter, Gretchen, has been missing for seven years."

"Gretchen is your older daughter, correct?"

"Yes."

The forefinger on Max's left hand began to tap a steady rhythm, a habit Ripley noticed he had when his mind was processing several trains of thought. "I was under the impression that she was doing missionary work in South America. At least, that's what's been on the church's social media feed. What was the post from yesterday? Ah, yes. Dinner with the remote tribes of the Amazon." Oh yeah, Max and Addison had done their research when they had received the reverend's request. "How could she be posting if she's been missing for six years?"

The older man's lips twitched in a thin line as he shook his head. "A ruse, I'm afraid."

He paused to take another breath, and his green eyes turned dark with worry. "Gretchen was the perfect child. She never fussed, never acted out, she was as calm and gentle as a butterfly in a rose garden. In school she was at the top of her class, and played guard on the basketball team. She was so talented on the court. When it came to the church, she was devout in her studies and generously volunteered her time."

He ran his hand over his tie again as his lip curled with disdain. "Unfortunately, like so many young girls, Gretchen had her head turned by a good-for-nothing hoodlum who was not from our congregation. He corrupted my baby girl, turned her against her family and God with false flattery and drugs. Together, they stole two hundred thousand dollars from the church coffers. As you can imagine, I didn't want to believe that my child could be a thief. I wanted to place the blame entirely on the boy. But my wife—this would be Gretchen's stepmother—suggested that she be the one to confront Gretchen, beseech her, woman to woman, to return the money and come back to the family." He sucked in a sharp breath, his eyes filled with tears. "They argued, and Gretchen killed my wife."

"Why?" Max asked sharply, then lifted his hand. "I'm sorry. I don't mean to sound as if I'm doubting your story or demeaning your loss, but you said that Gretchen was a model child. Why would she suddenly turn violent?"

The reverend nodded and brushed his hand down his tie again. "I understand your question. This young man, Sam, was drugging my daughter. I do not believe she was in her right mind, and when confronted, she became enraged. She and my wife were in her room, and I could hear the shouting downstairs in my office. There was a crash and then sudden silence. I raced up the stairs and found my wife on the floor. A lamp was next to her, broken and covered in blood. The window was opened, Gretchen gone. I haven't seen her since."

Max leaned forward in his seat. "What did the authorities do?"

"I never called them." He lifted both hands and shook his head, his lower lip quivered. "I know what you are thinking, but I couldn't. I just couldn't. She is still my daughter. I know that in her heart she is sorry for what happened. She was scared and not in control of her own mind. Her crimes were against me and the church, and that is where her punishment lies. Also, the destruction to the congregation would be irreparable. How would it look if their own leader could not manage one teenage girl, his own daughter? No, it was best for all to contain the incident amongst a few trusted individuals."

Max motioned at the man who had stood like a statue at the reverend's side. "I'm guessing that Deacon Winston here is one of those people?"

"Yes. If you will, Deacon Winston." He pointed at a briefcase that rested next to the empty fireplace. "He has been leading the search for Gretchen, but it's as if she's disappeared off the face of the earth. She had very few friends outside of the church community. I don't know where or how she could have gotten far. That is why I am seeking your help, Maestro. I've heard about the success your team has had on missing-person cases. I'm also aware of the low profile you prefer to keep. I am hoping that you can find my daughter and bring her home safely, quietly."

Ripley watched Max out of the corner of his eye. His friend sat almost motionless, brooding. His finger kept up the tapping motion as he appeared to ruminate on the reverend's story.

The team was very selective about the private cases they

accepted. They had no need for money or fame, doing what they could for the betterment of man and to help those who couldn't help themselves. But above all, they tried their utmost to remain within the boundaries of the law. To bring in a fugitive and not release her to police custody could be very damaging to their cause if word got out.

"Here is everything we have regarding the incident." The reverend retrieved a large file folder from the case Winston held open for him. "Her schedule at the time. Known associates. The evidence of the theft, and the last photo I have of her."

Max accepted the folder and opened the cover. His sudden stillness set Ripley on alert. The subtle flare of Max's nostrils was the only hint that he was alarmed.

Ripley peered over the arm of the chair and looked down onto the smiling face of the pretty young blonde in the photo. His heart stopped before slamming into a pounding beat in his chest. His muzzle twitched, fighting the impulse to howl in denial.

This innocent young girl could not be the cold-blooded killer the reverend spoke of. She couldn't be. Ripley whimpered in his throat.

Alisia.

CHAPTER TWO

WHOEVER CLAIMED THAT a cold shower would cool the libido was full of shit.

Alisia stepped onto the slate floor and reached out a trembling hand for the thick peach bath towel hanging on a nearby rack. The soft cotton felt like sandpaper against her beaded nipples as her teeth chattered an erratic beat. Her breath stuttered in her lungs while her skin fought the freezing effects of the icy shower. Inside, however, she was molten lava, a burning, aching puddle of lust that nothing seemed to quench.

"Goddamn him," she gritted between clenched teeth and tiptoed into her bedroom.

This was all *his* fault. That son-of-a-bitch shifter with his big, muscled, golden body and simmering cornflower-blue eyes did this to her.

She dragged a pair of fuzzy wool socks over her pale feet before shimmying on jeans and a T-shirt. She zipped a dark blue hoodie up to her throat then jumped up and down, slapping at her arms in an attempt to increase the circulation of her blood.

This need, this hunger, to climb Ripley like a tree and ride him was getting worse by the day. If only his surfer-boy good looks were all she found appealing about him she might have been able to resist the attraction, but she found *everything* about him fascinating. The man moved with a sensuous grace that made his every muscle ripple in a hypnotic sway. And his smell, holy hell, dark chocolate and spice. Just being within breathing distance made her insides quiver and heat.

He was smart too, and funny, oh so funny. Many times she found herself working in the lab and suddenly burst out laughing at something he had said or did earlier. And the way he looked at her. Like he could lick her from head to toe and she would love every second of it and beg for more.

The energy that pulsed between them was intense, too intense, which was why she tried to keep him at arm's length. The last time she let herself go and said damn the consequences, horrible things happened. She had to be smart, had to keep vigilant, and never lose control.

The damp towel landed in the hamper with a soft thud. She picked the hairbrush off the dresser and attacked the long blonde strands as if they were the cause of her frustration.

It had been easier to ignore the attraction when she first met Ripley the year before. Working at the medical clinic with Dr. Megan Kelly had brought them into contact on only a few occasions. He would come in, bleeding from wounds sustained from what she had thought were illegal activities, he'd ask her out, she'd say no. A cycle that had become as annoying as a broken record.

It had actually been a relief when she had learned the reason for his injuries was not due to shady dealings but because of his ability to shape-shift into any mammal. Falling for men with dubious backgrounds was a weakness she thought she had beaten, and desiring Ripley had been making her wonder if there was something mentally wrong with her that drove her to the bad boys. Was she always going to want what she shouldn't have?

Who says you can't you have what you want now?

She paused with the brush in mid-air.

Yeah. Why *couldn't* she have what she wanted now?

As the only non-super member of the team, her position was tenuous at best. It was only by Doc's insistence that she needed Alisia to help with her research that she was allowed into the inner sanctum of the Evolutioneers. It still amazed Alisia that Max allowed her anywhere near his private lair, but there she was.

Over the last few months the mountain fortress had become her home, her haven, a place where monsters could never touch her. The team was an answer to a wish made years before that she had feared was never going to come true. But the dream did come to fruition, and the need for absolute secrecy was what compelled her to take the position. Security meant more to her than anything, and it was a commodity she would pay any price. Suppressing her most illicit desires was a small fee easily paid if it meant not engaging in activity that would jeopardize her position with the team.

That wasn't to say she didn't have her moments of going batshit crazy confined within the fortress. Yes, the mountain gave her shelter, but the rooms dug deep in the earth were crowded, sometimes stifling.

Leaving the mountain to let off some steam was never an easy option. At any time their location could be discovered, so any activities outside of a mission were allowed only if the rest of the team was notified, and even then Addison gave out trackers so everyone could be electronically trailed.

True privacy existed only within the confines of your

sleeping quarters, and outside the four walls of her room was the temptation of Ripley. Now that constant thoughts of him were invading her inner sanctuary, her control was beginning to fray. Remaining in strict check of one's emotions was exhausting. If she didn't release some sexual tension soon, she was afraid she was going to do something pathetic, like sprawl spread-eagled across his bed and scream, "Do me."

She tossed the brush onto the dresser with a disgusted chuckle. She lived in safety now. And this burning ache she carried had to end. Really, what was the worst that could happen if she gave in to the heat in Ripley's eyes? More than likely they'd have a passionate affair that flamed out before it began. Okay. A manageable awkwardness if that came to be. At least she would be able to put the thoughts to bed for good.

There was also the possibility that the sins of her past would surface and she would be forced back out onto the street. Did she want more regrets than she already had by hanging on to her stubborn fears and not take a chance on him?

Her and Ripley. Together.

In the mirror her cheeks were flushed and her green eyes turned smoky as a colony of butterflies settled behind her ribs.

Holy hell, she was really going to pursue him.

Between her thighs she turned liquid, her body already preparing for Ripley's possession. And he would possess her, of that she had no doubt. There was no halfway with the man. That blasé devil-may-care attitude he projected to the world hid the animal inside him, the beast who would devour her whole. Take and take until she was drained.

Heaven help her, that was just what she needed.

Her fingers shook as she dabbed on a touch of lip balm and smoothed down a wayward strand of hair. A smile flirted on her lips and she shivered, anticipating the intense union as she padded on her stocking feet down the hall on the hunt for her man.

The Evolutioneers made their home in a labyrinth of caves deep in the rock of the Cascade Mountains. Each member had their own living quarters, with Alisia and Doc sharing the wing that held the lab. Over her head, motion-sensor lamps that mimicked natural sunlight came on as she moved down the tunnel. She quietly slipped past the partially opened door to lab where Doc was working and headed straight for Ripley's room.

She knocked on his door, her rap matching the pounding of her heart as she waited. And waited. And waited.

"Ripley?" She cleared her throat and tried again. "Ripley?"

Hmmm. Maybe he was in the gym.

But the workout room was empty, as was the kitchen. In the common room, Chase stood alone with a game controller in each hand. His fists were a blur as he pummeled his holographic opponent in front of him. The computer was no match for his superhuman speed and the boxer fell in defeat in seconds.

Chase heaved a bored sigh. His breath came easy and his skin wasn't even slightly damp with sweat.

"Is that even fun when your games end so quickly?" Alisia asked while the game reloaded.

He shrugged. "Fun enough. Addison is working on a simulator so that we can all practice our powers. It will be sweet once it's done." He smiled in that boyish way that was pure smartass. "But that will not get you out of our training sessions. If you're gonna try to kick my ass, it's going to be face to face."

"Try?" She popped a hand on her hip. "I cleaned your clock yesterday."

"Lucky shot," he groused and fingered the faint blue mark on his square jaw.

Alisia was grateful that she was allowed to train with the others on the team even though her primary job was working in the lab with Doc, searching for the origins of how they had obtained their powers. When the others were on assignment, she assisted Addison in the communications room. The likelihood of her being in a situation that required hand-to-hand combat was slim, but Max believed that they all should be prepared for any possibility. Hey, who was she to refuse such valuable instruction?

The game signaled its readiness and Chase fell into a combative stance. A bell rang, and he was off.

She looped her thumbs in the top of her jeans and strove for her most nonchalant tone. "It's really quiet around here. Where is everybody?"

"Doc's in the lab, Crystal is taking a nap. Addison is in the comm room watching Max and Ripley. They're out in Lacey on a call."

"Lacey?" That was almost an hour and a half away. "What are they doing way out there?"

"They're meeting with some reverend. Howell, or Powell, or something like that."

Alisia's heart stopped so fast it hurt. She forced air into her lungs, her head going dizzy with the effort. "Lowell? Reverend Creed Lowell?"

"That sounds right."

She locked her knees to keep her legs from buckling. "When will they be back?"

"Don't know. They left about an hour ago."

"Oh," she managed to eke from her tight throat. "Well, I'm just gonna…go."

Chase was absorbed in the game and barely acknowledged her departure with a quick, "See ya."

Panic welled like a lead balloon ready to burst as she tried not to run to the comm room.

No, no, no, no. Shit, shit, shit, no.

She slid in her socks along the smooth rock floor, passing the entrance of the communications room. Peering around the door jamb, she spotted Addison at the helm. One hand propped up her head, while the other held a handkerchief to her nose. Two monitors flickered in front of her. One showed an image from Max's glasses as he entered the low-lit interior of an old farmhouse. From the second monitor was a similar image, but from about thigh height, from Ripley's necklace.

Addison blew her nose with a delicate honk, drawing her attention.

"Hey." Alisia approached on legs seemingly made of Jell-O. "Are you okay?"

"Dumb allergies," Addison answered. Behind her wireframe glasses, her red, teary eyes blinked slow and heavy. "I'll be fine. Doc gave me a decongestant. I think it's starting to kick in."

Alisia nodded at the screens. "What's boss man and Fido up to?"

Addison stifled a yawn. "Meeting with some reverend from up north. You know, the one on TV with the big fancy church near the river."

"What does he want with us?" She focused all her energy on appearing only mildly interested on what the boys were doing, when in reality she wanted to press her nose to the glass to watch the conversation.

"They've just been exchanging pleasantries. He probably wants us to repent our wicked ways and renounce our powers, like that quack who called us a few weeks ago." She blew her nose again.

Alisia was always ready to pounce on an opportunity when it presented itself—a trait that had saved her life on more than one occasion. "Sweetie, you don't look so good. Why don't you go lie down and I'll take over here?"

Addison sniffed once, twice, then sneezed into her handkerchief. "Are you sure? I don't want to ruin any plans you may have."

Too late.

"Like I'm allowed to have any plans. If I even think about stepping off the mountain, his royal beastliness pitches a fit." Not like that ever stopped her from sneaking away to get in a ride or two on her bike every once in a while.

Addison's shoulders slumped further with relief under her navy cardigan. "Thanks. I'm so tired. Okay, they're at a farmhouse just south of Lacey. Besides the reverend, there are two other men on site. Just shut everything down but the mainframe when they're halfway home."

Lacey. Her stomach clenched. Ah yes. The House of Penance. A location she was more than familiar with. "Got it. No problem."

It felt like forever passed before Addison dragged her sick body out the door. Alisia immediately sank into the captain's chair and slid on a headset. Usually when they worked they allowed the sound to fill the room, but she couldn't risk any of the conversation to be overheard by the others.

The first voice she heard made her blood freeze. That timbre, that cadence, she would recognize anywhere. Max's camera relayed images of the man sitting opposite him. A man she hadn't laid eyes on in seven years.

Her father.

He was looking good for a man pushing sixty. Sure, a few more lines bracketed his mouth, and his blond hair was thinner and showing more gray. But he still carried that air of piety, of sincerity. He was the people's preacher, their confidante. Following him, he told them, would lead them all to the arms of the Lord.

Motherfucking, son-of-a-bitch liar.

A man moved near his right and the bile rose in her throat when she recognized Deacon Winston. Tears obliterated her vision but she refused to let them fall. That man had taken everything from her. He took her life. Took away her beautiful, precious Sam. Oh, how she wanted to repay him in kind.

She swallowed against the pain of reopened wounds and tried to follow the conversation. Her father handed Max a folder and the camera panned down as he flipped over the cover.

Alisia didn't recognize the smiling girl in the photo. Dark blonde hair fell in a solid sheet past her shoulders, falling to her waist if the frame had been larger. Her emerald green eyes sparkled with youth, innocence, vitality. That girl lived in a community that embraced her, gave her comfort and security. She had the love of her family: a stepmother who helped her grieve the loss of her mother to cancer, a younger half-sister who tormented her as much as made her laugh. And a father who she believed was put on the earth by the hand of God himself.

She was a lamb guarded by wolves and had paid for it with her life.

The muzzle of a German shepherd appeared on the screen, looking down upon the picture.

A sob escaped her lips and she snapped her teeth together to hold her emotions in check. What lies were that monster spouting to Ripley?

"That photo was taken a few months before she disappeared. She was just about to graduate from high school," her father said and nodded to the flash drive in Max's hand. "That drive has all of the information I have on my daughter. Class schedule, a list of all her associates, evidence of the money she stole, everything."

Max's long fingers sorted through the papers, his hand paused after revealing a photo that had Alisia gasping while her stomach clenched in remembered horror.

Even devoid of color, the black and white image couldn't repress the violent brutality of the one of the worst moments of her life. The woman on the floor could have been an angel with her platinum blonde hair fanning under her like gossamer wings. Only the lamp lying shattered at her side and the large puddle of blood told the tragic story. Pale eyes stared sightlessly from her vacant face, as cold and brittle as the lying, manipulative heart that once beat inside her.

"And you're positive that Gretchen was the one who killed your wife, Reverend?" Max asked as he closed the folder, waking Alisia from the grip of her past. "You didn't have any other enemies?"

Reverend Lowell shook his head and heaved a sad sigh. "As much as I would like it to be otherwise, it was Gretchen. She was the only other one in the room."

Max nodded. In the lower corner of the monitor she saw his finger tapping the folder in a steady rhythm that matched her frantic heartbeat. "Let me make sure that I understand what is being asked of my team. You want me to locate your thieving, murderous daughter and *not* take her to the authorities, but to you directly. Am I correct?"

The reverend winced. "I wouldn't put it into those exact words, but yes. That is why I came to you. Compared to your recent exploits, this should not be a difficult task, even with the long length of time that has passed. I just want to make sure that my daughter is all right. I am the wronged party here, and I will see to it that Gretchen will repent the way God intended, in the church." He raised a hand in supplication. "Please, Maestro. I am willing to pay anything to get my child back."

Max snorted. "We'll discuss payment after I locate Ms. Lowell."

Hope sparked in his eyes as his nostrils flared in excitement. "You'll do it, then?"

"I'll find her."

Lowell sagged in relief, melting into the recesses of the chair. "Good, good. The moment you find her, call me. Day or night. If I am not available, Deacon Winston will respond. Between church activities and the upcoming wedding, I am never at rest. But do not hesitate to call."

"Wedding?" Alisia breathed at the same time Max asked, "Are you remarrying, Reverend?"

"No." He smiled and gestured to Winston. "My younger child, Mary Beth, is marrying Deacon Winston at the end of the month."

"No!" Alisia jumped to her feet, banging her knees on the desk.

Whatever discussion the men continued to have was completely lost as Alisia jumped up and down, then bent double in a silent scream. Blood filled her mouth as she bit her lip to keep from shouting every curse word she had learned on the street.

How could he! Her baby sister was just a kid, she would've barely turned seventeen, and that bastard was giving her to that vile *thing*. Winston would destroy her, if Mary Beth was lucky.

Alisia paced the four feet of available floor space, struggling to keep it together. When she'd left home, her sister was still in grade school. Her father's cruelties had never extended to them as children. She'd thought Mary Beth would be safe until she was able to break her out of that cultish existence.

But she never went back.

Right.

Alisia sank, defeated, onto the chair. She had thought about it. Tried to make plans. During those nights when she had been able to sleep in a real bed, she had plotted, tried to strategize on a way to break Mary Beth free. Once she had even made it within a mile of the church compound before she drew up short at the first glimpse of a church van coming down the road. Money, lack of skill, and the fear of what would happen if she ever returned had kept her from following through. Fear kept her running and ignoring what she had left behind.

Tears of shame fell from her eyes. And now her sister was going to pay for her failure.

Two car doors slamming shut brought her attention up. Ripley and Max were in the Rover, backing out of the drive and turning onto the dirt road back to the highway. Max placed his glasses in the center console, obscuring the view, but she could still see out of the windshield from Ripley's pendant.

"I don't believe him." Ripley's low rumble vibrated over her headset and sent chills down her spine.

"She lied to us," Max stated in a flat, cold voice.

"I don't—"

"No," Max snapped. He pointed a finger in warning. "Just because you want to fuck her does not make her innocent. We trusted her and she lied."

"Maybe she had a reason."

"Like she was a thieving murderer?"

"I—I…" There was a sigh, then nothing.

The ensuing silence was a knife to her heart. Her chest ached as she held her breath, waiting, waiting for Ripley to continue, to defend her. But there was nothing.

He didn't believe in her. Did he really buy the horrible image her father painted?

Her head dropped into her hands as she wrestled back more tears. What did she expect? Her past was littered with people who turned on her. Protectors that became villains. Not one person had ever been there for her.

Sam was there for you.

Sam was dead.

What had she done to deserve this misery? All her adult life she had fought, battled for a better existence. Every time she struggled, broken, bleeding to stand on her feet, fate or God struck her down. Why?

Her fingers curled, her nails biting into her flesh as she

choked down a wail.

She had been a good girl. She obeyed her elders, done well in school, prayed daily, and it wasn't good enough. Why? She beat her fists on the countertop. Why?

Max spoke again. "I'm not saying I trust Lowell either. Something about him tweaks my sensors, but we can get to the bottom of this in two minutes. We'll have Crystal read her past. *Bam.* All of our questions will be answered."

"Fuck," Alisia bit out.

Not only was Crystal an amazing psychic, but if she touched your skin, she could see your memories from the past. Once she found out the ugly truth, Max would give her up to Lowell, or throw her in jail before her next breath.

She had to move. Now.

She threw down the headset and quickly shut everything off. Erasing any data would be a waste of time because Addison could use her powers to connect directly to the mainframe and retrieve any lost information.

Her room felt miles away as she sprinted down the hall, her stocking feet slipping on the smooth surface. She burst into her room and shut the door, grabbing her leather jacket hanging on the wall and slipping on her boots. She knelt to reach under the bed where she hid a packed bag for just such an occasion.

There was always the chance that she would need to make a quick getaway. The Evolutioneers were wanted people, and Alisia had been forced to run for her life more than once. It was habit for her to be prepared. They all had a backpack ready, equipped with supplies for two days, a weapon, and a GPS device. That bag sat on the floor near the door where it was going to stay. Now, she gathered a few last-minute items to stuff into her secret pack.

She picked up her hairbrush and paused, staring at the bristles. Less than an hour before, she had thought that if she had to leave, she would regret never being with Ripley. She had been right. She was leaving and her heart hurt with regret. She regretted ignoring her common sense and starting to trust him.

Even if she did give him the benefit of a doubt, she didn't have the luxury of waiting for his return to see if he'd call her a liar to her face. Max for sure wasn't going to understand. He'd have her in her father's clutches before dawn.

She ignored the rush of fresh tears that burned her eyes as she slung the pack over her shoulders and slipped back down the hall. Only the whisper of her breathing broke the silence as she followed the familiar path out of headquarters. Before, she would sneak away from base to escape the intensity of being near Ripley. To have a few minutes alone where his spicy scent didn't tease her to arousal.

This time, she ran for her life.

CHAPTER THREE

"ALISIA IS NOT a murderer. I'll never believe it," Ripley growled. A constant rumble of displeasure vibrated in his throat.

His hands shook and his claws wouldn't retract, tearing holes in his pants as he struggled to Velcro them back in place. He jerked his shirt over his head, seams popping with his agitation.

Max sighed long and deep and rubbed a hand over his face. "I like her too, Rip, but we have to proceed with caution. Why don't you run that drive through the scanner and let's see what we've got?"

Ripley swallowed down his anger and focused on sorting through the bullshit that had dropped in their laps.

From under his seat, he pulled out a laptop and inserted the drive into the center console to be scanned and debugged for viruses. While the computer booted up, he looked at the photo of the young Alisia that had been in the file. Guilt over every dirty, lewd act he had ever fantasized about her heated his cheeks. She looked so pure, so sweet and wholesome, his teeth hurt.

The flash drive was clean, and Ripley went to work. His large, thick fingers slowed him up as he typed on the tiny keyboard. Each new piece of information made the muscles around his nose and mouth twitch as the low rumble resumed in his chest.

"Anything good?" Max risked a quick glance in his direction as he pushed the Rover to ninety miles an hour.

"Depends on what you mean by 'good,'" Ripley muttered, watching a section of footage from a security camera.

The quality was dark and grainy, but it was clearly Alisia taking money from a church safe. Also on the drive were more photos that showed her with a boy who couldn't have been older than twenty. They were photographed at what appeared to be a school or some type of community center. That must have been the boyfriend Lowell mentioned.

Grrrr.

Ripley's gums burned as his teeth lengthened into fangs and the hair on his arms thickened and stood on end. He shook his head to clear the red that clouded his vision and focused on the intel Deacon Winston had gathered.

Sam Connor was tall and scarecrow-thin in his green flannel shirt and Converse sneakers. He wore his dyed black hair long and tucked behind his ears, which made Ripley snort. He wouldn't have taken Little Miss Sunshine for a girl who went for the alternative rocker type, but then again, he apparently knew nothing about Alisia.

From the video footage of the theft, Alisia appeared to be on her own. Whether or not her shit of a boyfriend put her up to it was not clear. Either way, it wasn't looking good for his girl. Was he so blinded by his desire for her that he had missed the obvious?

No. There was no "obvious." There couldn't be. His instincts about her couldn't be that wrong.

Could they?

"She definitely stole some money," he finally reported. The words were bitter on his tongue. "But nothing that looks like the amount Lowell indicated. That much cash is heavy, and she would have needed to have a super large suitcase with rollers, or someone to help her, in order to carry it."

Max hummed in thought. "We'll get Network to do a more thorough investigation on the reverend and Deacon Winston too."

"Shit, Network," Ripley gasped and exchanged an alarmed look with Max.

In the midst of their emotional turmoil, they both forgot the other party listening in on their conversation. A party who was good friends with their new target.

"Network? Are you still there?" Max spoke into his earpiece. "Network?"

Nothing. Not even the sound of breathing could be heard.

"She was pretty sick when we left. And you did tell her to go to bed after we left the house. Maybe she fell asleep or left early because she thought we were good to go." Ripley's excuses sounded lame the second they left his lips.

Max shot him a glare that questioned his intelligence as he activated the Bluetooth on the Rover. "Call Network."

With each unanswered ring, the speedometer climbed higher and higher.

Ripley slumped in his seat when the voicemail picked up. "Leave a message. If I know you, I'll call you back."

"Call Intrepid," Max commanded, cruising past freeway traffic at nearly double the legal limit.

"Yo, what up, boss man?" Chase answered.

"Hey, Chase, Addison was monitoring our visit but I can't reach her. Where is she?"

"Oh that." He popped a yawn. "She wasn't feeling so hot, so Alisia took over for her and she went to bed."

Ah fuck.

Ripley's sharp inhale was drowned out by Max's muttered curse. "Where's Alisia?"

"I don't know."

"Find out." Max's order brokered no argument.

With each second that passed, Ripley's heart pounded harder and harder.

"She's not in the comm room," Chase reported. "Let me check her room."

Ripley stared out the windshield, his claws digging into the upholstery of his seat. He couldn't meet Max's gaze. He didn't want to see the condemnation he knew was in those cold blue eyes. He didn't want to believe that his woman could be guilty of the horrible crimes she was accused of.

"Her room is empty, but her escape pack is still here, and so is her cell," Chase reported.

Max grunted, obviously not convinced. "Gather the team together. We'll be there in thirty minutes. We have a case we need to jump on immediately."

Defiance shot along Ripley's nerves, bunching muscles and tightening sinew. His animal wanted to protect his mate, to jump out of the car and race home to confirm her safety.

If she wasn't on that mountain when he returned...

His vision blurred as his eyes shifted from man to beast and back again. He would chase her down and never let go until she ceded control to him. He wanted answers and so help him, he wouldn't stop until every part of Alisia belonged to him.

In his mind, he pieced together all his encounters with Alisia. What could he honestly say he knew to be true about her? The Alisia Caldwell he knew had a quiet reserve he had attributed to shyness, but that might have hidden an intense watchfulness of her surroundings. She never was a sharer about anything, and she wasn't the chatty sort. She was calm, an ice princess with the subtle heat of cinnamon when she let her guard down around him.

Added to that, the girl was clever, not just smart, but incredibly clever. More than once she managed to sneak off the mountain without alerting anyone or tripping any of their alarms. No one but Ripley knew about her late-night escapades and he hadn't found a time to confront her about it where he wouldn't have done something stupid, like rip off her clothes and fuck her.

Acid burned in his gut as he wondered what she had been up to all those times. Was she meeting with someone? Sam Connor, perhaps?

Ripley's throaty rumble marked the time on the long drive back as both men fell into an uneasy silence that belied their normal jovial banter. The two men had nothing else in common besides wielding a power no one else possessed and carrying the inbred honor of protecting those they called family. Their friendship had been forged through a series of one-upmanship and pranks, each one more outrageous then the next. Max could always rely on Ripley to watch after Crystal when faced with danger, and Ripley knew that his friend would do the same for Alisia.

At least he used to.

Could Ripley trust that Max would do right by Alisia, wait to act until they heard her side of the story? Or would Max toss her out in a knee-jerk reaction thinking he was protecting the team?

When it came to Crystal's safety, Max was legendary at flying to extremes. Unfortunately, Ripley couldn't fault him for his hair-trigger reaction. Watching the woman you love die, then come back to life would do that to a man.

Max turned off the highway and crossed the unmarked border of their mountain hideout. Thick hemlock trees and long-reaching arms of vine maples swallowed the Rover whole as they plowed deeper into the dark vegetation. Max used his powers to cover their tracks as Ripley yowled an animalist call out the open window to his four-legged sentinels for news of any disturbances. A wolf howled in response, reporting that Alisia had been seen striding through the woods earlier in the night. Since the wolves considered her a member of Ripley's pack, they let her pass without incident.

He kept that piece of information to himself and jumped out of the car the moment they pulled into the garage. "I'm going to search her room. See if I can catch a scent."

Not waiting for a response, he strode into headquarters, head lowered, ears alert, and followed his nose down the rocky corridor.

Alisia had definitely been at the controls of the comm room. Ripley sorted through the different scents of earth and ozone and found the gentle pheromones of his woman underneath. The imprint was faint, but he could pinpoint the vapor trail of her emotions like a map. Shock was hot and spicy, like a shard of pepper caught in the throat. Outrage hit him like a brilliant tomato red flash in the eyes that left a salty coating on the tongue. Her fear was a deep murky green, bitter and sour as it stole his breath.

She had traveled with great urgency to her room, where nothing appeared to be amiss in the rather austere space. In Ripley's eyes, her living quarters looked more like a hotel room with nothing indicating Alisia's style or personality. No photos sat on the bureau. The sink area wasn't cluttered with her cosmetics. There were no knickknacks, no mementos, nothing. It was as if she never really lived within these walls, just passed through as though a stranger.

Fear for her safety tightened his chest as anger at himself boiled in his veins. Did he never notice how sheltered she lived, how alone? He should have pushed, should have gained her trust so that she would have confided in him. Perhaps she wouldn't be in this position if he made a bigger effort to be her friend and not her lover.

He sucked in a harsh breath and froze. Under her citrus and musk scent was the heady, rich aroma of her arousal. It was on the air like a heavy perfume that made his body harden and his animal rush to the surface, ready to take his mate.

Tracking the sweet vivid fragrance like a kid after a batch of brownies, Ripley followed her escape route out into the forest. Standing at the edge of the wood, his instinct screamed at him to continue on and run after her, but he needed to know what the others were discussing. Max would be formulating a plan, and Ripley had to be the one to implement it. He wasn't going to give her up without learning all of the facts.

The night air burned his lungs as he sucked in a large breath. His fists tightened as his gaze shifted with a laser-like focus. He would get her back.

All talking ceased the moment he stepped into the great room. Max was front and center, standing before the widescreen TV. The light from the screen of the photo of Gretchen Lowell painted his dark clothes in hues of blue and gold. The others turned in their seats to stare at Ripley with bated breath.

He shook his head. "She's gone."

Doc released a tiny whimper, her dark hair slapped her cheeks as she vehemently shook her head. "I can't believe this, any of this. I can't believe that that"—she gestured wildly at the photo—"girl, my friend, killed anyone. I just can't."

Ripley shared her denial, but the evidence was damning. "Crystal, when you had the vision of Max and me at that meeting, what else did you see?"

She pushed a heavy fall of her hair off her face. Her eyes were rimmed in red with unshed tears. "Not much else. I saw the house, those velvet chairs, and you sitting by Max. That's all."

"And you never once saw anything in Alisia's past?"

"Never." She paused, her brow furrowing. "Well, not really. Once I caught a glimpse of her walking down a street. It was in the city, and dark out, she was alone, but that was all."

"Addison, what have you found?" Max asked.

"A whole lot of I don't know." She pushed her glasses further up her red and congested nose and furiously pounded on the keyboard. While her fingers sorted through the information on the desktop, her mind suctioned the information from the keys and downloaded information directly from databases and networks from all over the world, Ripley knew. She then sorted the information and relayed it back out in tidy graphs and spreadsheets.

"Reverend Lowell's first wife died from leukemia when Gretchen was seven. He remarried a year later to Jillian, who was a member of his congregation. They had one child, Mary Beth, who is seventeen. Reports say that Jillian died of a brain tumor seven years ago, but the only records are from a family doctor. The body was never taken to a hospital or a coroner's office." Images reflecting the information flashed across the screen for all to see. "It was a few days after the funeral that word spread that Gretchen moved to South America to do missionary work for the church. There are no photos of her from that time. It's like she ceased to exist, except in virtual form on the church's social media pages."

Chase raised his hand like a good student. "I don't get it. How could Lowell keep up a lie like that for years? And where did Alisia, I mean Gretchen, well—her, how did she elude him for so long?"

Max rubbed his chin. "I'd like to know that, too. It would be nice to have her here to ask those questions. Addison, what do you have on Sam Connor?"

"Sam Connor was from Scappoose, a small town near the church's compound. He was a year ahead of Gretchen in school. There isn't much on him. His dad's serving twenty years in Walla Walla for manslaughter, his mom is a waitress, extended family is in Portland. Connor was reported missing about the same time Gretchen disappeared. There is absolutely nothing on him since."

"Doesn't really mean anything. There's nothing on Gretchen either," Max pointed out.

"Not necessarily. I traced Alisia's driver's license number and found this from about ten years ago."

Addison brought up a copy of a license issued to a sixteen-year-old new driver. The information was identical to the one issued to Alisia, except for the photo. The teenager pouted with sullen entitlement, her makeup dark. Dirty-blonde hair spilled from a ponytail high on her head.

"Who is that?"

"Alisia Caldwell. Her parents were killed in a car accident when she was a kid and she lived with her grandmother. She dropped out of high school at sixteen, but received her GED two years later with almost perfect marks. That's quite a turnaround for a student who was receiving D grades, don't ya think?"

Chase raised his hand again. "I'm confused. Are you saying that somehow our Alisia became that Alisia? How? And where's the original?"

"That's why we need Gretchen now. Right." Max clapped his hands. "Here's the plan. We're—"

"No," Ripley barked. "I'm going after her. Alone. There is too much here that is not making sense and she trusts me." A tiny lie. But she for sure trusted him more than she would Max. "You dig up more info on Lowell and I'll get Alisia."

"Ripley, I know you care for her. We all care for her. But we have a duty—"

"Fuck duty," he interrupted Max again. His vision shifted as his pupils dilated, his animal growing anxious to leave. "Lowell isn't what he seems, I can smell it. And that Deacon Winston isn't right either. What kind of father gives his seventeen-year-old to a man at least twice her age? What kind of man, reverend or not, allows his wife's murder to go unreported? I don't trust them, and I'm not letting you hand her over to them to do who knows what."

Max raised his hand in an attempt to steady the beast. "I know. I don't trust him either. I told him that I would find her. I didn't say anything about letting them near her. Look, Reverend Lowell is a very well-known and influential man. He's a trusted member of the community and we have to tread carefully. He came to us in secret, but that doesn't mean it will stay a secret. The safety of this team comes first, and right now there is an unknown. I don't like unknowns."

"I will find her," Ripley vowed.

Max sighed and shared a glance with his wife, who nodded. "You have forty-eight hours. Your time starts now."

CHAPTER FOUR

S HORT-SHORT-SHORT, LONG-LONG-LONG, SHORT-SHORT-SHORT.

Alisia released the doorbell and cast another glance over her shoulder to scan the dark empty parking lot for any observers. In typical Northwest fashion, a low cloud cover obliterated all moonlight, making anything that lay outside a pool of lamplight look as welcoming as a black hole. So dark was it that one couldn't see the rain that fell, only hear the patter of the steady drizzle as the drops hit the pavement.

A soft whirling sound drew her attention up to the security camera where she offered a sheepish smile and tiny wave.

"State your business—oof," the pleasant voice of the receptionist over an intercom was abruptly cut off.

"Go directly to my unit. Do not pass go. Do not collect two hundred dollars," the familiar voice of Jameson Alinari directed in a tone as smoky as the whiskey she was named after.

Alisia picked up her gear and waited for the buzz that allowed her entrance into the inner sanctum of the Evergreen Domestic Abuse Shelter. From the outside it looked like any other brick and glass office building in the industrial district of the city, and that was the point. Only the women and children who lived and worked there and a few select law enforcement officers knew what went on inside those walls. There were a lot of deranged people out there, which Alisia was more than aware of, and secrecy meant the difference between life and death to these women.

Another set of doors guarded the true entrance to the shelter, where the first floor was made up of offices and a small medical center. The second floor was a dormitory for the single women, with the remaining two floors sectioned off as individual apartments for families. Alisia strode to the set of stairs that led down to the basement, past the laundry room, and down the long hallway to the lone unmarked door.

She raised her hand to knock when it suddenly opened, revealing a small, muscular woman. It was as if a tinier version of Lara Croft herself had come to life and blocked the entrance with a fierce frown turning down her lips.

"What are you doing darkening my door?"

Alisia couldn't help but smile at the ridiculousness of what she was about to say. "The Evolutioneers are after me."

Jameson's dark brows lowered further when she realized nothing else was forthcoming. "No shit?"

"No shit."

"Then get in here." She grabbed her arm and hauled her inside.

The moment she crossed the threshold, Alisia released the first easy breath she had taken all night.

Once upon a time, this two-bedroom apartment with second-hand furnishings and paint-by-numbers artwork on the walls had been her home. A refuge from the horrible nightmare her life had become. She was safe within these walls. Protected by a community of women who wore their battle scars not only on the outside, but inside as well. Security was not guaranteed now that she was back, but for the moment it was a small reprieve.

Her bag and motorcycle helmet hit the wood floor with a smack as Jameson tackled her in a huge bear hug. "You look so good and healthy."

"Thanks. So do...you?" She raised a brow as she got a good look at the friend she hadn't seen in over a year.

Jameson's dark sable hair was plaited in a thick braid down her back. A black leather corset covered a tank top and matched the pants seemingly sprayed on to the lower half of her curvy body. Fingerless black gloves covered her hands and combat boots covered her feet.

"Am I interrupting anything?"

Jameson waved a hand. "Naw, I have business to take care of, but it can wait. Can I get you anything? Have you eaten?"

A shot of whiskey sounded awesome, but was probably not the best thing to ingest. "Tea would be nice."

Alisia followed Jameson to the kitchen area and slid onto a stool next to the Formica-topped bar. She ran a finger across the worn, cracked surface and smiled. How many nights had she and Jameson sat in this very spot, drinking hot tea and watching Jameson's mother cook an Italian feast? Maria Alinari had never rested until she was satisfied that all the girls in her care were well taken care of. Her love extended from her own daughter to the children of her heart that came through the shelter, both young and not so young. As the center's director, she worked tirelessly to provide a safe environment and a new life for everyone who wished for the opportunity. That devotion was passed to her daughter, who took on the role when she retired a few years earlier.

"How's your mom doing?"

"She's good," Jameson tossed over her shoulder as she placed a cup of water in the microwave. "Loves Albuquerque. She's taking pottery classes and flirting with a widower. I think she's beginning to understand that retirement is a good thing. But you are not here to talk about my mother. Why are the Evolutioneers after you?"

"Creed Lowell hired them to find me."

"That bastard?" she hissed.

Jameson was the only person who knew Alisia's entire sordid history. Theirs was a sisterhood that was stronger than blood, forged by rising from the ashes of tragedy to stand side by side and demand a better life. When one needed, the other provided, even if it meant skirting the edges of the law to do so.

"I thought he gave up the search for you." Jameson set the cup of tea before her.

"He won't give up until he personally sees my body. He never gave up. He just didn't have anyone smart enough to find me. Until now."

"So how did you hear the Evolutioneers were involved?"

Alisia cupped her hands around the warm mug and blew across the scalding surface. "I work for them."

"What?" Jameson screeched. "Hold the phone." She sprinted around the kitchen island and jumped onto the neighboring stool. Snatching a bowl of fruit from the counter, she hugged it to her chest like a bucket of popcorn. "Start at the beginning."

"You have to take the oath first."

Jameson rolled her eyes. "Are you kidding me?"

"Deadly serious."

"Fine." She jostled the bowl into the cradle of her arm and held up her left hand, holding three fingers up in the shape of a "W." Any impatience she displayed died as she solemnly recited, "Upon the honor and blood of the warrior women who fought and died to free me from the oppression of the patriarchy, I vow that whatever confidence is bestowed upon me will go with me to the grave and beyond."

To some, the oath might appear childish, but to the two women the vow was sacred. If broken, the punishment meant death. Well, maybe not to that extreme, but a serious ass-kicking resulting in a lengthy hospital stay would definitely be expected.

"Thank you." Taking a deep breath through her nose, Alisia began. "Do you remember my friend Megan, the doctor I worked for?" Jameson nodded and took a bite from an apple. "Well, she has super powers."

"Seriously? What can she do?"

"Not important. Anyway, when she met a few others who also had super powers, they decided to form a team. She asked if I would join them to help her with research and provide additional medical assistance. I'm single, have no real obligations, and she thought I would be a good fit. Of course, I figured what better place to keep low than in a secret hideaway surrounded by a bunch of super humans? It was a no-brainer."

"Where *do* you live? What are they like? How did they get their powers?" Jameson's eyes grew wider the faster she shot out the questions.

The question of the century. How did the Evolutioneers obtain their powers?

At this point all they knew was that when the human

body absorbed certain elements from the environment, it created a cosmic cocktail that required a burst of adrenaline to hit the body so hard and so fast, it ignited the person's natural abilities, creating the super power. For years Doc Kelly used her own body and what samples Ripley would give her to try to determine exactly what factors in the environment contributed to their creation. With the discovery of other supers, she had enlisted Alisia's help with the research. For every question answered, six more appeared in its place. But the one thing Alisia was certain of was that she herself was not a super. She'd been hit, chased, even stabbed once, enough adrenaline-inducing events that should have triggered something if she had had the right combination of toxins in her system.

Not having powers didn't bother her too much. With her luck it would have only added to the disaster that was her life.

Alisia shook her head. "I can't tell you that. But they're really great people. They truly want to help others, and what they do is very dangerous work. The living conditions are…interesting, with us all being in one location, but I was used to that from growing up on the compound. And it's not all serious all the time. We have fun, too. I thought they were my friends…" she trailed off, not able to keep the hurt out of her voice. Her vision swam and she angrily blinked away the tears. Crying had never helped her in the past. "Um. Right. Well, earlier tonight I heard that a few members of the team were meeting with my father. We always monitor whenever anyone goes out on a call, so I was able to hear what was going down."

Jameson popped grape after grape into her mouth, riveted to the story. "So they knew you were listening?"

"No. One of the others was supposed to be at the board, but she was sick and I sent her to bed. They didn't know I was listening."

"Nice."

Alisia gave a non-committal hum and told Jameson what transpired during the meeting. It was difficult to accept that she had become complacent, that there had been no word made public about what was going on at the church over all these years, that there had been a change, that her sister might be spared. That after all these years of running, of never letting her guard down, she had allowed herself to think that the past was a distance nightmare. It figured that the moment she had begun to entertain the notion of letting go, of finally saying yes to Ripley, and having something her heart truly wanted, the horrors of yesterday would come clawing back, ripping her security to shreds.

Jameson ditched the healthy food and went for the big guns, pouring them a big bowl of Moose Munch. "I can't believe your sister is marrying that murderous asshole. Do you think she's being drugged too?"

"I don't know. Possibly." Alisia rubbed her eyes. The stress of the night was wearing her down. "I just don't know anything anymore."

"So, what's your plan to take the bad guys down and clear your name?" Jameson asked, munching a piece of chocolate-covered popcorn.

"What?" Alisia choked on her tea.

"Punkin, I've read the newspaper. You have super humans who know who you are, and they know you know who they are, coming after you. What's their success rate?"

She tried to swallow down the bitter taste in her mouth.

"Perfect."

"Hmm, yes, thought so." Jameson placed her hand over Alisia's icy one. "Alisia, you are the smartest woman I know. Running has worked for you so far, but the rules have changed. What will happen if they find you?"

"They'll take me back to *him.*"

"And what will happen to Mary Beth?"

This time Alisia couldn't stop the tear from spilling down her cheek. Her mouth fell open but her vocal chords wouldn't function. The atrocities Deacon Winston were capable of were too horrible to speak of.

She was going to have to fight, take the offensive. Up to now, her entire survival strategy had been to run and hide in a protective shell, like a turtle, until danger passed. She never went after anyone.

At least Max had his super powers and the support of the team when he had gone after his psychotic father. And even then, Crystal had lost her life and only Doc's powers had brought her back from death. Alisia would be going in alone to face the devil and his minions. A mission that was certain suicide if she took one tiny misstep.

More tears burned the back of her achy throat as she debated her next move. She was so tired of running. Why couldn't she be allowed to just live? All she wanted was to wake up in the morning and do the work she loved. She wanted to go out with friends and not constantly look over her shoulder. She wanted to love a man, and have him love her in return.

A snarl curled her lip, but she smothered it with a handful of chocolate caramel peanuts she shoved into her mouth. How stupid was she to think that Ripley could have been that man? It had taken two seconds for him and Max to believe she was guilty and take Lowell's money. If she were to succeed in revealing the truth, she'd be able to leave that jackass and the rest of the team behind and start over again with a clear future.

She turned toward Jameson, her stomach pitching the popcorn and tea she had consumed in a storm of nerves. "I'm going after Lowell."

Jameson's smile stretched from ear to ear as she nodded. "That's my girl. What about the Evolutioneers?"

Her breath blew out in a rush. "They're going to be on my ass, and quick, too. I may be able to keep one step ahead of them for a little bit, but it won't be easy."

"And what about after you clear your name?"

"After?" Her laugh was low and bitter. "Screw them. Anyone who could so easily believe those lies about me can kiss my ass."

"Well, technically—"

"No." Alisia raised a finger in warning. "There is no technically. And a good friend would not even go there."

Jameson held up her hands. "Sorry, just keeping it real. But as a good friend, I will help you however I can."

She jumped off the barstool and pulled open one of the kitchen drawers, removing the silverware tray and setting it on the counter. From under a false bottom Jameson withdrew two knives, a baby Glock, and several clips of ammunition. Tucked under the dish towels in another drawer was a holster for the gun.

Alisia raised a brow. Of course. Why wouldn't the director of a women's shelter hide weapons in a hidden compartment in the kitchen? At least, that's what she hoped was the reason behind the cache.

"I'm going to assume that these are legal," Alisia said

with an upward lilt.

"I'm going to assume that you know how to use them, and have obtained training and a permit through your recent employment, not that it really matters."

"The answer is yes and yes."

Jameson clapped her hands. "Excellent, and of course these are legal. One more thing." She disappeared down the hall.

Alisia picked up the Glock and checked the chamber. Taking a life was not, and never should be, an easy decision to make. However, with the hard plastic warming in her grip, anticipation raced through her at the possibility of aiming the barrel at Arnold Winston's black heart and pulling the trigger.

"Here you go." Jameson tossed a cell phone at her. "Number's taped to the side, it's all ready to go. If anyone tries to trace it, the number leads to a pizza shop in the U District."

Alisia stared at the items on the counter. "Seriously. What is with all of this? And your outfit? What have you gotten into?"

"What?" Jameson ran her palms down the slick surface of her corset. "You don't like my new look?"

"Jameson."

"Alisia," she mimicked the chiding tone. "I'm just doing a little security work. You know we can get some undesirables sniffing around here."

True. But there was definitely more going on than met the eye. If only she wasn't neck-deep in her own troubles, she'd grill Jameson more on the topic.

"Thank you for these. And the phone will only be used in an emergency. This group can locate the source on anything." Alisia reached for her pack to store her loot and pulled out a bag of her clothes. "Here. I have a small…donation. Could you get a few of the girls to wear these tomorrow?"

Jameson laughed, a warm rich sound that always made Alisia smile. "Absolutely." She quickly sobered. "I wish I could go with you."

"I know, and the fact that you would means so much to me." Alisia enveloped the shorter woman into a hug. This might very well be the last time she saw her best friend, and it hurt. "Love you."

Jameson squeezed her so hard, her spine popped. "Love you. If I don't hear from you in two days, I will come after your ass."

Alisia smiled through the tears she refused to allow to fall. "Okay."

"Damn, I wish I didn't have plans to go out tonight."

"I understand." She tugged on Jameson's braid. "You take care, too."

A cold, anticipatory light sparked in the other woman's dark eyes. "It's not me you should be worried about. Make yourself at home, take what you need. I'll try to be back before you go."

After a final hug, Jameson slipped out the door, leaving Alisia wondering what sort of mischief her friend was up to. The woman was a warrior and whatever it was, Alisia was certain a social injustice was involved.

She rubbed both hands over her face and behind her neck. If she was going after Goliath, she needed all the knowledge she could gather to arm her brain the same way she was now armed with weapons. Swiping the bag of Moose Munch off the counter, she headed to the computer, ready to settle in for a long night.

CHAPTER FIVE

H E WAS GOING to throttle her. He was going to hug her, tie her up, fuck her, shout at her, then hug her again.

Ripley pulled his battered Chevy Silverado into the parking lot of a hole-in-the-wall pub and slammed to a halt next a black Honda CB 919 motorcycle. The squealing tires sprayed gravel in all directions, the resulting ping of rock hitting metal sounding like firecrackers. His nostrils flared as he dragged in a deep calming breath, then another as the steering wheel threatened to crack under the force of his grip. He had to tamp down his temper. If he came at her with all the fury rioting inside, she would bolt for sure.

Mist blanketed the area in a thick gray cloud. His blood boiled so hot in his veins, he was surprised steam didn't rise from where the moisture touched the bare skin of his arms.

How galling was it that a little slip of a woman was able to elude him for so long. He had been certain he was right on Alisia's tail, her scent growing stronger and stronger until he found the women's shelter.

The building reeked of her. At least eight women he saw coming and going were wearing her clothes. But the shelter's director was as forthcoming as a statue. Nothing and no one got past the fae-looking woman who he thought missed her calling as the gatekeeper to hell.

Jameson Alinari's only saving grace was that she was obviously protecting Alisia because she cared. She turned every one of his questions back on him, and refused to give up any information on her friend. That level of loyalty would have been admirable, if it wasn't working against him.

After a few fits and failures, he had finally been able to get a lock on Alisia's scent. Luckily, the weather had cooperated by staying dry when he needed, which enabled him to make up some time for her head start. Of his forty-eight hours, he had already eaten up eighteen, and no way was Max going to allow him one minute more before taking action.

Inside the dim interior of the pub, Ripley's predatory gaze sharpened as he hunted for his prey. The stench of beer and greasy food filled his lungs. Underneath that was a clean, musky scent of woman that hardened every muscle in his body. His woman.

A husky chuckle drew his attention to the corner were the pool tables were located. Alisia tossed a smile over her shoulder at the two men standing behind her as she chalked up her cue. Her dove-gray sweater gaped in the front when she leaned over to take the shot, revealing the peach-soft swells of her breasts. A curtain of wheat-blonde hair draped down to the green felt obscuring his view. A growl rumbled in his chest, drawing a curious glance from the patrons closest to him, but he paid them no heed.

He stalked through the Friday night crowd to where she held court, entertaining a passel of yokels who were staring at her as if she were the first female they had seen live and in the flesh. As she bent over to line up the next strike, her heart-shaped ass turned up at him in invitation.

Jesus, woman. He wiped his hand down his face several times and drew in a steadying breath. What full-blooded male could turn away from such perfection? Why didn't she just wave a flag and demand trouble to come and take a go at her? Judging by the hunger in the men's gazes, one of them was going to make a move. And soon.

Not on his watch.

He waited until she finished the stroke then strode up behind her to press his hard length along the curve of her body.

"Hey! Back off." She turned to glare at him with her arm cocked and ready to throw a punch when recognition dawned and she froze. Her lips pinched tight and her throat worked as she swallowed. "Oh. It's you."

He let her slip away to the side. "We need to talk."

"I'm busy." She bent for another shot. The cue ball struck with a solid crack and rocketed across the table.

"Now." His heart was racing a million miles a minute. How could she be so calm? She must have known someone from the team would be after her. That's why she ran, right?

"Hey, buddy. Leave the lady alone." One of her suitors placed himself before Alisia.

Ripley stared hard at the man. A low rumble vibrated from his throat, sending a shiver down his own spine. The man paled and picked his jaw off the floor as he took a hasty step back.

Alisia stifled a curse and sighed. "May I have fifteen seconds, please?" she asked Ripley with all sweetness.

He nodded and remained where he stood with his massive arms crossed over his chest. "But only fifteen."

"Fine," she huffed.

Clack, clack, clack. Ball after ball fell into the pockets until the table was cleared.

She picked up a stack of bills from under a beer stein

and touched them to her forehead in salute. "Thank you, boys."

The men's gaze jumped to and fro, and they looked as though they didn't know what to be more upset about: losing their money or having their eye candy taken away by the big, beefy guy.

After the cash was tucked into her back pocket, she reached for her leather coat and shrugged it on. A cool mask settled over her features. She was going to make this as difficult for him as possible.

"So talk," she said.

"Not here." He tipped his head toward the door.

Her gaze scanned the room while he waited with hair-thin patience. She could look for exits all she liked, but the only way out was with him. She sighed again and preceded him to the parking lot. The moment they were out of earshot from those inside he grabbed her arm and pulled her around to face him.

"I—you—why—" All thoughts of staying cool went to hell now that he had her alone. While the animal in him demanded that he haul her over his shoulder and claim her body until she learned to never disobey him, the man, concerned for her well-being, wanted to hold her until she melted in his embrace. The man won.

He let go of her arm. "Are you all right?"

Those big green eyes of hers blinked at him once, then twice. She opened her mouth to speak then snapped her teeth together and shrugged with indifference.

"Do you know how worried everyone is? Why did you run away?"

She snorted, eyes wide in disbelief. "Maybe because you and Max were planning on wrapping me in a big bow and delivering me to Satan and his right-hand man."

So, she had been listening to the conversation at the farmhouse. "That's not true."

"Ha," she sputtered. "Don't lie. I heard you."

"Well, you didn't hear enough. We wanted to talk to you first, hear your side of things."

Her eyes narrowed. "I don't believe you."

"It's true. Look, I know Max can get a little overzealous when it comes to protecting the team, but he, all of us, are willing to listen. Please, let's go home and straighten all of this out."

"No. You and Max can go to hell. I have things to do." She moved to step around him.

"Don't be stupid, Alisia. I'm not letting you walk away. We're going home."

"Fuck you." She pointed a finger in his face. "I'll never go back. Not to the mountain and not to that church. You can't hold me. The moment you blink, I'll be gone."

He placed his hand on the wall near her head and trapped her between his big body and the building. He lowered his head till they were nose to nose. "There's one thing you forget," he purred. "I will always come after you and I will find you every time. No matter how many ways you try to trick me, I will know your scent anywhere. It's embedded in my soul, because you are my woman and I will always find you. You belong to me."

"I belong to no one," she snapped, her body trembling. Her gaze remained fixed on his collarbone.

His lips brushed her cheek and her trembling grew. "You know you're mine but you continue to fight it. Why? Why do you fight me?"

She braced her hands against the solid wall of his chest,

her fingers flexing then releasing as if she couldn't decide to pull him closer or push him away. "I—I don't—"

"You do. And I'm not letting you run anymore." The fingers of his free hand cupped her behind the neck to tilt her face up for his kiss.

Dear Lord, he shuddered and pressed harder. Her lips were soft. And sweet, oh so sweet. His tongue swept into her mouth to coax and tease. The flavor of the cider she had drunk earlier and the subtle notes that were pure Alisia burst on his tongue.

A whimper joined the music of their heavy breathing as she kissed him back. Her lips moved slowly, carefully like a teenager breaking curfew and afraid of being caught at any moment.

How had he gone so long without this? Without her kiss? His lips burned a path down her swan-like neck. The ache in his cock created a fiery path up his torso to his gums, where his eyeteeth lengthened to sharp points. The scrap of his fangs over her pulse caused her to gasp and arch into him, the sexy sigh spurring his lust higher. Why was it that he had to focus his energy in order to shift, but any time he thought of Alisia, his animal stirred, changing parts of his body to bite her? Mark her. Claim her as his for eternity.

He nipped her skin and fought the urge to maul her like a beast. "Talk to me, Alisia. Be mine. Let me love you. Let me protect you."

She sucked in a deep breath and jerked out of his arms so violently her head smacked into his jaw, his fangs cutting his tongue.

"No." She pushed against his chest. "No. You're work-ing for *him*. I can't believe anything you say." Her lips swollen from his kisses quivered then pressed into a thin line.

The lost, haunted look on her face cooled his ardor. "Of course you can believe me."

"No, I can't!" she shouted and slapped at his hands when he reached for her. "Stop, just stop, Ripley." The green in her eyes turned emerald with unshed tears. "Leave me alone."

He gripped her cold leather-clad arms and gave her a little shake. If only she would let him in, he'd make everything better. "How can I help you if you won't let me?"

"Ugh." She covered her face with her hands. "Shut the fuck up, Ripley. You are so clueless."

"Is there a problem here?"

Ripley squinted into the mist. A deputy stood near his cruiser stopped in the middle of the parking lot. The beam of the headlights bounced over them.

"No, officer," Alisia replied with a shaky smile. "My, uh, brother here just told me that there is an emergency at home. It's a little troubling."

With his superior vision, Ripley saw clearly the officer's disbelieving frown as he asked, "Will you be needing any assistance?"

"Oh, no." She waved him away. "Family issues. You know how that goes. Actually, I was leaving now." She wrenched out of Ripley's grasp and jumped onto her motorcycle parked near them. Strapping on her helmet, she shot him a glare as frigid as the evening air. "See you at home, bro."

"Alisia." His warning went unheard over the rumble of the bike. With a little wave, she shot out of the parking lot and onto the road.

Damn. She was certifiable if she thought he would leave it at that. He spun on his heel and headed for his truck.

"Do you need me to follow you home?" the deputy called out to him.

"No, thank you."

"Then you wouldn't mind giving the lady a few minutes' head start, now would you?" he asked, laying a not-so-subtle hand on the butt of his gun.

He's just doing his job. He's just doing his job. He's just doing his job.

The mantra rattled in his brain as the two began a staring competition. "You did hear her say she was my sister."

"Well, where I'm from, we don't go kissing our siblings the way I saw you two going at it."

Harrumph. The man had him dead to rights there. Guess he should count his lucky stars he hadn't been arrested on sight.

But oh, the agony of waiting until the officer finally gave the nod for him to depart with a pleasant, "Have a good and safe evening, sir."

"You too, officer," Ripley said as he jumped into his truck and tried to control the squeal of his tires on the gravel as he tore out of the parking lot.

The misty air was like ice on his nose as he drove with the window rolled down and his face stuck out of the opening. The scent of exhaust, rain, and dirt filled his nostrils, for mile after mile until the heady, subtle musk of Alisia filled his lungs and began the thaw.

There she was. Just turning onto the interstate.

The interstate. Oh, great.

"Hold on, baby. You can make it," he cooed and stroked the dash of the shuddering Chevy. His girl was old and rickety, built more for hauling and less for speed.

A high-pitched squeal pierced his concentration above the rattle of pipes and the whine of his engine, hitting his sensitive ears and making him flinch so that the truck swerved on the highway. "Ow. What the hell?"

"Sorry, Ripley," Doc's voice came across his earpiece. The tiny transmitter was nestled in his ear canal and was capable of sending and receiving signals. "This communications equipment is not my field of expertise."

He rubbed the area under his ears to relieve the pressure. "Where's Addison?"

"She's in her quarters digging up information on Lowell. She doesn't know I'm in here."

Hmmm. Having Doc reaching out to him via the earpiece and not the cellphone was not necessarily a boon of good fortune.

"What's up?"

"I saw you found Alisia, so why are you heading away from the mountain?"

"Did you turn on the GPS on my necklace?

"Of course."

"Damn it, Doc." Which meant she also turned on his camera too, which is why she knew he had located Alisia. Great, a witness to his humiliation. "Yeah, I found her. But as you might have seen, she slipped away before I could convince her to come back. I'm on her trail, don't worry."

"I'm worried about her, Ripley."

"I know."

"Do you…do you think she's innocent?"

"I'd bet my life on it," he replied with one-hundred-percent conviction.

"Good. I just can't believe she would do anything like

that man claimed. And I trust your instincts."

"Yeah…about that." He scrubbed his hand over his face. "You know that little matter I was having you help me on? About me turning…" He swallowed hard. "Feral? It's getting stronger. More frequent. Especially when I'm near Alisia."

"Really?" Concern over her friend left her voice and was replaced by the scientist. "Describe your symptoms. Anything new?"

"Not new, just stronger. And it feels like at any moment the beast will take over. I—I can't have that happen. Especially not now."

"I hear ya. Let me do some research. Run some more tests, see what I can find. In the meantime, stay focused. And quit trying to kiss her or engage in sexy stuff. Keep to the task."

"Yeah, yeah."

"I mean it, Ripley. Keep your dick in your pants. You two have enough to worry about without dragging sex into it."

He squinted through the windshield at the worsening weather. "Doc, I gotta go. Thanks for the update."

"Be careful, both of you. And don't have sex."

"Got it," he shouted as she hung up.

Rain poured through the truck's open window, drenching his left side. Alisia's trail grew fainter as his heart rate escalated with each second that passed.

"Where are you?" he muttered. "Wait. Whoa. Whoa!" He jerked the wheel to the right, skidding across two lanes as her scent took a sharp turn into a rest stop.

A few remaining picnickers were scrambling to pack away their gear as rain fell in fat drops. Ripley parked the

Chevy in the rapidly emptying parking lot and scanned the area for her little black Honda. When only a van and his truck remained, he jumped out. Where was she?

He drew a deep breath, sorting through the scent of drenched vegetation and exhaust fumes to follow the citrus and spice musk to the door of the women's restroom. A silver-haired woman stepped through the open door, glancing behind her with a furious frown.

She jumped when she ran into Ripley's solid frame. "Oh. What? Damn weirdos," she exclaimed as her scowl deepened and she rushed to the waiting van.

The wind picked up, drowning out his footsteps as he crept into the restroom. Alisia's motorcycle rested against the concrete wall. She sat under the row of sinks with her back to the bricks and her knees raised, her head on her crossed arms. She was still, so still, she could have been another cold fixture in the room, until she shuddered and her fingers dug into her elbows as she choked back a sob.

"Ah, sweetheart." He held out both arms, entreating her to confide in him.

She flinched and looked up with a gasp. "How did—?"

"I told you. I will always find you."

Her lashes lifted to reveal emerald eyes blazing up at him through the fringe of her damp hair. "I'm not going back."

He pushed his wet hair off his face and released a long sigh. He took a half step back to give her space as if she were the wild animal. "Alisia, baby, you can't keep running."

"You're crazy if you think I'm going to let you hand me over to those killers," she spat.

Ripley froze. Now they were getting somewhere. "Then talk to me. We don't think Lowell is being completely honest. Tell me your story. Look." He removed his earpiece and crushed it between his fingers, tossing the bud into the trash. Next, he tucked his pendant behind his shirt.

A second later his cell phone shrilled. He didn't have to look at the display to know it was headquarters wondering what he was doing. They were probably shitting themselves silly at his actions.

Shutting down the phone, he slipped it into his pocket. "I'm listening."

She scoffed, unimpressed with his gestures. "And then what? Max will never listen to me."

"Let me worry about Max. Besides, all of this can be cleared up in two seconds. If Crystal reads your memories, she can confirm that you're innocent of what Lowell is accusing you of. The truth will set you free."

"The truth?" Her sharp bark of laughter echoed against the concrete. "Oh, she'll see the whole ugly truth. Did I steal money from the church? A little bit. Did I kill my stepmother? Hell yeah. And if given a chance, I'd stake that bitch again."

CHAPTER SIX

O NE WOULD THINK that sitting on the floor of a public restroom about to spill some of the worst details of your life to a man, a man whom twenty-four hours ago you were intent on stripping naked and licking from head to toe, would rank as the lowest moment of your life. For Alisia, it barely broke the top ten.

Was this the most spectacular hiding place she could have chosen? Of course not. But the rain had made speeding down the highway suicidal, and she had hoped the drizzle had provided enough coverage to fool Ripley. Apparently, fortune was still not on her side.

She peered up at the shifter through the wet clumps of hair hanging in her face. Her little bombshell of a statement might have momentarily stunned him, but she was so exhausted, she lacked the strength to stand, let alone make a decent escape.

Water trickled in an icy stream down her back, and her fingers, nose, and ass were numb from sitting on the cold concrete. She couldn't stand if her life depended on it. At the moment, it likely did.

His Adam's apple bobbed once, then twice. "You killed your stepmother? Why?"

She rested her head back against the wall. "I found out the church was a sham and she was going to drug me to keep me complacent. We fought and I hit her."

"So it was self-defense?"

She shrugged and closed her eyes. "You could say that."

Fuck. Even she wasn't sure exactly how it went down. Everything had all happened so fast. The syringe coming at her. The weight of the lamp in her hand. The blood. So much blood.

In the days and weeks after that night, she had been convinced that the incident had all been a terrible accident. A shock-induced nightmare that warped her memory. She wasn't a killer. She had been raised to value and respect life. It was up to God to punish those who did wrong as he saw fit, not her.

But as time went by, and that moment replayed itself over and over in her mind, a deep-seated conviction had taken root that if she were to relive the scenario, the result would have been the same. Yes, she was sorry she took a life, but in no way did she regret ridding the earth of someone so manipulative and evil.

A warm hand settling on her knee made her jerk to attention. Ripley knelt before her, gazing at her with those deep blue eyes that made her heart race and an ache bloom deep inside.

Although her mind was determined to ignore her desire and sent signals to her nerves to move away from his touch, her leg remained in his hold, enjoying the slight contact. Apparently nothing over the last several hours was going to discourage her body from craving his touch. Traitor.

"Alisia," he murmured, low and husky. "Please."

The soothing timbre of his voice combined with the chill in the air ratcheted up the shivers coursing through her. She clenched her teeth to keep them from chattering, as a snarl curled her lip with a surge of frustration.

So he'd listen. And then what? What made him possibly think he could ever understand what she went through? As if he ever had a moment of strife. He was always going on about how great his childhood was, how his parents supported and loved him. Yes, he had seen some truly terrible things since they formed the team, but to Ripley, those horrors were part of the job.

The only horrible thing that had ever happened to him was being attacked by a bear, and that event triggered his powers. Even in defeat he ended up ahead.

He lifted his other hand to brush the hair out of her eyes. "You're freezing and I'm soaked. How about I load your bike into the back of my truck, we'll grab some dinner and you can tell me the whole story. I want to help you, Alisia."

"Why?" She sniffed. "I just told you I'm a murderer."

"Because I've known you for years. I think there is more to your story. You're not a murderer."

"You know shit about me."

He pressed his finger to her lips. The pad stroked lightly over her skin. "Let's get dry and fed. I know you're hungry. I can smell you have low blood sugar."

She slapped his hand away. "I hate when you say things like that to me, about how I smell."

A smile flirted with his lips. "I can't help it. If you won't talk to me, I have to gather information in other ways. Besides, I love how you smell. You smell delicious."

Air lodged in her throat at the sensual look that stole over his face. His eyelids lowered, sheltering the swirling blue depths of his eyes. Despite the cold, a flush stole over his cheeks and his tongue swept over his full lower lip. His nostrils flared slightly.

Oh God. She shuddered again. Could he smell her arousal, her need, the fear she felt of not being able to resist him?

His rough fingertips trailed down her cheek and neck to linger on her frantic pulse. Suddenly, he sucked in a sharp breath and stood.

His hand trembled as he held it out. "Please, come with me."

Alisia stared at his giant, callused hand for several long minutes as she dug her fingers into her crossed arms. His big hand looked so strong, so capable. The temptation to say fuck it all and let Ripley take control coated her tongue like spoiled ginger.

As she had begun to form her plan of action, it had become ridiculously obvious that it would be near impossible to clear her name on her own. Somehow, some way she was going to need assistance. And now Ripley was there, offering just that.

Dear Lord, she was tired. Tired of running. Tired of everything. Dare she trust him? Dare she give in to the desperate need to say yes?

No more debating, Alisia. Get off your ass and act.

She slid her palm along his, setting off another round of shivers, and allowed him to pull her to a stand.

This wasn't giving in to his wishes, she tried to placate the strong, independent woman part of her brain. This decision was of her own free will. If he went back on his word, she would run, simple as that.

Ripley released a huge sigh and squeezed her hand before he let her go. "Go on and I'll follow with the bike."

She nodded and hugged her arms tighter. God, why couldn't she stop shaking?

The chatter of her teeth set a macabre musical sound-track to their gait as she led Ripley as he wheeled her bike out of the restroom and into the downpour. A snort of laughter escaped her as she watched the ease with which he lifted the heavy machinery onto the flatbed of his Chevy as if it were nothing but a toy.

Once the cargo was tied down, he lifted the hem of his shirt and wiped his face, exposing his washboard abs. Her mouth went dry at the sight, which was crazy. She'd seen him naked at least a hundred times when he shifted. Well, she had seen him naked on a small monitor, so his potency was diminished, but seeing those muscles in the flesh... Lord have mercy.

His intense gaze found her where she stood huddled under the thin awning of the building, ogling him like a maroon.

Some men may have preened and pressed their advantage over holding her attention in such a way, but not Ripley. His gazed softened to a smolder and he held out his hand. That was all. No quip about how he caught her staring or if she liked what she saw. He simply held out his hand, and as if he were a magnet, he drew her to him one slow step at a time.

Like a gentleman, he held the passenger door open for her. As she slipped past him, she was careful to avoid brushing against all that chiseled hardness.

The inside of the cab immediately turned into a sauna as steam covered the windows, yet she continued to shiver even when Ripley turned up the heat and aimed all the registers in her direction.

Seconds later, he merged onto the interstate. The next exit was four miles away and with it, the turnaround back to headquarters.

They remained silent with nothing but the scrape of the windshield wipers and whirl of the heater making conversation. She was dying to ask him his intentions. Was he going to give her up to Max or keep his word? Did she want to hear his plans of betrayal from his lips, or experience the disappointment that she put her faith in the wrong man as it happened?

With each second, the exit drew closer and closer. Her chest tightened as her heart pounded. Was he going to slow down? She held her breath. Was that *click-click* the sound of his turn signal?

They approached the exit—which flew by without a pause. Within seconds, the green sign was nothing but a streak in her window.

She practically melted against the vinyl interior as relief unhinged the stress in her limbs and they continued to travel north, farther away from headquarters. Holy crap. The beast was keeping his word.

For now.

Two more exits passed before Ripley was the one to break the silence. "You did know that you were heading *toward* the church, right?"

She peered at him from the corner of her eye. Ah. Here it was. The question and answer portion of the program.

"Yes," she drew the word out slowly. "That was the idea."

"Oh," he replied in surprise. He tapped his fingers on the steering wheel and she held her breath, waiting for the rest of his response. But he was the one to surprise her by changing topics. "What were you doing in that bar?"

She sighed and shifted in her seat. That was a much

easier situation to explain. "I needed seed money."

He glanced at her in alarm. "You were hustling?"

"Of course. It wasn't like I could use a cash machine." Hell, Addison would have been on her the second the plastic card even approached the machine, not that Ripley would have been much further behind.

Hustling was one of the many skills she had learned on the streets. As much as it burned her to admit it, there was a lot she learned on the streets that had saved her life more times than anything she had ever learned in a classroom. It wasn't that she enjoyed hustling, but she was all too aware of what happened if you didn't take advantage of every opportunity.

When it came to her survival, nothing was off the table. Still, she didn't need Ripley's disapproving frown to add to her regret of having to revert to her old ways. "I haven't had to do that for a long time."

"You looked like you were doing pretty well. Man, if I'd known you could hustle, we could have used those skills to get Chase to do all sorts of things."

She snorted. "I didn't think you noticed much about me."

"I noticed. I notice everything about you."

She refused to respond to the husky rasp in his voice and look directly at him. The heat in his glances always made her temperature soar and reminded her of the illicit things she wanted to do to him. What she still wanted to do to him. Oh, they were going to burn the house down.

Stop it. She opened her jacket and pulled the damp cotton of her T-shirt away from her overheated skin. *Keep your mind on the mission, Caldwell.*

A familiar red and white sign appeared in the distance,

setting her stomach to rumble. Food. Good. Hunger was always a good distraction.

Without saying a word, Ripley pulled off the highway and into the drive-thru. When she was growing up on the compound, there had been no such thing as fast food. Gooey cheeseburgers and crispy fries were some of the few joys she had discovered after she ran away, but was only able to enjoy on a rare occasion. The fact that he knew this was her favorite told her how much he paid attention to her.

"Double cheeseburger, no onions, fries, and a root beer. Right?" he asked her.

Okay. He paid *really* close attention to her.

After ordering enough food for ten people, he parked the truck in a faraway corner of the parking lot. Alisia took her time munching on one French fry at a time, chewing each potato wedge fifty times before swallowing.

Yes, she was stalling. Ripley was only going to wait so long before he'd demand answers. And once he heard her story, he'd lose what little respect he still had for her and probably wish he'd taken the exit back to the mountain.

The odd thing was she could handle it if he lost his desire for her. Lust was a drug that usually led to disgrace and embarrassment once the craving was fed. Sex didn't stand by you when monsters pounded on your door and you needed a shoulder to cry on.

She hated to admit that while she longed for his compassion, it was his respect that meant the most to her. If by the end of the day the light in his eyes did turn cold, she would have no choice but to mark him in the adversary column.

Finally, her last fry was consumed and the straw in her soda gurgled nothing but air. Her heart rate tripled when he turned in his seat to rest his back against the door. White flakes fell from her cup as she scrapped at the wax with her thumbnail. She could start chewing on the plastic, but that was only putting off the inevitable.

The sordid tale of how Gretchen Lowell had become Alisia Caldwell was a story she had shared only once. The circumstances had been just as awkward, but explaining her past to Ripley was much different than when she had done so with Jameson. Her friend had crawled through hell herself and understood that sometimes choices were made from necessity, no matter how abhorrent they were. Ripley wasn't as perfect as he might believe. He took advantage of every opportunity available, but there were some things even he would find objectionable.

Unable to bear the silence, she opened her mouth and her throat closed up. The elephant in the room sat on her chest, forbidding her to acknowledge its existence. She closed her eyes to fight against the rising tide of panic. Breathe, breathe, breathe.

The air exploded out her lungs and escaped her lips with a surprised gasp when he laid his palm over her trembling hand. Her eyes flew open at the touch and her gaze was immediately ensnared by the sight of the back of his big, broad hand covered in crisscrossing scars from his run-ins with wildlife. She had seen this same hand rip men apart. It delivered death. But at that moment it was offering comfort that she grabbed onto like a lifeline.

"I don't know where to start," she barely managed to whisper as her fingers intertwined with his.

"Start at the beginning," he whispered back.

Tears welled in her eyes as she sucked in one breath, and then another. "In the winter of my junior year, I met a boy."

CHAPTER SEVEN

G RETCHEN'S FINGERS WORKED feverishly to remove the band from her heavy braid. Her secret midnight journey from her house to the farthest corner of the church's property had taken longer than expected and Sam was going to be there any minute.

The elastic snapped between her fingernails and the thick locks spilled free. Braids were for children and the way she felt about Sam was in no way childish.

She might have grown up under the sheltering umbrella of her father's church, but she wasn't completely naïve. She knew about sex, although most of her education had come from watching the farm animals mate. Then there were the girls at the youth center where she volunteered who gossiped on end about the boys they had or wanted to sleep with. Boy, some of the scenarios they mentioned would make a porn star blush. Or so she imagined.

In her father's teachings, it was firmly impressed upon Gretchen that intercourse was only between a husband and his wife and a way to honor God's blessing of the union while propagating the congregation. Yep. Propagating. Those lessons made an act that should be the deepest expression of love sound as exciting as a jog up a hillside.

Not so according to the girls at the center. They made sex sound wicked and lusty. And as for them being in love, heck, even being in like was optional.

Gretchen knew that the truth had to lie somewhere in the middle. The feelings she had for Sam were in no way lewd or tawdry. And when two people who loved each other as they did came together physically, no way could their passion be described as bland. In her heart she knew that sex between her and Sam was going to be stars and fireworks. Once they were married, of course.

She smoothed the ends of her hair over her shoulders then fiddled with the top button of her blouse before releasing the catch, exposing a sliver of skin and her gold cross. She refused to compete with the low-cut shirts and up-to-there skirts the other girls wore, and Sam didn't seem to want her to, but she did want to look her best for him.

A nervous giggle bubbled from her lips. Dear Lord above, what was she doing? If her father found out she was hiding in the woods at night waiting for a boy, he would have her on her knees in prayer until the grain in the wooden floor was permanently imprinted on her skin.

Even now she couldn't believe what she had done. She lied to her father. Shock and disbelief made her sober with a hard swallow over having actually lied to her father for the first time.

He thought she was at the youth center helping the staff prepare for Easter festivities, which wasn't entirely untrue. She had been there. Just four hours earlier.

Lying was wrong. And she knew she would have to atone for her sins later, but she needed more than the few stolen moments she and Sam managed between her tutoring appointments and his basketball practices. Her entire life was about pleasing others: her parents, God, her teachers, the congregation. Sam was the one thing in her life that belonged solely to her. Her most treasured secret.

It wasn't that she was ashamed to be seen with a boy whose mother struggled with drug addiction and whose father was a convicted murderer. Sam was the gentlest, sweetest soul she knew. The fact that he rose above such adversity to try to stay in school and go to college was a testament to his strength and courage. However, her father would not see things the way she did. For all his preaching about reaching out to the meek and humble, he would never approve of her relationship with someone of such…colorful parentage. Not to mention, Sam wasn't even from their congregation!

Although Sam did not attend church three times a week, okay, maybe even at all, he was spiritual and lived with God in his heart. That was enough for her.

The tinny rumble of a Honda motorbike weaving through the woods reached her ears. A huge grin stretched her lips as little zaps of electricity zipped over her skin. The first time she rode behind him, she was so nervous she had almost puked all over his Doc Martens.

Sam had thought he was being so cute, daring the little church girl to ride with him around the block. He never expected she'd take the bait and agree.

She hadn't believed she said yes either, until he handed her his banged-up helmet and gestured for her to hop on. The dents in the hard-plastic shell provided no confidence in his ability to keep her safe, but she hiked up her long skirt, exposing a scandalous amount of thigh, and settled onto the seat. The moment she wrapped her arms around his lean waist, every thought about crashing and burning across the blacktop disappeared as the world as she knew it changed forever.

It was the closest she had ever been to a boy physically.

She didn't realize that they were so different. His lightly muscled stomach was firm under her clasped hands, his hips were lean between her thighs. The bike vibrated against her mound, sending lust racing in her veins as quickly as they tore down the street. It was so sinful, so decadent.

And she'd never been so terrified in her life.

Who knew that being so close to another person could feel so incredible? Laughter and tears pricked her eyes as a million new sensations bombarded her seventeen-year-old mind and body. The sensation was an exhilaration she had only experienced before in church, and it rocked her sense of self to experience it while clutching on for dear life to a fallen angel from the wrong side of the church fence.

Many months and several bike rides later and the sound of the Honda still sent goose bumps along her arms and a tingle straight to her secret girly spot. Behind her white cotton bra, her breasts grew heavy and sweat broke out along her hairline.

As the light from the headlamp bounced through the trees along the path toward her, she wiped her damp palms against the sides of her skirt. "Dear Lord, please grant me strength to withstand temptation. Please grant me the wisdom to express my love without giving up my virginity."

Sam cut the engine as soon as he entered the clearing and rolled the bike closer. "Are you sure no one can hear us out here?"

She nodded. "My dad and the deacons are at the church arranging Easter services. There's always a spike in attendance during a holiday, so they like to make a good show."

He chuckled and swung his long leg over the bike. After removing his helmet, he shook his head, his thick dark hair fell to his shoulders like a satin cloak.

Sam had the sullen teenager look down to perfection. He was a master at sitting still, appearing completely unimpressed with his surroundings for hours. But not with her. When Sam looked at her, the tightness around his lips softened and his brown eyes glowed with an amber light as he gave her the slightest smile. A smile he reserved only for her, which made her love him all the more.

She shivered with a mixture of nerves and excitement as he strode toward her. Technically this was their first date, since they usually spent their time at the community center. Because of the secrecy of their relationship, she couldn't rely on the traditional rules of courtship. She didn't have the luxury of a movie or being at a restaurant full of other people to take the focus off their being alone. The last thing she wanted was to come off as an inexperienced little girl.

"You look like an angel standing here in the moonlight." He brushed his fingers through the length of her hair.

She opened her mouth to speak but nothing came out. The light in his eyes hypnotized her as his head grew closer and closer until his lips settled against hers, firm yet soft. Oh, now this was heaven.

Gretchen melted against him, as pliant and sweet as warm taffy. He pulled her flush to his body, his tongue breaking through her lips to taste her as no man had done before. His fingers gripped her hips, holding her still, igniting her soul. This was the way a man kissed a woman. His woman.

Was she ready to be a woman? The ache between her thighs said "Yes!" But in the eyes of the Lord, this was wrong. So, so wrong.

"Sam," she gasped. "Please, stop." She clutched his

wrists and pulled. Her vision swam and it was difficult to hear over the pounding of her heart. "I—you. Wait. I can't think."

She laid her cheek against the downy flannel of his jacket. Under her ear, his heart beat strong and fast, and she smiled, relieved at not being the only one affected.

"Sam, I've broken so many rules for you already, but I can't break that one, not even for you. If you keep kissing me, you're going to think I'm a tease, and I don't want that."

He stroked his palm up and down her back. "I don't think you're a tease, Gretchen. But you're so pretty. All I want to do is kiss you. Do I want more? Hell yeah, but I'm not gonna to talk you into doing anything you don't want to." He released her with a sigh and wiry grin. "That's why I'm going to think about you later when I'm jacking off."

"Sam!" She pushed him away. Her face flamed so hot her cheeks stung. "Don't say things like that. That's just, it's just—gross. And it's a sin."

He laughed and tugged at the ends of her cardigan sweater. "It is a sin, because you won't be there with me."

"Stop it." She slapped at his hands.

"Come on. Don't you ever think of me that way? When you're alone in your room. Do you touch your pussy and think of me inside you?"

"Sam!" His words shocked her at the same time every-thing female pulsed and clenched with want. She would never touch, or even think about touching herself that way.

Darn it. Now that was all she could imagine. The image of Sam, alone, in his bed, naked and with his hard—thing—in his hand and her name on his lips.

No, no, *no*. That was so bad. "If you're just going to be crude then I'm going home."

She pivoted on her Keds and stomped back to the trail with Sam's laughter following. She made it all of three steps before he wrapped his arms around her middle and dragged her back into the curve of his body.

"Gretchen, stop. Hold up." He hunched over to press his cheek to hers. "I like watching you get all flustered. You're so cute when you turn red."

"You're not funny." She pouted, feeling the heat in her cheeks deepen.

The creep laughed again, hugging her tighter. "I joke because I have to. Damn, Gretchen, I want you so bad that I think I'll explode. But I mean it when I said I won't pressure you. The first time we have sex, your last name will be Connor."

The world stilled. Even the crickets stopped their chirping. Her shoes felt as if they had turned into cement as she stumbled trying to turn around to see his face. He didn't mean... "What?"

He touched their foreheads together. "I mean it. When we're done with school, I'm going to marry you."

"Why?" she asked in confusion.

"What do you mean, why?" he asked with a chuckle.

"Why me?" Not that she wasn't thrilled that Sam wanted to marry her, but she knew that how she was raised and living on the compound made her...different. She grabbed a lock of her hair and played with the ends. "There are other girls out there. Worldly girls that know so much more than I do. I'm just a preacher's daughter who needs permission to walk out the door."

He trailed his finger over her cheek, knocking aside her hair and exposing all of her face to his soft gaze. "You are so much more. You believe in me, make me want to be a better person. And you remind me about the important things in life. Like love."

Butterflies took flight in her tummy. Were her dreams coming true? "Really?"

"Yes." He laughed and brushed a quick kiss across her lips.

"I love you, Sam," she exclaimed, giddy with love. "And I want to be your wife."

He picked her up and swung her around. "You will be, after I ask you properly. I want to surprise you and make it special, like you deserve."

He had no idea, did he? She swallowed down the tears of joy his simple words provoked. He had absolutely no clue that he had made this the happiest moment in her life. What more could he possibly do to make her feel more special than she did right then?

"You already have, Sam."

Even in the moonlight, she could see his cheeks had turned a ruddy pink. "Come here. I did bring you a surprise." He tugged her toward the bike, where he rifled through his backpack. "You keep talking about how much you'd love to see Paris someday, so I brought Paris to you. I have some crackers, and that weird cheese, and look, a bottle of not so fancy wine."

"You brought me a picnic?" Gretchen peered into the bag, stunned that this man who wouldn't know a baguette from a bidet went out of his way just to make her smile. "Oh, Sam, I love it. Where did you get all of this?"

"Uh, that would be a store," he joked.

She pinched his arm. "Ha ha. I mean you're saving money for school. You didn't need to spend money on me. And where did you get the wine?"

"Angel, you're never any trouble. And I bought the wine."

"How did you buy it?"

"My cousin Mike made me a fake ID."

"Your cousin Mike who's been to jail, and smokes pot, and tries to get you to do stupid stuff?"

"Yeah."

A sinking feeling settled in her stomach at the ease with which he answered. "Why do you need a fake ID?"

"So I can buy you wine?"

"Sam," she admonished and crossed her arms. "I'm serious."

He shrugged and smoothed his hair behind his ear. "I don't know. No one will hire me to play in their band because I'm underage. I might have a chance if people think I'm older, then I can earn extra money. It's no big deal."

"It *is* a big deal. Sam, you can't go around breaking the law because it suits you. That's wrong."

"Gretchen, calm down. I'm not going to do anything illegal."

"Having a fake ID and buying alcohol when underage *is* illegal."

He rolled his eyes. "Okay, then I won't do anything else illegal. Jesus, Gretchen, give me a little credit here. It's not like I'm dealing drugs or stealing. It's just a piece of plastic to get me into the clubs." He tried to smooth away her frown with his thumb. "Trust me."

Trust him. Oh, she was trying. But the whole situation was so morally wrong, how could she allow such a thing to continue?

"It doesn't feel right. I don't want you to get into trouble."

"I won't." He settled her arms around his neck. "Stop worrying. Look, forget the wine. This is our night and I don't want you upset about stupid shit, uh, stuff. I just want to lay you out on a blanket, feed you grapes, and feel you next to me."

She allowed him to hug her closer. "I can't help but worry. You've had so many bad things happen in your life, I don't want it to be worse."

"How can anything bad happen when you're by my side?" He nipped at her lower lip.

The sharp pain made her gasp with unexpected arousal. She never knew that love could be so all consuming, so intense that she would lose the ability to think the moment he touched her. His skin was so warm, his mouth so hot, she plastered herself to his body, afraid to lose an ounce of his heat. She took a deep breath through her nose, inhaling his Lava soap and shaving cream scent. Her fingers tangled into his hair. The long strands covered her hands like a luxurious coat. She was so lost in his kiss that it wasn't until she tasted salty water on her lips that she was able to pull away.

"What the heck?" she exclaimed and looked up at the dark sky. While they had been floating in hormonal euphoria, storm clouds had rolled in, obscuring the full moon, and unzipped their cargo upon the earth.

Rain rolled down her neck and soaked her clothes at the shoulders. "Oh no, our picnic," she moaned.

"Let's get under the trees." Sam led with his bike while she jumped puddles chasing after him.

They took shelter under a copse of pine trees with Gretchen sharing Sam's flannel jacket, their arms wrapped around each other.

"I'm so sad. I was having such a lovely time."

His chuckle rumbled under her ear. "You're the only person I know who uses the word 'lovely.'" Water collected on the needles to fall on them in big drops. "I guess I should head home."

"Isn't riding your bike in the rain and darkness dangerous?"

"Yeah, but staying out in this weather is just as crazy."

Sam was right, but she didn't want this magical time to end so soon. "I have an idea. Follow me."

She took his hand and led him along the darkened path. On the fringes of the compound sat several outbuildings that stored extra supplies for all aspects of the church community. From furniture and building supplies, to groceries and almanacs, the compound strived to be self-sufficient and provide as much for the congregation as possible.

They dashed under the eaves of the nearest white-washed shed. The door was locked and the windows were too tiny to crawl through. Sam knelt and withdrew a metal pick from the inner pocket of his jacket.

"Sam, what are you doing?"

"Picking the lock. You ask a lot of obvious questions."

"I'm sorry, I normally don't see people breaking the law." She shivered, secretly hoping he would be successful so they could at least get in a drier environment.

The door swung open on silent, oiled hinges. "And you're welcome."

It was surprisingly warm inside as she stepped through the door and fumbled for the light switch. A plume of noxious fumes poured out of the opening, smelling like a thousand cats drank gallons of drain cleaner then relieved themselves wherever they wished.

"Oh my goodness." She held a hand over her nose, fighting the urge to retch. "What is that stench?"

"Holy shit," Sam exclaimed behind her. "Gretchen, who's cooking meth?"

"What?"

Amongst the stacks of boxes were a few hard-backed chairs and a series of long plastic worktables. An impromptu kitchenette had been built in the corner, consisting of a wooden shelf and hot plate. The cracked utility sink was stained a rusty orange, and more orange saturated the coffee filters filling the trash bin under the table. Warehouse store-sized boxes of antifreeze and cat litter were stacked as high as the ceiling, along with more boxes of mason jars she recognized from the church's preserve-making parties.

Sam batted her hand as she reached for a baggie. "Don't touch that."

"I don't understand. What is this?"

"Either your father, or someone he knows, is making meth. Drugs. Narcotics," he added when she continued to look at him in confusion.

She knew the meaning of each individual word, yet as he strung them together in one sentence, all comprehension was lost. "Why? How? I mean—why?"

"Money, probably. What's in these boxes?" He gestured to a row of boxes with the name of a Christian communion supplier printed on the side. Reaching into the box, he pulled out a smaller package. "Hey, aren't these those Jesus crackers?"

"Eucharist wafers." She rolled her eyes. "This makes no sense. Why are Eucharist wafers and drugs being stored together?"

"Oh," Sam breathed, his eyes darting around as his

brain puzzled out the question.

He raced around the expansive shed, opening boxes and humming in consternation after each inspection. With each grunt, she pulled her damp sweater tighter around her body as the shadows in the room stretched out with long fingers to wrap around her chest, restricting her breathing. An evil presence pricked her skin and it made her want to run for safety.

"Sam, I want to leave." As he continued to open boxes she shouted, "I want to leave now."

"At what part of the services do you eat these wafers?" he asked, completely absorbed in his investigation.

"Near the beginning. Right after the opening prayer." She tugged at his jacket. "Please, let's go."

"And how do you feel during the rest of the service?"

"I feel fine, now let's go."

He latched onto her forearms. "I mean it, Gretchen. How do you feel during the rest of the service? Happy, sad, euphoric?"

"I-I—it's indescribable. It's as if God is in the room with me and anything is possible."

"What about everybody else? Do they react the same, like they're rising out of their bodies? Or like you can see every individual molecule of air?"

"Some people say that God physically touches them, that they can actually see his light shine down upon them. We are truly blessed."

He snorted, but not with laughter. "No, you're truly high. Baby, you're being drugged."

Again, Sam was speaking English, yet she didn't understand. "What?"

"See, this looks like special K. Some of my cousin's

friends take it. And look at all of these boxes and boxes of those cracker things. All of the packages on this side of the room are intact. All of these ones over here have been opened and resealed. You are being drugged."

She shook her head before he finished his sentence. "No. I don't believe it. Why would someone want to drug the congregation?"

"It's like I said, money. A person under the influence is more susceptible to suggestions. They'd be more willing to part with their money, maybe give more donations. Plus, when you get them addicted, they have to come back for more. Yeah, I bet that's so it. All those people get home from an amazing day at church, have their roast chicken dinner, and then—wham!—they hit this funk. Their lives aren't as shiny happy as it was when they were swaying with their peeps and praising Jesus. So they have to go back. They need that fix. And your dad is more than willing to give it to them."

The idea was so horrible, so preposterous, she couldn't fathom the reality even as it was staring her in the face. "That's crazy. Maybe, maybe my father doesn't know. Maybe it's someone else."

"I hope it's your dad."

"What?" she screeched.

"My dad's a convicted felon, your dad's a drug dealer. It kind of balances out."

"Sam." She slapped at his arm. "This isn't a joke. This is—this is apocalyptically bad. People can get hurt, or die. Oh my gosh," she gasped, slapping both hands over her mouth.

People had been dying. Lately, it seemed as if there was a funeral at least once a month with someone passing away from a heart attack or stroke at much too young of an age. Could those deaths have been facilitated by the drugs they unknowingly ingested?

Bile rose up her throat. No. It wasn't possible. It was inconceivable that her father had a hand in such a nefarious plot. He was a servant of God, not a peddler of sin and vice.

"Sam, I want to go. I don't feel well." She doubled over as her stomach cramped.

He hugged her around the shoulders. "I agree."

Sam led her to the door. As he reached for the doorknob, the sound of a vehicle braking in the gravel outside shrieked over the patter of rain on the tin roof like a vulture squawking over prey. He snatched her back and dragged her between a row of boxes in the farthest corner of the outbuilding. Pushing her into the darkest corner, he stood between her and whomever was at the door.

"I don't know who left the light on, but it wasn't me," a voice Gretchen recognized as Deacon Ryan grumbled as he opened the door. "Goddamn, it's wet out. I hate rain."

"Language, please," Gretchen's father, Reverend Lowell, admonished. The footsteps of who knew how many others plodded onto the cement floor. "Let's make this quick. I still have a sermon—" he suddenly broke off.

Gretchen dug her fingers into Sam's wet jacket and pressed her face into his back. Too many seconds passed without anyone saying a word. Her ears strained over the escalating pounding of her heart for any little sound. She bit her lip and tried to keep her breathing slow and shallow as the absolute silence stretched on and on.

"Sir, we have mice issues," Deacon Winston announced from two feet away from their position.

She peeked over Sam's shoulder and gasped at the sight

of Deacon Winston standing before them aiming an ugly-looking black gun at Sam's chest. He gestured with his free hand for them to step forward.

"Gretchen," her father exclaimed after they inched into the light. "What is the meaning of this? Explain yourself."

The ridiculousness of the question slapped her in the face. "Explain myself? Why don't you explain yourself? You are hurting people. Why?"

Her father shook his head. "You are a silly little girl who knows nothing." He turned his attention to Sam. His gaze turned frigid as the corners of his mouth turned so far down, they practically touched his jaw. "Who are you?"

"I'm Gretchen's boyfriend," Sam replied in a low, hostile tone she never heard from him before.

"Gretchen doesn't have boyfriends. Especially those as unworthy as you." He heaved a deep sigh as he pinched the bridge of his nose. "Stupid, stupid girl! I'll call the house and have it prepared for Gretchen. Arnold, take care of this."

Have the house prepared for *what*?

"Wait! Father, what are you talking about?" she yelled at his back as he marched out the door without a backward glance.

Deacon Winston grabbed her arm as she moved to run after her father. His fingers dug painfully into her skin. "Ow!"

"Let her go!" Sam reached out, then pulled back when Deacon Winston swung the gun in his direction. "Don't hurt her."

"I can do whatever I want to her." He dragged her to his front, his arm a steel band across her torso. "She belongs to me."

His possessive tone shot ice through her veins. "I do

not."

"Oh yes, you do," he breathed hotly against her cheek. "Your father has promised you to me. On the day you turn eighteen, you will be presented to me to do with as I please. And I will please a lot." He cupped her breast in his palm, pinching her nipple through her sweater.

"Get your fucking hands off her!" Sam growled.

The next few minutes of her life passed as quickly as a single heartbeat, yet moved as slowly as a movie being watched frame by frame by frame.

Sam lowered his head and charged. His long hair obscured most of his face, except for the feral topaz glow of his eyes. One shot, then a second, and a third burst from the barrel of the gun. Spent casings and gun powder discharge seared her skin as she jumped in Winston's grasp. Sam's shoulders jerked, his knees buckling as he crumbled to the cement floor.

His name ripped from her soul, shredding her vocal chords, but she couldn't hear for the ringing of gunfire in her ears.

"No! No, no, no, no! *SAM!*"

All of her muscles turned to jelly, allowing her to slip from under Winston's grip. She stumbled and fell beside Sam. Her hands flailed with no clue as to what to do. Color leeched from her vision, turning the world into blacks and grays, except for the sinister river of crimson pooling on the floor.

Fear clouded Sam's eyes. His mouth worked up and down without sound.

Blood covered her hands and smeared his pale skin as she gripped his face. "Don't leave. Please. God."

A hiss eased from his lips. His brow relaxed as emptiness filled his gaze. Blank. Nothing.

Shock robbed her sense of touch as she collapsed over him, beating on his chest, willing him to respond. Her tear-soaked screams echoed off the metal ceiling and vibrated over every surface with her pain. This was not happening. This. Was. Not. Happening.

"Will you shut up!" Winston hauled her up by her hair and slapped her across both cheeks.

Her wailing died to a whimper, but her gaze remained on Sam's unnaturally still body. Even when Winston tossed her over his shoulder, her gaze stayed locked on Sam's vacant stare.

"Clean up this mess," he ordered Ryan.

She was dumped onto the back seat of a sedan, where she instantly scurried to peer out the window, her nose pressed to the glass. The outbuilding door slammed shut, but her gaze remained fixed as if she could see through the wood.

Her hearing returned enough so that the wounded mewling of a tortured animal filled her ears. It would be weeks later when she realized the agonizing cries had come from her.

The cold glass stung her enflamed cheeks, her tears blended with the condensation, yet she could not look away even as the car turned the corner and entered the residential area.

One hundred families made their homes on church property. One hundred cookie-cutter ranch-style houses, all in shades of cream and tan, with lush green lawns lining deserted sidewalks. The weather had driven all sane people indoors to their comfy wall-to-wall carpet and gas-heated homes. Did anyone hear the gunshots? Did anyone hear her screams? Did anyone know that a beautiful, innocent life had been viciously ended? Would they even care?

They passed the massive stone and glass structure of the church, a hulking black mass in the dark without a single warm light to welcome parishioners. It was as if God refused to acknowledge the people who would blindly follow a madman.

She had. She had believed that her father was a good, honest, compassionate man, who loved his followers and took pride in showing them the way to enlightenment. Nothing and no one could have convinced her any differently.

That blind devotion and naïveté killed Sam. Why was he the one to be punished for her sins?

Numbness set in all over her body. Her teeth chattered, yet nothing registered. She floated in and out of consciousness as someone lifted her out of the car and carried her up the stairs into her childhood home to deposit her on a bed. She curled into a ball, pulling her knees as deep into her chest as possible, wishing to disappear into nothingness.

"You look like a walking nightmare."

Her eyes flew open at the sound of the sharp, biting voice spoken in her ear.

Confusion continued to slow her thinking as Jillian, her stepmother, stood at her bedside with her arms crossed and a frown drawing down her red lipstick-stained mouth. Creamy white pearls hung around her slim neck, standing out against the navy-blue silk dress that fell to her knees. For it being so late in the evening, her stepmother appeared ready for a night out with not a hair out of place from her platinum blonde French twist. She was so clean and pressed that the dirt and sweat covering Gretchen's body made her itch from being exposed to such purity.

Jillian had been a good, if strict, mother to Gretchen. She led by example and held her position in the church with a regality reserved for a queen with her subjects. She was the type of wife and mother that Gretchen strived to become. To see her stepmother brimming with such hostility at the darkest moment in her life was beyond a shock.

"A boy, Gretchen?" Jillian snapped. "All this trouble for a boy? Did you fuck him?"

The accusation lashed Gretchen like a razorblade. Stunned by the vulgarity, she could do nothing more than shake her head and whisper, "No."

"You better not have. You're no good to me unless you're a virgin," she huffed.

A universe of grief pressed down on her as yet another angelic mask fell off a person she trusted.

"You know," Gretchen forced from her ruined vocal chords. "You know about the drugs."

"Of course I do. Whose idea do you think it was in the first place?" The calculation in her eyes reminded Gretchen of Lady Tremaine from *Cinderella* as she pursed her lips in consideration. "Don't think that I'm going to let you and your stupid teenage curiosity ruin all of my hard work. I got rid of your mother and I can do the same to you. I would have already if not for Winston. He wants you as payment, although I have no idea why he'd want someone as plain as you." Jillian flicked a dismissive hand and turned on her heel.

Gretchen slumped against the wall. "My mother had leukemia."

"That's what it looked like in the end. Your father wouldn't divorce her and I couldn't be his mistress forever.

But, as they say, patience is a virtue, and I just had to wait for the poison to take hold. Your father is much better off."

Gretchen pressed a trembling hand to her aching heart. Her eyes burned, unable to produce any more tears. No way could she survive one more infliction of betrayal.

Why? Why was this evil allowed to touch her family? Why did God forsake her mother and Sam? All they had done was love unconditionally and they were ripped from the earth, while that creature—she glared at Jillian flitting around the room—was allowed to live.

Gretchen lifted her heavy eyelids and watched Jillian prepare a syringe. More drugs? Poison? Was Jillian going to kill her too?

The notion that she was about to die loosened the constraint on her soul.

Oh yes. Please kill me. End the pain of having to face a day without those I love.

Who would mourn her if she died? That whisper of a thought pierced through the veil of her agony. As it stood, it appeared that Jillian, and her father, and Winston would carry on as if nothing disrupted their perfect world.

Mary Beth might mourn her. They were as close as any two sisters could be. But if Gretchen died, her sister would be left defenseless. No one would be around to avenge Sam and her mother. If she gave in, evil would win.

But if she lived—oh, that would seriously mess with Jillian's perfect existence. If loving Sam had taught her anything, it was to never let anyone get the best of you. She would not let him down now.

The muscles in her legs and arms jerked out of concert as she struggled to her feet. An armor of detachment wrapped around her, separating her mind from her body.

Jillian did a double take and frowned when Gretchen stood. "Don't bother getting up. This will help you rest, and when you wake up, this will all be a forgotten memory."

"No." The word floated in the air as eerie as a wraith.

"Don't be stupid, Gretchen. Either I drug you into submission, or you die."

Her head lowered in challenge. "Then I guess you'll have to kill me," she rasped.

Jillian's face pinched as if she was dealing with an annoying fly and reached out for her arm. Gretchen spun away as if she were accepting a bounce pass to head down court, a move she practiced thousands of times during practice. She pivoted again when Jillian reached out, her fingers curled into pink-tipped claws. Gretchen slapped at the grasping hands, knocking the syringe away, and continued to attack, striking out with flailing limbs. Silk tore, hair was pulled as the women grappled.

With her throat damaged from her earlier screaming, Gretchen's breath burst out in animalistic grunts. Her lips pulled back in a snarl as Jillian grabbed her by the hair at her nape. In response, Gretchen reached out, her fingertips brushing the lamp on the nightstand. Her fingers wrapped tight around the porcelain column. She struck once at the arm holding her hair, the second blow at her stepmother's head. The third broke the lamp, the pieces falling to the floor faster than Jillian's body.

The sudden silence snapped Gretchen from her trance. She stared in horror at the growing pool of blood on the carpet. The canvas of the lamp shade soaked up more blood as if it were tissue paper.

Her hands flew to her mouth in shock. She had committed murder, a mortal sin.

She glanced around the room, frantic as to what to do. Someone must have heard the commotion—she need to escape. Now.

On her dresser, a photo that had been taken a few days before snagged her attention. She stood in the sunshine with her Sunday school class. Smiling, clean, pure. She was a girl who had the world at her feet. Her gaze rose to the mirror and her mouth fell open at her reflection.

Green eyes rimmed with puffy red skin peered out from between twisted strands of wet hair, tipped red with blood. More blood of the innocent and guilty covered her rumpled, torn clothes. Bruises and scratches marred her face.

She looked back at the photo, and her features hardened into an expressionless mask as the light inside her flared out. Reality calmed her racing heart and focused her perspective. This room belonged to a girl who had lived in a fantasy, to a girl who no longer existed.

Gretchen Lowell was dead.

CHAPTER EIGHT

A LISIA JERKED AT the touch of paper scratching against her face. She turned her head, startled to realize that it wasn't rain pounding the windshield that was obscuring her vision, but her tears.

"I've got you," Ripley whispered and continued to dab at her cheeks with the napkins from their meal. He reached under her knees with his free hand and draped her legs over his lap to cradled her in his heat, his arm strong against her back.

"It was my fault," she choked. "If we had stayed out in the rain. If I let him go home when he wanted. If we had gone to any other shed. Sam would be alive."

"Ah, honey. You can't do that to yourself. The what-if game will destroy you."

Her throat burned, and in the rearview mirror she saw her blonde hair hanging in tangled strands over her red, swollen eyes. Just like that night.

"How did you escape the compound?" he asked softly.

"I-uh—" Her mind struggled to break free from the cobwebs of her memories. "I took the money from that morning's collection deposit. Sam's bike was still in the woods. I jumped on and just drove."

"Where did you go?"

Bile rose in her throat. "Sam's backpack was still with the bike. His phone was inside, so I looked up his cousin

Mike. He was the only person I could think of that might be able to hide me. Fortunately, he knew who I was from Sam's stories, and he helped me because he liked Sam. He made me a fake ID and a disguise."

"That was lucky for you."

Lucky nothing. He told her that she owed his family a blood debt for Sam's death, and his help cost her one hundred dollars and her virginity. Although she cried the entire time, she endured the humiliation without protest. It was a small sacrifice for her part in Sam's murder and any form her punishment took, she met willingly.

She drew in a deep lungful of air, then another, wiping the ends of her coat over her cheeks as she scooted back to her side of the bench seat. No way was she going to dive into those details with him. That was enough confessing for one night.

Torn leather caught on her jeans. "What happened to the upholstery?"

"Uh, nothing." He swiped at the small tufts of foam smattering their pants.

She smoothed her hand over her face one more time and finger-combed her hair. Telling her story to Ripley was a thousand times more difficult than when she had told Jameson. Then it had been two women sharing the horrors of their past in a bond of sisterhood. With Ripley, she was ripping open wounds that had only recently scarred over, and exposing the ugliness to his judgment and criticism.

She didn't know why, of all people, his opinion mattered so much. Why she needed him to understand why she hid and took someone's identity. Since the night Sam died and she sold her soul, she lived her life not caring what others would think of her. To do so hadn't been an option, for if she had, she wouldn't have survived her most desperate moments.

Still, she craved his approval. He was the only man who looked at her as if he saw *her*, the girl she once was. He also reminded her of all that she lost, and she feared seeing the disgust in his eyes when he found out the truth.

She tensed when he settled his hand over hers. God, please don't let him say something trite to avoid sparing her feelings.

"Alisia, I'm so sorry."

Ah, crap.

"Don't be. You had nothing to do with any of it."

He squeezed her hand when she tried to pull away. "No, Alisia, I don't mean it that way... Well, of course I do, but I'm sorry that you felt like you couldn't tell us the truth. Couldn't tell me the truth."

"Oh, sure, 'cause that would have gone well. Hey guys, can I join your gang, even though I'm a murderer and a whor—thief."

"We would have understood. You didn't have to run."

She shook her head, refusing to believe him. "I killed someone."

"Hey," he barked. "Look at me."

She stubbornly kept her gaze on her dirty knees until he pinched her chin between his thumb and forefinger and forced her head up.

"I've killed. Max has killed. We understand."

"But I'm not sorry I did it," she whispered.

Felt sorrow, yes. Sorry that she did it—never. For years the overwhelming layers of guilt had crushed her spirit, but with Jameson's help she finally came to accept that she was the victim and that the events of that night were beyond her control. Her choice had been life or death and she had chosen life. Or at least survival. She wouldn't call what she did those months afterward as living.

Ripley closed his eyes and let out a long sigh. "Baby, I wouldn't be sorry either. If it was me, I wouldn't have stopped with your stepmother. I would have ripped apart your father, Winston, and anyone else involved." His slid his fingers to the back of her neck and his thumb rubbed circles under her ear. The motion melted her tension and she relaxed in her seat. "We don't want to kill, but sometimes it's the only choice. We can be sorry for doing the action, for having to make a decision, but never be sorry for choosing to live."

Biting her lip, she tucked her hair behind her ears. Her throat closed up and tears came to her overtired eyes in the hopes that maybe Ripley did understand.

"Look, it's getting dark and we've had a hell of a twenty-four hours. Why don't you sit back and I'll take us someplace safe for the night. We'll worry about tomorrow later."

Still unable to speak, she nodded. Her plans had not changed. She was going after her father. But Ripley was right, whatever role he might play in her scheme could be decided after a hot shower.

Her head fell back against the seat and her eyes drifted shut. It wouldn't be so bad letting Ripley take the lead. For now.

✧　✧　✧

RIPLEY UNCLENCHED HIS teeth and let his shoulders relax when he finally heard soft snoring from the woman in the seat beside him. He wiped the sweat from his forehead and willed his claws to remain sheathed.

Listening to Alisia tell her story tore him in a thousand directions. Jealousy, anger, grief, and sorrow prodded the animal inside him to defend its mate. Alisia had been so lost in the past that she never noticed that he channeled all that aggression into his innocent leather seats.

"Sorry, baby," he murmured and patted the dash.

He snuck a glance at Alisia and pressed his lips together with regret. How could she have thought that he wouldn't understand? Of all the people. When she helped out Addison in the command center, she had a front row seat, in high definition to the lives he ended.

When she had learned her father was after her, Ripley should've been the first person she came to, and it hurt more than he expected that she didn't trust him. He was a smart guy. He had a frickin' PhD in veterinary medicine, the kindest and most compassionate profession on the planet. Of course he would have understood.

Her days of running were over. She had him now, and her tutorial in accepting him as her mate and protector began immediately.

Step one: Gain Alisia's trust. Objective already in motion. Never again would she question who had her back.

Step two: Get the rest of the team on board, namely Max. He still believed Alisia was a threat to the team. Now that he heard the true story about the crimes against her, that meant Lowell was the real threat, Max was just going to have to trust him to take care of the situation.

Ripley couldn't contain his dubious chuckle. Max relinquish control? Yeah, that was going to be the hardest obstacle of them all.

The Chevy's headlights cut through the night like beams of butter, illuminating the small log cabin residing along the shore of Lake Baker.

Alisia continued to sleep even after he cut the engine. Her gentle snore chirped in harmony with the crickets residing in the brush. She had pulled her knees up on the seat and her face was smushed against the back window.

He slowly opened her door and caught her in his arms before she tumbled out. The moment he straightened his knees, she jerked awake, arms and legs flailing until he dropped her to the ground.

"What are you doing?" they shouted at the same time.

"We're here," he replied. "I didn't want to wake you."

"Oh." She shoved her hair off her face. "Sorry. Got a little disoriented. Where are we?"

He pulled their gear from the flat bed. "One of the cabins shared by the University of Oregon and the UW. Students come out here to study the salmon migration. The season hasn't started yet, so it's locked up, but we can still get inside."

"Is there hot water?" She followed him.

"Yep."

"Sweet."

Ripley dug a finger into the soil of a hanging flowerbed full of dried stalks and fished out a key. He opened the door with a flourish and gestured with an open palm. "My lady."

She glanced up at him through her lashes and entered, careful not to brush against him as she passed through the door. She didn't need to bother to be so cautious. Her heat reached out to caress him like a velvet glove, stirring his lust just by being within breathing distance.

"Can I turn on a light?" she asked from the darkened interior.

"Yeah, but not too many. If anyone is on the lake, they

could see it."

The flick of the switch turned on the desk lamp, exposing the sparse interior. A lumpy futon and matching chair huddled in the center. A large worktable ran the length of the entire wall with half a dozen surge protectors peeking out from underneath.

"As you can see, the kitchenette is there." Ripley pointed to the amenities. "Over there is one bedroom with the other on the opposite end. The shower is through the door in the middle."

Alisia looked around, her thumbs hooked in her back pockets. "It's pretty cozy. I take it only a few students at a time can make use of the space."

"Three, maybe four at a time." He set her pack on the couch. "Go ahead and take a shower. I'll go do a quick scout around the perimeter just to be sure no one else is around."

She nodded then ensnared him in a gaze so deep it reached out and grabbed hold of his heart. God, he could sink inside her forever. "Thank you, Ripley."

The simple words were spoken so quietly, yet the sheen in those emerald eyes and the press of her lips conveyed so much more.

"Any time. I mean that."

She nodded again and took her pack into the bathroom, shutting the door behind her. A thin wooden door. That was the only thing between him and her soon to be naked body.

His claws arched over his fingertips. Gritting his teeth, he grunted and tried to force back the change crawling through him as he stumbled out the front door.

The misty night air was bracing against his overheated skin as he strode several long-legged paces away from temptation. The woman had bared her soul to him. He refused to add to the list of betrayals she had suffered by backing her against the wall and grinding them both to orgasm. He would hold on to his honor, even if it killed him.

Fortunately, he knew of one surefire way to cool his ardor.

He pulled out his phone and hit the call button on the last of the extremely long list of missed calls on the display.

There was an answer on the first ring. "This better be good."

Ripley sighed. "That depends on your definition of good."

He told Max Alisia's story, sticking only to the pertinent details. The facts were grisly enough without interjecting Alisia's and even his own personal reactions. Max remained quiet, with an occasional thoughtful hum until Ripley fell silent.

"Does she have proof?"

The question hit him like a kick to the head. "Proof? Proof of what?"

"That Reverend Lowell is, or was, manufacturing drugs and giving them to his congregation, or proof that Deacon Winston murdered Sam Connor."

"Are you fucking kidding me? This is Alisia, whom you've lived with and worked beside for months. You know her. Of course she's telling the truth."

"I thought I knew Anthony, too."

Ripley flinched at the mention of Max's former mentor. Anthony DeMateo faked his own death so he could implement Max's father's plan to stage a military coup. With father pitted against son, Anthony was setting himself up to rule the country. *Clusterfuck* was not a strong enough word to describe the shit that had gone down and left a lot of people dead.

"Okay. I see your point. But Alisia's different."

"Uh-huh. What was she doing when you found her?"

"She, uh"—was hustling pool—"she had stopped for fuel."

"And where was she going after that?"

Well, damn. He forgot to ask. "We didn't talk much beyond why she ran. I believe she's going after Lowell."

"To confront him or kill him?"

"Does it matter? I'm going to kill the son of a bitch myself the next time I see him."

"Easy, boy. Despite what people have read, we are not judge, jury, and executioner."

"You sure about that, sledgehammer?"

Right. The man could talk about staying calm and in control all he wanted. The bloody pulp DeMateo had been turned into after Max had literally pummeled the man into the ground told the tale.

Max grunted. "Look. We've all learned our lesson. We collect evidence, give it to the proper authorities, and let them take care of the bad guys. We do not go around killing people, no matter how much we want to. Or if they deserve it. Or if they provoke it—look, let's keep the death toll to a minimum."

Ripley chose not to answer rather than make a promise he totally intended to break. "What has Addison dug up?"

"As incredible as it sounds, very little. For the most part, the compound is self-sufficient. Cell phone usage is low, land lines bring up nothing. They use an ancient version of QuickBooks to manage the church's finances, and they have that lone social media account. Lowell might as well be using quill and parchment to run his business for all we know."

There was a pause and a sound as if Max scrubbed his hand over his face. "Right. Okay. Reverend Lowell hired us to find his daughter, not to expose his extracurricular activities. If there is a paper trail, it's not electronic, which means we will need to investigate personally. If word gets to him, or his men, of what we're doing, he can make it ugly for us publicly. I'd rather not have the People's Pastor on the evening news saying that the Evolutioneers are in league with a thief and murderer."

"I am in complete agreement. That's why I have a plan."

"*You* have a plan?"

"Of course." Why did he sound so surprised? Just because Ripley had a thick neck did not mean he had a thick head. "Have Addison keep digging on Lowell, Winston, and Deacon Ryan. You continue looking the ruse of looking for Gretchen. In the meantime, Alisia and I will go search the compound. She may have an idea where any evidence may be stored and I can check out that shed. Hopefully they're still using it."

"It's a decent plan. I just have one concern. Can you keep your dick out of the mission?"

Ripley chocked on a sputter. "Seriously? Hello? Wait, there's a call on the other line. It's the kettle saying to shove it up your pot-bellied ass."

The line went quiet for several beats before Max burst out laughing. "Is that supposed to instill confidence? Ripley, I understand where you're coming from, believe me. But you cannot lose focus for one second, or one or both of you will end up dead."

Ripley rubbed at the tension in his neck. "Got it. You know, it was a whole lot funnier when you were the one with women issues."

"Take comfort in the fact that when it's Chase's turn, we can gang up on him. Are you in a secure location for the night?"

"Yeah, we're good."

"Take care. And…and bring our girl home safe."

Ripley's knees buckled a little. Thank God Max was coming around. "Will do. Thanks, Max."

He pocketed his phone and strode back to the cabin. As he turned the doorknob, Alisia's sweet scent carried over the air. Lust shot from his clenched teeth down his spine, flexing his biceps and hardening his cock. *Christ almighty, give me strength.*

Alisia stood freshly scrubbed and as ripe as a peach in the doorway to one of the bedrooms. Stretchy pants and a tank top in pale pink conformed to her every curve. The shadows of large, cinnamon-colored nipples poked through the thin cotton, making him froth at the mouth. Only her rapt attention on the phone in her hand broke through his lust.

Wait. A cell phone?

"Who are you calling?" he asked.

Her head snapped up. "Oh, you're back."

"The phone. Who are you calling?"

"I'm not calling anyone."

"Then who are you texting?"

"No one. And it's none of your business."

"Alisia." Her name came out in a frustrated growl. "We can't be an effective team if you are keeping secrets. You have to start trusting me."

"We are not a team."

"Yes, we are."

"No." She slashed her hand in the air. "No, no, no. You are not getting involved."

"Baby, I became involved the moment your father hired me."

"Do not call me 'baby.' "

"Why are you arguing with me? Geez, woman, you are being stubborn over nothing. You are in need and I can help you. I want to help you. It's what people do when they care about each other."

"I don't want you to get hurt."

He laughed at that. "Baby, I'm the baddest thing out there. Don't worry about me."

"Ripley, thinking like that will get you killed."

"I can take care of myself. And I can take care of you too. But I need you to trust me. Who were you texting?"

It better not be a man. If it was a man, oh…

He bit back a snarl and lowered his head. The two of them locked gazes in a battle of wills that was one for the ages.

She was good, he'd give her that. Barely a blink in, how long were they at it now? One, two, twenty minutes? But he had experience with the bad boys. Wolves, cougars, and other predators who were bred to wait out their prey. He was prepared to hold out forever.

The muscles in her jaw ticked before she let out a sigh. "Fine. It's a friend who would be concerned if I didn't check in."

Ah. That gave him an idea. "Would that friend be that whack-job Jameson?"

She gasped. "How do you know Jameson?"

He tapped his nose. "You knew I would follow you. That's why you gave your clothes to all those women at the shelter to throw me off your scent. Jameson is quite the guard dog."

"She can be a little intense."

"She pulled a blade out of her bra and threatened to feed me my balls if you got hurt."

A smile tugged at her lips. "I believe that. I'd do the same for her."

"Good. I'm glad."

"What?"

"Not everyone is lucky enough to have a friend who would fight to the death for you. I'm glad you have someone like that in your life. I hope you know that I will fight for you too."

Her pale eyebrows arched high over her wide green eyes that shimmered with gathering tears. "Ripley," she whispered.

His nostrils flared on a deep inhale. Citrus and dark rich spices filled his senses in a heady combination that sent heat racing through his veins.

Ah shit, she was in heat.

Fangs erupted from his gums as his vision shifted, signaling the change. Every muscle in his body flexed and bulged as his hearing picked up the pop of seams in the fabric around his growing cock. He couldn't tear his gaze away from the pulse beating in her neck. Imagining the sweet taste of her blood coating his tongue as she screamed out his name. The animal wanted its mate.

"I'm going for a run," he mumbled around his enlarged teeth and shot out the door without waiting for her response.

Bones snapped as black fur rippled over his skin, shredding his clothes. Damn, he loved that vintage AC/DC shirt.

The two-hundred-pound panther dropped to all fours and released a snarl before racing into the night. If he couldn't feast on the woman in the cabin, he'd have to find sustenance elsewhere, even though he knew a tasty little rabbit was not going to be nearly as good.

CHAPTER NINE

CRYSTAL WATCHED MAX as he ended his phone call with Ripley. Clutching the phone in one hand, Max dropped his head in the other and sagged in his chair.

Her husband would never admit it out loud, but the Evolutioneers were his family. When one of them was in danger, the stress of worry took a physical toll on him, robbing him of sleep, stealing his appetite. Not the best trait for the leader of a group of superheroes to possess, but it made her love him all the more.

She stroked her hand along his back while Doc Kelly vibrated by her side with agitation. They had all been listening on the call, anxious for news. Doc paced a tiny circle in the small amount of available space in the cramped command room. Chase and Addison hovered near the door, wearing matching grim expressions.

"Why didn't she ever tell me?" Doc tucked her hair behind her ears. "She's my friend. I thought she knew that."

"She suffered a trauma," Max answered in a voice deep with strain. "Everyone she ever trusted betrayed her, and the only one who didn't end up dead. That's a pretty big obstacle to overcome."

He reached up and squeezed Crystal's hand. Max, better than anyone, would understand exactly the betrayal Alisia might've experienced.

Crystal lifted her gaze to focus on a spot in the distance.

Her vision blurred as she sought out answers in the future. Since her near-death experience, her psychic ability had become easier to manage and no longer incapacitated her when the visions occurred. If she pressed her powers, she could even call on visions if needed.

Although her predictions were almost always accurate, any change of action by any one person could change the vision. And she was well aware that sometimes the future was not meant to be changed, that an act of prevention might ripple into chaos due to interference. It was a fine line between fate and coincidence, and Crystal tried to keep her influence to a minimum, thinking of her role as more of an oracle than fortune-teller.

But in life and death situations, she needed to know the future, just a little, for her own peace of mind.

As her focus turned inward, the cramped room faded away and Crystal found herself standing behind a row of young women. Ripley was crouched low, frozen halfway between man and beast. His clothes hung in shreds from his body. Each muscle rippled and flexed as if controlled individually. His nose and mouth were stretched into a muzzle and blood and gore dripped from his fangs as he let out a howl.

"Crystal."

Crystal snapped back to the present. Four pairs of eyes watched her intently. Max held her hand tight between both of his.

Those cool blue eyes she loved so much darkened. "What is it? Is it a vision?"

"No," she lied. To reveal the details of a scene she didn't understand might cause the others to panic. "I'm just thinking, and I'm worried. It's exhausting."

Max pressed his lips tight together. He knew how protective she was about divulging too much about the future and wouldn't push her for answers, no matter how much he'd like to otherwise. "You are looking a bit pale. Why don't you rest? Addison, I want you to dig deeper into all of the church's employees. Chase and I will question some extended family members. Make it look like we're searching for Gretchen."

"Do you want me to go and see if anyone has memories of Lowell or the drugs?" Crystal offered.

He kissed the back of her hand. "Not if you're too tired."

"I'll be fine." She brushed a lock of hair off his forehead. "Give me a moment to put up my hair and change."

She pressed a brief kiss to his lips, then another, longer, lingering taste before stepping away and out into the hall with Doc on her heels.

"So, when are you going to tell him?" Doc asked when they were a good distance away.

"Tell who what?"

"Max that you have a gumball-sized embryo in your belly."

Crystal stumbled into the wall as her heart fluttered. "Really?" Her throat closed up, making her light-headed. "I wasn't sure. The tests were never consistent. I—oh, oh boy. Is the baby all right? Any signs of anything…different?"

"My powers detected you have a perfectly healthy, and normal, eight-week-old bun in the oven." Some of the worry left her eyes as she smiled. "When are you telling Max? I can only sit on news like this for so long."

"Well, I can't tell him now. He'll never let me out of the cave, especially not until this thing with the reverend is over. He has enough to worry about as it is."

"True. He does get a little overprotective with you."

"A little?"

"Give the man some slack. He watched you die."

"I *know*. Believe me, I know. That's why I need to proceed with caution. I'll tell him. Eventually."

"Right. Just make sure it's before you go into labor. Okay?"

"Yeah. Sure. Of course I will," she exclaimed when Doc gave her the side-eye.

"Good." Doc sighed and bit her lip. "I don't suppose you've had any sort of vision about Alisia?"

"Nothing substantial, but I have a strong sense that there will be some sort of impending action soon."

"Oh, how frustrating." Doc smoothed her palms over her long, dark, hair. "At least I know Ripley will do anything to protect Alisia."

Crystal's smile faltered. That was what she was afraid of.

✧   ✧   ✧

ALISIA LET OUT a long, shaky breath and rubbed her palms over her chilled arms. Outside, a mournful yowl of a great jungle cat penetrated through the windows, making her jump and her skin pebble. An expected reaction at hearing an unfamiliar and dangerous sound. But her reaction was not from fear. Oh no. Normal people would feel fear. She on the other hand knew that was Ripley in animal form and now she had an uncontrollable urge to chase after him and taunt the beast.

What would've happened if Ripley hadn't bolted out of the room when he had? It seemed that the longer they had stared in each other's eyes, the larger Ripley appeared to grow, both in height and in his jeans. His pupils had changed into slits, resembling the cat she had just heard, and she swore she saw a bit of fang.

Her nipples beaded and another tremor rattled her teeth at the thought of those fangs nipping and teasing her skin. She wanted to do the same to him, and bathe every gorgeous inch of his flesh with her tongue.

"Oh my God," she groaned and stumbled into the bedroom.

This intense sexual hunger was not like her. Never in her life had she ever been driven to throw herself on the floor, spread her legs, and beg a man to bang her. Yet there she'd been, a heartbeat away from doing just that when Ripley ran.

Hey. Why did he run?

She paused, hand in mid-air as she laid out a sleeping bag over the bed.

All the signs of sexual attraction had been there. Red cheeks, harsh breath, want and need darkened his eyes. He had been after her for a year, and she was positive that if she had looked in the mirror, she would have seen the same wanton expression on her face. The same hunger, signaling her desire. Yet he found the strength to ignore his primal urges. Why now? Did her past effectively place her in the "friend" column now?

A sharp, shooting pain of loss ignited in her chest, surprising her with its intensity, though she knew it was probably for the best. There was still a lot about her he didn't know. To give him her heart only to watch as disgust extinguished the light in those dazzling blue eyes...

She blinked away the tears that blurred her vision. No, Ripley wasn't Sam. She didn't love him like she had Sam. Watching Ripley walk away would hurt, hurt like hell, but she wouldn't shatter like she had when she lost Sam. She wouldn't allow it.

The chill of the sleeping bag against her skin did little to cool her overheated skin. Alone in the dark with just her thoughts, she twisted in the confines of the bag, searching for sleep that eluded her like shedding those last ten pounds. Silky nylon taffeta tickled her exposed skin, making her long for Ripley's rough caress. An ache settled between her thighs, burning hot and deep until ignoring the need became impossible. Licking her lips, she glanced toward the window and the starry night sky.

Ripley would be out for who knew how long, maybe even all night. Leaving her alone. All alone. Did she dare take care of her needs on her own?

A giggle slipped past her lips as she slid her palm slid over her abdomen and under the band of her cotton pants, remembering when Sam had teased her about taking care of his own needs in such a way. But now she understood exactly how he had felt. Oh, this was naughty. So naughty. The tip of one cold finger parted the lips of her sex and dipped inside. Holy crap, she was wet.

In her mind she replayed the kiss Ripley stole from her outside the bar. He tasted like Irish coffee and his skin smelled like the fresh outdoors. Being surrounded by all that man and muscle had made her feel sexy, feminine, protected.

Instead of fighting the attraction as she had then, this time dream-Alisia wrapped her legs around his lean waist and ground against the cock straining the fly of his jeans.

Wait. Even better. Now they were naked, and hot, and sweaty, and her girly bits were getting acquainted, very acquainted with all his manly parts. She knew what he was packing, having seen his cock when he shifted. The man was beastly, even without his powers.

Oh yeah. This dream was getting good. Her legs fell open, her fingers slipping with ease against her clit as she became lost in the fantasy.

Bam!

The bedroom door blew open, practically ripped from the hinges. Alisia jerked upright, mouth agape at the sight of Ripley standing in the doorway with his blond hair falling to his shoulders like a lion's mane. Silvery moonlight bathed his naked body like silk on marble. The bulge of his muscles created dark shadows and grooves she ached to explore with her fingers. His legs stood strong, rooted to the floor, and his cock rose hard and thick from his body, so heavy it curved downward. Her lips parted and her tongue darted out, ready to lick the glistening tip.

"Do you have any idea what you're doing to me?" he rasped in a low, gravelly voice that sent chills from her breasts to her pussy.

He took a halting step forward, then another. Grasping the bottom of the sleeping bag, he whipped it out from under her like a magician performing a trick. The bed creaked under his weight as he crawled between her sprawled legs.

Alisia couldn't move, couldn't breathe as he lifted the hand she had been pleasuring herself with and leaned close to inhale. His tongue flicked out, licking her cream from her skin. His tongue was rough, scraping deliciously into each crease. The sensual look on his face and the trembling in his shoulders as he licked her clean was the most erotic thing she had ever seen. Afraid to blink and break the intensity of being the focus of such ardent sexuality, she felt her eyes burn as she stared.

He kissed his way up her arm to hiss in her ear, "I can smell you. Smell your desire. Your need. I was a mile away and I could smell the heat of your pussy like a fresh-baked pie." He pulled down the strap of her tank top, exposing one puckered peak. Cupping the weight in his palm, he ran his tongue over the tip and groaned. "I couldn't stay away. You smell so fucking good."

The carnality of his speech, the fervor in his touch held her immobile as she panted in anticipation of his next move.

His nails were more like talons, leaving faint red lines on her hips as he removed her leggings. Then his big hands held her thighs wide apart, open to the blue flame of his gaze. "I have to taste."

The breath burst from her lungs at the first touch of his mouth on her too-hot skin. That wonderfully wicked tongue of his swirled and teased, driving her passion to the edge of insanity. She threaded her fingers through his hair and hunched her hips, silently begging for more. He responded by reaching up to twist her nipple and plunged two blunt fingers into her sheath.

The sensual assault, both inside and out, was too much. Behind her ribs, a fuse ignited, smoldering hotter and faster until her heart detonated. She cried out, part ecstasy, part disappointment of reaching the summit too quickly, while her body bucked in his grasp.

And still she hungered. Even as she rode the wave of the most intense orgasm she'd ever experienced, she wanted more.

"Please." She dug her fingertips into his firm shoulders. "Ripley. More."

He stalked up her body, pausing to suck a pouting nipple between his teeth. His throbbing cock settled over her opening, the rigid shaft slipped over her drenched folds. So close yet so far.

Her hips writhed, desperate for release. "I need you inside me."

He whimpered against her breast, his big body shuddering. "Can't. Must. Protect. You."

The breath rushed out of her lungs as her head fell back. What an idiot. How could she be so foolish? "Right, condoms."

He stilled. "What?" He raised his head. His brow that was once creased in confusion cleared with hope. "Condoms. Yes. Condoms."

Leaping off the bed, he attacked the drawers of the nightstand.

"Please, please, please, please. Yes! What? No, too small." The packet hit the wall with a smack. "Come on. Yes."

The foil sparkled briefly in the moonlight before being torn asunder and tossed to the floor.

She didn't get the chance to admire the flexing of his forearms as he rolled the latex over his weeping erection before he flipped her onto her belly and pulled her backside high into the air. She pressed her palms to the mattress, tensing to lift, then fell back down with a strangled cry when he pressed the plum-shaped head into her tight sheath.

They both groaned as he worked the shaft in short jabs deeper and deeper. Stretching, filling, consuming.

Tears leaked from her tightly closed eyelids. How could anything feel so incredibly good? His possession rippled along every nerve, leaving no part of her untouched.

Finally, the last inch sank home. The head of his cock

pressed snug at the neck of her womb for several glorious seconds. Then he pulled all the way out and lunged. Again, and again, and again.

He draped himself along her back, hips thrusting hard and fast. "Incredible," he growled. His hot breath washed over her neck. "So fucking perfect."

She curled her fingers into the mattress and hung on for the ride. His tongue lapped at her pulse and a rumble worked in his chest, the vibrations streaking down her spine to her pussy. But it was the scrape of his fangs on her neck that shoved her over the edge. A howl ripped from her throat as she exploded, back arching to send him deeper. Without knowing exactly what she was doing, her head dropped, offering him her submission as her inner muscles constricted.

Ripley jerked up with a roar, his claws sinking into her hip to puncture her skin and hold her still. The head of his cock swelled, locking them together as he came with a howl of his own.

Aftershocks raced over her body while behind her, Ripley jerked and spasmed as he collapsed on top of her and his cock continued to stake his claim.

She was now officially addicted to the beast.

CHAPTER TEN

R IPLEY WOKE THE next morning with the warmth of the sun on his face and a heavy weight of *what the fuck just happened* filling his chest. Joints popped as he stretched his sated limbs beyond the confines of the tiny bed he occupied all by himself.

He jerked up, heart racing. Had Alisia run again?

From the other room he heard the tread of soft footfalls on the wood floor as the scent of citrus and cloves tickled his nose and sent heat racing through his body.

He sank back on the bare mattress with relief. She was still there. That must be a good sign, right? Whatever had happened the night before hadn't scared her off.

What the hell *did* happen the night before?

Lifting his hands, he inspected the thickly veined backsides and the callus-roughened palms. Both appeared to be normal.

With trepidation he reached down and gripped his morning-erect shaft, lightly stroking up the entire length around the head and down to his balls. Again, all felt and looked normal.

Normal. Ha. Nothing about how he had felt and behaved had been close to normal. Hotter than hell? Yes. Normal? No fucking way.

The moment he had scented her arousal in the air, another power had come over him. The cock in his hand had ruled his every action with the singular goal of mating with his woman. Ripley had disappeared and the beast had been in control. The panther's claws and fangs had never receded, and he remembered puncturing her hips as he held her still for his frantic thrusts. It had taken every ounce of strength he possessed to keep from mauling her. And as he came, the knot formed, locking them together. As if he were a dog.

It was not lost on him that the last word that could be used to describe him was ordinary, but at least he had been able to keep the dual sides of his nature separate, calling on the shift when he required. Now the line between man and beast was blurring. Even now his gums hurt and his skin tingled with the compulsion to settle unfinished business riding him hard.

In Alisia's arms, his body had found release, but the animal inside him was pissed that his mate did not carry his mark. And what did *that* mean? Obviously, skin to skin contact was not enough, and no way was he going to mark his territory and urinate on her. What more did his animal want?

Under his flexing fingers, smooth skin glided over the springy tissue of his erection, giving him a pretty good idea of what his animal wanted. But would the knot form every time he had sex or was it being with Alisia specifically that brought out the beast?

The remembered pleasure of her sheath suckling his swelling shaft hardened his cock to granite even as shame filled his heart. Such a beastly act should not be so intensely satisfying, but it had blown his mind. He wanted to do it again, claws and all. And this time, without a condom.

God help him, he was a fucking pervert.

Self-loathing left a bitter taste in his parched mouth and his limbs trembled as he pulled himself away from the allure of self-pleasuring. He dragged himself to his feet to shuffle to the door.

Opening the door a crack, he spotted Alisia sat at the worktable with her back to him. A half-eaten protein bar sat at her elbow as she intensely worked at whatever she was writing on a pad of paper.

He shifted into his panther form and stealthily strolled across the room and used his fangs to retrieve his duffel from the exact spot he dropped it the night before when they had first arrived. Great protector he was, he hadn't even taken the time to properly see to her basic needs before rutting all over her.

Slipping into the bathroom, he nudged the door shut and shifted back to human and stepped into the shower.

A strangled scream locked in his throat as the ice-cold water hit his skin. Motherfucker, was that painful. But he so deserved it for his behavior the night before. In fact, that little sting was nothing more than a slap on the wrists.

With sharp jerky movements, he washed the sweat and cum from his body while debating the best way to approach her. He was going to have to leave the bathroom at some time. Alisia wasn't stupid. She probably thought that he had slinked past her like a coward, which was only slightly true. Okay, it was totally true, but there was no way he could face her covered in their…well…them.

Skin still damp, he tossed on a pair of tear-away pants and a T-shirt, then opened the door to find Alisia coming back into the cabin with the remnants of the clothing he had shed the night before in her arms.

"Good morning." His voice was rough with a desire he

believed would never abate.

"Morning. These were on the porch." She dumped what was left of his clothes on the couch and returned to packing her backpack. She had released her ponytail and the wavy blond strands covered her face, obscuring her expression.

Anxiety tightened his chest as he stood waiting for her to acknowledge him. A word, a glance, anything that indicated her mood.

Huh. So, it was up to him to make the first move, was it? Sure. No problem.

He sucked in a breath, then another.

Come on, man. Just do it!

"So…how are you feeling?"

"Fine," she said in that way women did that could mean anything from *All is well* to *I'm one heartbeat away from ripping your head off.*

"Alisia." He took one more encouraging breath. "About last night, I'm sorry."

She held up her hand, still refusing to look at him. "Don't be. It was just sex. No big deal."

"Just…sex?" A punch to the kidneys didn't hurt as badly as her cavalier shrug. "No, it wasn't."

"It's all right, Ripley." She crossed to the kitchenette and used a paper towel to wipe away imaginary crumbs from the counter. "I was horny, you were horny, we were handy."

The hair along his arms bristled and his cock hardened, testing the limits of the Velcro closures of his pants, eager to show her that the night before was more than just two people getting their rocks off. "That was not what happened and you know it."

She sidestepped him as he advanced, keeping the couch between them. "I'm a big girl. I don't need morning-after chit-chat. Let's just forget about it and move on."

"How can I move on? It was one of the most intense moments of my life."

"Right," she scoffed. "That's why you're sorry it happened."

"I'm sorry that I hurt you." They continued the dance around the furniture. "My pleasure should not cause you pain."

"You didn't hurt me."

"Don't lie to me. I know I did."

"Why are you being so weird?" she yelled.

"Why are you shouting!"

"Because you are!"

A lion's roar ripped from his throat, making her jump with a squeak onto the worktable. The rumble moved to his chest, which rose and fell, matching the pace of her rapid breathing. As his heart rate slowed, he held out his hands in supplication.

"Last night was amazing, but I hurt you. I clawed you and knot…" He couldn't even finish the word. "To hurt you is like dragging a dull blade through my skin. I can't stand it."

"But I liked it," she admitted in a voice so soft he almost missed it.

"I took you like an animal."

"I know. That's what I liked. The scratching, the way your…" A blush stole across her cheeks as she licked her lips. "…Cock swelled. All of it."

Lord have mercy. She was telling the truth. The sultry scent of her dampening pussy filled his senses and made his eyes roll in pleasure.

Ripley crossed the distance separating them and her

scent deepened.

"I know. It's weird," she continued, worrying her lip. "Sex and me. How I've grown up. What I've been through. Society standards of what a woman should and shouldn't be into. It gets all muddled and jacked up. But I liked it. What we did. A lot. But we're not supposed to be having sex. We're supposed to be taking down the bad guys and saving the day. Not daydreaming about crawling back into that bed and having sex all day."

"Alisia. Look at me, please." He tilted her chin up with the tip of his fingers.

The green in her eyes sparkled with the need she was trying so hard to compress. Always so vigilant and on guard. When was the last time she had lost herself in the moment and enjoyed?

"You mean so much to me," he said softly. "Whatever you want. Whatever you need. I want to provide for you."

Her chuckle held little humor. "I have no idea what I need. Don't even know where to start."

"What about with what you want?"

"Want?" Her lashes lowered and her cheeks pinked. "I want…too much."

Her lush lips parted, ready for the kiss he couldn't deny her, and she melted against him like chocolate under a hot marshmallow, sweet, rich, and oh so decadent.

The kiss went from zero to sixty as her knees gripped his flanks as he bore her back along the table. Hands groped, clutched, and smoothed over fevered skin, both his and hers, as his hips ground against the juncture of her thighs, desperate for the release only Alisia could give him.

Tearing her mouth away, she looked up at him with confusion on her brows. "What's that sound?"

Ripley closed his eyes and forced his attention away from the soft press of her breasts and writhing hips. The rush of blood in his ears mellowed, and he heard the lumbering growl of a V-12 engine in need of a tune-up. Through the window he spotted a dirty, black Ford Explorer slow into the clearing and park next to his truck.

"Shit. We have company." He pulled her to her feet.

Alisia whipped on her jacket. "Anyone you know?"

"Possibly. But I think it's best if you weren't seen."

"I agree." She grabbed her pack. "I'll go out the bedroom window."

"Hey." He brushed a kiss on her cheek. "Be careful."

Her smile was brief but filled with warmth. She slipped into the bedroom and shut the door.

Ripley stepped out onto the porch to greet the portly man who climbed out of the driver's seat. Three more people inside the car created shadows on the windows.

"Dr. Yasbeck?" Ripley asked in disbelief. Hell, when was the last time he had seen his former professor?

"Ripley." The doctor squinted up at him through his bifocals. "My, what a surprise. What brings you this far north?"

Ripley shook the outstretched hand. "I'm doing an environmental impact study for a private company over in Boise. Research ran late last night and I started drifting off. Then I remembered the cabin and thought I'd borrow a cot for the night. I hope that was all right."

"Oh, fine, fine." Yasbeck waved him away. "I heard you left the zoo last summer. Pity for them, but a boon to whomever snapped you up. Students," he addressed the young people who had piled out of the car and were now staring up at Ripley with eyes wide. With his shirt off and in the morning sun, he knew he cut quite a figure. "This is Dr. Jorgensen, one of my brightest, as well as the biggest pain in the ass, student I've had."

"That never stopped you from eating all of the brownies my mom sent for our research trips."

Yasbeck laughed and patted his generous waistline. "You had your uses."

"Let me give you a hand." Ripley helped unload the Explorer, carrying a massive trunk in each hand up the stairs. "This looks like more than a simple research expedition on salmon spawning."

"I got a call this morning of a report of a possible large cat in the area. Farmers said they thought it was a panther."

"Panther? In Washington?" Ripley set the bags in the corner farthest away from the bedroom.

"I know." Yasbeck chuckled. "It was probably a cougar, but there is the possibility that someone had an illegal pet that got loose. We'll do some scouting around, alleviate some fears, then get down to some real research."

Ripley nodded absentmindedly, wondering if he'd left any tracks that might lead back to the cabin. "Well, let me get out of your way. I was about to leave when you pulled up."

He gathered his pack and stepped into the bedroom to gather the sleeping bags. The glitter of the gold foil on the floor distracted him for half a second with memories of the night before. Right. A used condom would be just awesome to leave behind. He pocketed the evidence and finished dressing.

After doing another quick roundup of the cabin, he joined the professor on the porch.

"Send me your contact information," Dr. Yasbeck said.

"I'd love to have you come talk to the students about black bears. I still marvel over how you survived that mauling without any permanent damage. It was truly a miracle."

"Don't I know it." Ripley set the bags in his truck and shook the professor's hand. "I'll be in touch, sir."

Dr. Yasbeck waved from the door as Ripley backed down the trail. When the Chevy hit the smooth pavement of Highway 2, the slim back window of the cab slid open.

"So. Your mom bakes?" Alisia curled her fingers over the frame and rested her chin on the backs of her hands.

"Yeah." He glanced in the rearview mirror at her reflection. It was the first time she had ever expressed any interest in anything close to his personal life. The soft, inquiring expression on her face tugged at his heart and reminded him of the photo of young Gretchen. "She could give Martha Stewart a run for her money."

A small smile curled her lips. "My mom baked too. She had a way with pie that was amazing."

"You're pretty good yourself. That cranberry-apple one you made at Christmas was great. I ate the whole thing by myself."

"That's right." She chuckled. "I thought you did that just to be nice to me in the hopes of getting into my pants."

"I ate one slice to be nice. I ate the rest of the pie because it was that good."

He reached over his shoulder to snatch her hand and bring it to his mouth for a kiss. When he let go, she laid it on his shoulder and kept it there as they trundled down the highway.

For a moment, just a moment, all was right in his world.

CHAPTER ELEVEN

CRYSTAL MADDEN FOLDED her arms across her chest and leaned against the doorway to the garage to admire the denim-clad backside bending over the trunk of the Range Rover. Joy spread through her like a warm toddy as she watched the muscles in her husband's arms tense and bulge while he held a pipe in place with both hands. A pneumatic drill floated in the air and lodged into place to tighten down the nuts and bolts. Ever since the night she had died and returned to the living, his control over his powers had become almost second nature.

What was it about a man installing a grenade launcher that gave her the teenage giggles and made all her girlie parts flutter?

"I can actually feel your gaze stripping the clothes from my body." Max's teasing baritone drifted from inside the trunk before he tossed her a cocky grin over his shoulder.

The sparkle in his cool blue eyes and the dimple near his quirked lips never failed to stop her heart and make her grateful to have this fantastic man in her life.

"I can't help myself." Her own grin stretched and she flicked her tongue over her lower lip. "You are a very sexy man, Mr. Madden."

He winked at her then turned back to directing the tools. "They're going to be all right, you know."

"Who?"

"Alisia and Ripley." He straightened and searched through the tall tool chest by his side. "They're going after a big piece of evidence today. Soon Lowell will be behind bars and they'll be tucked back here in their own beds. Or Ripley's bed, if he has anything to say about it."

She bit back a giggle. "I know. Remember?"

He lifted a monkey wrench in victory and tapped it against his thigh. "How much do you know about what happens next?"

"Enough to not be worried."

"Care to share?"

She pinched her lips together and motioned as if turning the key and tossing it over her shoulder.

"Not even a little hint?"

And threaten the possible outcomes? "I admire your persistence, but no."

He laughed, holding her gaze for several long seconds before laying down on a shuttle and sliding under the Rover. "Then what is it that you *are* worried about?" He raised his voice over the pop and clang of working power tools.

Her breath caught and she had to swallow before asking, "Why do you think I'm worried?"

"Your eyes are topaz."

Damn her eyes and their mood ring ability.

She bit her lip and drew in a deep breath then let it out in a slow, steady ten-count stream while she considered her words.

Well, Max always said he appreciated a straight shooter. Better to just rip the bandage off in one swoop.

She pushed away from the door and straightened to her full five-foot height. "I'm pregnant."

"Wha—? Ah—ow!" Max jerked up, slamming his head into the chassis. Concentration broken, all the tools he had working crashed to the floor. The staple gun discharged as it hit the concrete, shooting rounds of staples across the room.

"Oh, sweetie." Crystal rushed to his side. "Are you all right?"

"I don't know." His voice quivered. He clutched his head and swayed as he sat up. "Did you say you're pregnant?"

"Yes."

"Then I'm not all right."

Tears of frustration, disappointment, and hormones immediately spilled down her cheeks. Why did her husband have to be such a man? "Just forget I said anything."

Even dazed and confused, Max managed to snatch her around the waist and hold her wiggly body on his lap. "I'm sorry. You caught me by surprise." He closed his eyes and rested his forehead against hers. "I think I'm going to be sick"

"You suck." She pushed against his chest.

"I have a head injury and am not thinking clearly." His eyes snapped open, pinning her in place. "But I love you."

All the emotions he hid inside were in the flames of his icy blue eyes. Fear was there, desperately waving a flag for help. There was also concern that she too shared if she dared to admit it out loud. Burning brightest, though, and what kept her temper in check, was his love.

The last time he had worn such an expression was when she was going on a mission that she alone knew she wasn't going to survive. He had let her go, even though his every instinct screamed to lock her away. He had let her go because he loved her and trusted she would do whatever she had to in order to come back to him. It was that love he had for her that kept her on his lap and not reaching for the wrench to give him a matching goose egg over the other eye.

He hands swept up and down her back. "I love you," he whispered. "But I'm scared."

"I'm scared too," she whispered back.

"I don't know if that makes me feel better or worse." He chuckled.

That was so not funny. "Max."

"Sweetheart, I'm trying to process all of this." He took a deep breath through his nose and let it out. "Is the baby okay? Are you okay?"

"We're fine. Doc did a scan. Everything is normal."

"Is she certain? We're not going to have a baby that will try to levitate your organs, are we?"

This time she couldn't hold back her laughter. "The baby is healthy. As for normal, we'll have to wait and see."

He grunted at that then frowned. Leaning back against the side of the car, he resettled her across his lap. "I can't even begin to describe how much I love you right now, but this is a scary time and the world is not safe to bring a child into it."

"I know. I feel the same way. But I'm not sorry it happened."

"I'm not either." He nuzzled her cheek then pressed soft kisses on her chin and down her neck to bury his face against her shoulder. In a tiny voice he admitted what she suspected was his real concern. "What if I turn into my father?"

"You won't."

"How do you know?" He pulled away and cupped her face in his hands. Anxiety pinched his mouth, creating deep groves. "Have you seen that in our future? Would you tell me the truth, even if it's bad?"

"Of course I would, but I don't have to, because you are not going to become your father. The fact that you're worried about it tells me that you're not." She grasped his wrists. "I could easily say the same thing about me and my father."

Max's chuckle held little humor. "You're stronger than I am."

"And smarter."

"True." He let out a sad sigh. "A murdering wife beater and a psychopathic, multibillion-dollar thief who tried to take over the world. Our kid is screwed in the genes department."

"They'll be fine, because they will have us, and we will raise them with love, understanding, and a firm but compassionate hand."

Admiration and wonder replaced the fear in his eyes. "You're going to be a kick-ass mom."

"Because you will be by my side."

"Always."

That one word filled with such conviction eased her worry. The kiss he placed on her lips was hot, strong, and more bracing than a cup of coffee with a healthy shot of whiskey. His arms, his hands, the way his tongue teased and tangled with hers, confirmed that he was her man and she could always rely in him.

"I love you, Max," she whispered against his lip.

"I love you, too. That's why I'm pulling you off the team."

"Motherfucker." She slammed both hands into his chest, smacking his head against the car door. She jumped off his lap and stomped away from potential weapons. Chase taught her so well, there were a lot of items she could cause some serious damage with.

"Dammit, Crystal." He wobbled to his feet and braced his hand on the roof of the car. "Look, sweetheart—"

"Don't sweetheart me. I knew you were going to pull some chauvinistic asshole move like this. You can't kick me off the team."

"Yes, I can. You died on me once. I will not lose you again, or the baby. Never again," and with that his voice broke.

"I know," she screamed.

With her power of touch, she relived his memories of her lying in his arms bruised and covered in blood every night as they lay side by side in bed. Every time they touched, she experienced the nightmares over and over as her heart gave out and she died as he begged her not to leave him. Her own memories of that moment were clouded from her pain, but Max's were as vivid as the moment it happened.

She closed her eyes and reined in her anger at Max's expected reaction. She understood why he was obsessive about protecting her, and didn't fault him one bit, but he had to believe in her.

She strode toward him in slow, deliberate steps, as his eyes grew wide and the line of his lips tightened, until they stood toe-to-toe. Breast to chest. Heart to heart. "I'm not going to do anything that will risk my life, but if I'm needed, I will go. And you cannot stop me."

He bit back a curse and looked away, an acknowledgment that on this, she would not bend. He wrapped his arms around her waist, pulling her in even tighter. "If you are threatened in any way, I will do everything I can to protect you, the success of the mission be damned. I will not let anything happen to you. My family comes first. Always."

The promise and threat in his tone sent a shiver down her spine. "The same goes for you, too."

Before her eyes, his image blurred and the breath in her lungs froze. In her third eye, the events in the future shifted and changed, terrifying her with their implication until the tethers snapped and she fell back into the present.

She dug her fingers into Max's shoulders, clinging to him as her knees gave out.

Maybe she should have waited a little while longer before telling Max about the baby.

CHAPTER TWELVE

"**S**TOP RIGHT HERE," Alisia instructed and jumped out of the truck before it came to a complete stop.

How many years had it been since she last stood on church property? Five? Ten? It felt like a hundred since she'd been in the craggy valleys dotted with fields of dry grass and clusters of evergreens. It was harsh and beautiful at the same time, with the rippling streams bisecting the rocky hillsides. Spring was forcing its way onto the landscape with bursts of green leaves on the once-bare trees. The earth was awakening. A time for rebirth, renewal. A time for new beginnings.

And a time to close the door to the past forever.

Being back on the church compound triggered a frantic rush of adrenaline that left her insides shaking. There would be no reminiscing on this trip. No pointing out locations of happy memories and longing for what should have been. The only objective was finding evidence of the drugs and getting the hell out of Dodge. Sure, enacting revenge on those that harmed her and getting her sister out safe would be stellar. But with their resources at a minimum, she'd have to stick to the basics.

"Why are we stopping here?" Ripley asked. "We can get closer."

"The truck is too wide. It won't fit much farther up the trail. We'll have to take the bike." She flipped open the tailgate and the door to the hardtop and dove for her backpack.

"The bike's too loud."

She donned her backpack, adjusting the straps. "Fine, then we walk."

"Jeez, woman, quit busting my balls." He gripped her by the hips and yanked her out of the truck. "Don't forget what I am."

He stripped off his clothes, and for a moment she was struck dumb by the sight of all those bronze ripple-ly muscles. For the love of all that was holy, it was ridiculous that a man could be so sexy.

The spell was broken when his body contorted. Bones cracked and popped as Ripley grunted with the shift. He claimed that he was used to the process and that it didn't hurt much anymore, but she'd bet her motorbike that it was agony. The sound alone turned her stomach.

But seconds later, the horror was over and a beautiful gold and yellow palomino stood in his place.

"Oh...wow." She slapped a hand over her mouth to hold in an explosive giggle. "That's impressive." The horse clicked its tongue and butted his head against her stomach. "I haven't ridden a horse since I was ten. How the hell am I going to mount you?"

The horse raised a brow and sniggered. Funny how even in animal form, Ripley's sense of humor continued to shine.

He knelt on his forelegs, allowing her easy access onto his back. Another giggle escaped her as she swung her leg over his massive back and settled in her seat.

"Thanks." She clutched fistfuls of his mane in her palms as he stood to his full height in a quick leap. "Whoa!"

Ripley snorted and pulled against the death grip she

held on his locks. "Oh, sorry."

He tossed his golden head and rolled his eyes before taking off at a gallop into the dense woods.

"Holy shit!"

Alisia flung her arms around his neck, her thighs gripping the bunching, rolling muscles that threatened to knock her to the leaf-covered ground.

"Okay. Stop. I get it. You're the man," she screeched into the side of his neck.

The horse whinnied and slowed to a reasonable trot.

"You're such a showoff," she groused, even as a smile flirted on her lips. If they weren't heading toward the place where her life had turned into a living nightmare, she would've better enjoyed the sun-dappled ride on the back of her lover.

Holy crap. *She was riding on the back of her shapeshifting lover.*

For all the weird shit she'd seen and gone through, this ranked right up there with the oddest thing she'd ever experience.

As a little girl she used to walk through these woods and daydream about marrying a nice man and becoming a mother. Her days would be filled helping the community, worshipping God, and taking care of her family. These woods had been magical and full of dreams. Now the dark shadows hid villains and devils. Men who acted as saints but were true demons feeding upon those who blindly followed their lead.

The trees grew taller and thicker the deeper into the woods they went. The clip-clop of Ripley's hooves was like a metronome, and a thick band seem to tighten around her chest, crushing her until she was forced to focus on her breathing or lose consciousness.

She thought she was ready to face her past. Hell, not only face it, but kick its ass. It was a bitter pill to acknowledge, even if only to herself, that she was glad Ripley was with her. In her gut she knew if she had been on her own as she had planned, she'd have probably taken one step onto church property then turned on her heel and run straight for Canada.

They emerged into a clearing and a bright patch of sunlight. Wild flowers had poked through the dirt and dried grass to display their pink and yellow petals to wave cheerily in the breeze. This was her and Sam's clearing. The place where she had believed all her dreams were going to come true.

Tears sprang to her eyes and she straightened. The hows and whys might have changed, but she was still living her dream. At least a small part of it. She was doing her part to help mankind. Sam had told her that she made him want to be a better person. Because of him, to honor him, she'd face down Satan himself. Sam deserved no less.

Old training kicked in and she used her thighs to squeeze Ripley's sides. "Hold up. We're coming up on the outbuildings."

She hopped down and stepped back to give him some room. The pop and snap of bones reshaping the mighty stallion into a magnificent wolf made her flinch, but she didn't look away even as the bile rose in her throat. He shouldn't have to be alone while enduring the pain of transforming, especially when he was doing it for her.

"Ripley. You don't have to keep shifting. I know that hurts."

Ripley gave a doggy shrug and nuzzled her hand, conveying in his way that he was all right and there for her.

So strong. So caring. He believed in her. And she needed to trust in him.

"If you want to check the area, I'll wait right here," she said.

He nodded and licked at her hand. It didn't take him long to do two laps around the perimeter before giving her an all-clear signal. She followed his alert tail and bent head as he led her to the door of the nearest shed. The fact he could nose the door open of the one where life as she had known it ended made her hopes plummet.

Empty. There wasn't a thing in the dark, dank interior. Well, nothing but cobwebs, a lingering chemical stench, and years of dust covering the floor.

Frustration, not the dust, choked her and made her voice rasp as she pointed toward the back. "They had tables set up there by the sinks. And there and there were rows of boxes." It was probably fruitless, but she took photos of the area with her cell phone. Perhaps Addison or Max knew of a magic computer program that might be able to spot evidence in a photograph.

Ripley set off for the far corner. His nose brushed the floor as he began a crisscross pattern. She moved to set off for the opposite corner and stopped short. Her foot hovered in midair, inches above a dark stain on the cement. Sam's blood.

The ball of ice in her chest expanded, stopping her heart. Before her eyes, the stain grew and began to glisten as if the blood had just been spilt as old screams echoed in her ears. At that moment she was the same as she had been then. Helpless. Weak. Her knees buckled and there was nothing she could do to stop the fall.

Ripley caught her in his arms and pulled her shuddering body close. "It's okay, baby. I've got you," he whispered in her ear. "I've got you."

Ripley...

His warm body against her back supported her, his strength and heat a vital reminder of the present, thawing her frozen lungs. Her next deep breath burned. The second one dragged her from the past.

She hadn't been able to save Sam then, but by God, she would avenge him now.

"I'll be fine." She dashed the back of her hand over her wet cheeks. Her breath hitched as she added, "I just really want to take these guys down."

"We will," he replied. His tone was low, solemn, with an underlying thread of commitment that he was behind her all the way. "Let's take a few samples. Doc may be able to find something to help us convict these rat bastards."

"Right. Ripley." She grabbed his hand as he stepped away and nestled it against her heart. "Thank you."

His blue eyes blazed as if lit from within. He bent and pressed a soft kiss to her forehead that made her breath catch again, overwhelmed by his tenderness.

"Let's do this," she said and searched for the vials and swabs, courtesy of Jameson and the medical room of the women's shelter, in her backpack.

The task at hand kept her from collapsing back into an emotional heap. Samples were taken of the floor, sink, and counters, with the hope that something would be found to verify that drugs had once been manufactured there. If they were lucky, they might be able to get a hit on some DNA as well.

After a final sweep of the building, Ripley shifted into

his wolf form and they stole back into the woods, setting off in the direction of her old family home.

The grand, two-story Victorian, which sat back from the road on a rolling green hill, used to remind her of a gingerbread house when she was a child. The white trim and curlicue accents looked like royal icing against the caramel-colored siding. Brilliant pinks and purples of peonies and rhododendrons added bursts of gumdrop colors.

In the morning sun, the house glittered as beautifully as she remembered. And like a gingerbread house, it was just as hollow.

"There are three entrances. One in the front, one in the back, and another through the garage," she informed Ripley as they hid in the cluster of trees about a hundred feet away from the brick-lined driveway. "At this time of day everyone should be heading to the church. If you live on the compound, attendance is mandatory, but I wouldn't be surprised if there was a deacon or two running around to make sure everyone is where they're supposed to be."

Ripley yipped and circled around her twice before nodding at the ground by her feet.

"I'm going with you," she said.

He yipped twice and stared at her expectantly.

"What does that mean? I don't speak dog."

He sighed, actually sighed, and rolled his eyes before pointing his nose at the ground then dragged his paw across the grass.

"Line. Lots of lines. One."

He yipped again.

"One. One what? One minute?"

Ripley nodded and tapped her foot.

"Okay. But just one."

He licked at her hand then took a few steps forward before glancing back with a frown, lowering his big bushy brows.

Across the distance she sensed his concern, but he didn't have to worry about her mental condition. Her moment of weakness was over. She was no longer the little girl who naively believed in the goodness of others, nor was she the terrified teenager who ran blindly into the night and into a hell she nearly died in. The woman now marching forward was a representative of justice, blind to everything except finding the evidence to put an end to those who would willfully harm others. She would not crumble.

"Go on." She shooed him away. "I'm fine. Really."

He trotted back to lick her hand one more time then dashed off through the bushes toward the house.

Having Ripley make sure she was taken care of while in his animal form touched her deeply. In her experience, she found compassion to be a rare quality in a man. Sad but true. To be the recipient of his care time and time again these last hours made her realize how truly exceptional Ripley was beyond his abilities.

Ripley barked the all-clear signal and she dashed across the backyard, slipping into the shadows on the back porch. Alisia knelt on one knee and extracted a slim case from her pack. Taking her favorite pick in hand, she went to work on the lock of the French doors. The tricks Jameson taught her with Sam's tools had come in handy on more than one occasion. Behind her, the sound of popping bones made shivers run down her spine.

"What are you doing?" Ripley whispered harshly in her ear.

She didn't dare pause in her work to peek over her

shoulder. She knew what she'd see, and she needed all her motor skills to work the lock. All those bulging muscles were definitely a distraction.

"I'm opening the door. Get your clothes out of the pack. A naked man will still attract attention, even with no one around."

"You're picking the lock?" he groused, jerking his slacks over his muscled legs.

"How else did you plan on getting inside? Kick the door in?"

"I had a plan. Where did you learn how to do that?"

"You learn how to do a lot of things when you're on the streets. Now hush up." The knob twisted easily in her hand.

"How do I look?" he asked and ran his palm over the wrinkles of his navy cotton shirt in a sorry attempt to smooth the fabric. The material stretched to the breaking point across his broad shoulders and emphasized his narrow waist. It was a tight fit, but the best they had been able to find during the quick trip to the thrift shop. Since he was an unknown, he was better suited to blend into the crowd gathering at the church, and his tear-away pants and T-shirt was not going to cut it for church clothes.

She couldn't hold back a chuckle. "You definitely look like you need to repent some sins."

Mischief sparkled in his eyes. "I'll only seek redemption from you." The frown returned to his brow. "Be careful in there. If you get into any trouble, scream, shout, whimper— I will hear you."

"I understand. No confrontations." She gripped him around the arm and squeezed. "That goes for you, too."

A snarl curled his lips. "I'll try. When it comes to you, my control is not at its best."

"Just remember, if you get hurt, die, or land in jail, you can't help me."

"I know." He smoothed a strand of her flyaway hair toward her ponytail. "But I can't help myself."

The deep timbre of his voice and the possessiveness in his gaze made her want to forget the evil in her past and risk building a future with him. But if the last few days had taught her anything, it was that the past always came back to bite you on the ass. Keeping vigilant about relying on no one but herself had been what kept her alive so far. Ripley made a very attractive crutch, but he was still a crutch. It would be foolish to give into temptation now.

Still, she couldn't resist the need to be intimate and placed a light kiss to his lips. "Good luck."

Ripley wasn't going to let her go with only a small peck as a good-bye. He cupped the back of her neck with his strong fingers while his tongue coaxed between her lips to tangle with hers, reminding her that as far as he was concerned, she belonged to him.

He pulled away with a whimper, his fingers flexing against her skull. "If you are not in that clearing in two hours, I will burn this compound to the ground looking for you."

With a last bruising kiss, he left her swaying on her feet as he disappeared into the woods.

"Holy shit." She ran the tip of her tongue over her swollen lips. That man had her running hot and cold so fast, she was surprised she hadn't succumbed to seizures due to the abrupt temperature changes.

Enough of that. She shook her head. Focus.

She checked the holster at her side to make sure her firearm was secured and at the ready before gingerly taking the first steps into the kitchen. The lingering odor of French toast and sausage from that morning's breakfast made her stomach rumble. Ah, the Lowell family pre-church tradition continued. That granola bar she gobbled that morning did not compare to a nice, spicy pork link.

The farmhouse kitchen with gingham curtains and cream with silver-flecked linoleum floor looked exactly as it had the day she left, as did the hall and living area she passed on the way to her father's office. It was almost as if she never left.

Or ever existed.

She pushed the surprisingly maudlin thought away and eased open the office door with a gloved hand.

Parchment-colored Roman shades filtered in a small amount of sunlight, adding to the already dim interior of dark wood furniture, floor-to-ceiling mahogany bookcases, and forest-green plaid wallpaper.

After a few rapid blinks, her eyesight adjusted and she crept farther into the room. With the cynical eye of an adult, she recognized the expensive artwork on the walls and fine antique furnishings as decorations no humble minister should be able to afford.

Walking into her father's office used to give her goose bumps, as if she were standing next to a Tesla coil. In this room she believed her father conversed directly with God. She had believed he worked hard to provide the best for his parishioners. Instead, he was gambling with those people's lives and profiting off their faith.

Those chills of old still skipped over her skin, only this time it was hatred that made her flesh crawl.

Scattered over the top of the desk were several drafts of sermons written in her father's heavy-handed scrawl, a few issues of *Christian Century* and *Christianity Today* magazines, and some congratulatory correspondence on Mary Beth's upcoming nuptials. Also on the desk were a few silver-framed photos. One was of Mary Beth as a pre-teen and another of her as a small child sitting on Jillian's lap. Smiling. Serene. Beautiful.

It didn't surprise her that there weren't any photos of herself on display. Not at all. but the sting that lashed her across the chest that her father didn't seem to acknowledge the existence of her or her late mother anywhere sucked the wind out of her lungs, leaving her hands shaking.

"Fuck him," she muttered, turning away. "Fuck him with a rusty nail and other horrible nasty things."

Grrrr. She slapped her hands on her thighs to bring her back from the past. Back to work.

A search of the two drawers came up empty. Not surprising, however it would be remiss to overlook the obvious places.

She set a penlight between her teeth and crawled underneath the desk. A litany began in her head with every gentle prod and push against the wood. *Please let me find something. Please let me find something.* As the sweat trickled down her back, her prayers grew more fevered.

Was it odd that she was praying to God to find evidence to bring about the end of her father?

Perhaps. But not as strange as the fact that she was praying at all. The last time she spoke with God was the night Sam died and she sold her body for a fake ID and a bottle of hair dye.

At first, she'd refused to pray because she had believed she was unworthy to beseech a higher power, but then had come the anger. God had forsaken her. Forsaken those she loved. In the eyes of the Lord she felt as if she were deemed unworthy, unclean, damned for all time.

She had only done what she had to in order to survive the challenges *He* threw at her. If anyone was unworthy, it should be Him.

So yeah. Her relationship with God was tenuous at best, so she didn't expect to have her prayers answered. Nevertheless, the litany continued to race in her mind like an old record playing at the wrong speed.

With the desk turning out to be a bust, she turned her attention to the dark oak bookcases. Their heavy weight didn't reveal a false wall as she had hoped, nor did the carpet hide a trap door to a secret room. If only she had Ripley's sense of smell, or Ripley himself, but they needed to split up to save time and take advantage of the house being empty.

The tick of the wall clock grew louder with each passing second, ratcheting up her heart rate. Panic fueled the desire to say fuck stealth and start ransacking the office, but she held the impulse at bay. Instead, she carefully stacked the books on the floor in a neat pile to re-examine the bookcases.

Her father's collection of Bibles was impressive in its variety, and laughable because he hadn't purchased a single one. Why people thought the perfect gift for a minister was a Bible was beyond her. One Bible was the same as the next with the only difference being the quality of the leather and the gold edging of the pages. Just another way people tried to buy their way into heaven.

The bottom row of the bookcase was lined with more humble editions of the Good Book, like the ones that resembled the versions occupying the nightstand at the local motel.

She picked up the last one and paused, the book bobbing in her grasp. The weight was different from the others. And the thickness felt inconsistent, even with her gloves on. Holding it up vertically against her palms, she let the pages fall open on their own, right to the section where someone had hollowed out the center to place a small notebook inside.

"Someone's been watching *The Shawshank Redemption*," she murmured. "You're a handsome fellow. What's your name?"

Names, dates and numbers, printed in someone's neat handwriting, filled the pages in tidy columns. What those columns meant was unclear, but her gut told her that it had to do with the drugs. She replaced the notebook with a stack of folded-up papers from the printer tray and set that Bible next to the others.

She knocked on the bottom panel of the bookcase and her hopes rose at the hollow sound.

"Yes," she hissed when the panel slid down and away, exposing the cubbyhole beneath.

Her penlight bounced off an unfinished pine box and collapsible file folder. The box was about the size of a laptop and four inches deep. Heavy, too. She needed both hands to lift the box out of the hole.

For its plain appearance, the interior was surprisingly sumptuous with crimson velvet lining. Among the various deeds and documents was another journal and a black jewelry box. The lid to the box opened with a soft *pop*. Nestled in the pearly satin was a simple, elegant diamond solitaire and gold wedding band. The fine leaf pattern on the band matched the detail surrounding the princess-cut diamond of the engagement ring.

Alisia swallowed down the anger that wrapped its fiery hand around her throat at the sight of her mother's wedding rings. Not only were they not buried with her mother as she had assumed, they were in the filthy hands of the last person on Earth who deserved such loveliness.

"Fuck that. He's not keeping these," she fumed as she jammed the rings into the front pocket of her jeans. "What other surprises will I find?"

Well, fuck a duck, she thought as she opened the file folder. Guess that answered her question. As she had suspected, her father had hired several investigators to locate her.

She figured there was no way he'd allow her to sneak off into the night without sending someone after her, a deacon or two at least. And there was at least one private investigator she knew of that she had managed to avoid when she lived on the streets. Fortunately, she had changed her appearance enough, and her acquaintances at the time had been too strung out to recognize the girl in the photo he was flashing.

But she had had no idea there had once been *five* investigators on her tail. How she managed to avoid them all was most definitely a miracle. However, what was more disturbing than the number of people hired to find her were the reports dated from just over a year ago from two more investigators. They had been closing in on her location and if she hadn't joined up with the Evolutioneers, it would've been only a matter of time before they stumbled across her.

Also among the reports were dossiers on Sam's family, and newspaper clippings of young girls who had been found dead from all over the Northwest, including the obituary of Samantha Hill.

Sam Hill. Alisia closed her eyes and leaned back against the bookcase. She hadn't heard that name in a while. The newspaper called the girl Samantha Hill because that was the driver's license Alisia had left in her possession. The girl's real name was Alisia Caldwell.

On that night long ago when she ran from her father, Gretchen knew she was going to need a new identity. Taking Sam's name had been a crutch she had needed to survive. His cousin Mike who made the fake ID for her thought the name Sam Hill was a hysterical play on words. Joke it might have been, the name served her well for over a year, and she had no reason to change it until an opportunity presented itself that she couldn't resist.

The real Alisia Caldwell had been a young, brash, selfish girl who stole her grandmother's pension checks and thought hooking was a fun way to earn money and get drugs. It was fun, all right, until a john killed her one night and left her among the trash in an alley. After stumbling across the body, it had taken Gretchen/Sam all of five seconds to decide to switch identities and never look back.

In the bottom of the box were returned letters from the reverend to Sam Connor's family asking about her location. She didn't know why he even bothered. They hadn't given a shit about Sam, so they certainly had no idea who she was. There were also letters written to Gretchen that were never mailed. Some were completed at several pages in length, others only a single sentence: *Gretchen, where are you?*

She held the stack of papers, debating, debating, debating, before stashing the bundle in her pack, and then got to her feet to set the room to rights. There were more rooms to search. More memories. More pain. Escaping this house of horrors could not come soon enough.

CHAPTER THIRTEEN

N OW RIPLEY UNDERSTOOD the emotional upheaval Max must've felt every time he sent Crystal out on a mission.

He rubbed his belly as his insides twisted. Alisia should not have been left alone, but she seemed so confident she could handle whatever she'd face next. She believed in herself, and he needed to believe in her, too. Ha. Easier said than done.

The best thing he could do for her was to accomplish his objective quickly and get back to her so they could blow this pop stand. The compound with its plain-cookie cutter houses and fields of crops gave him too much of a *Children of the Corn* feeling that was creepy as fuck. The sooner they got out of there, the sooner they could hand off their intel to Max and Addison to sift through properly.

The parking lot in front of the church was packed with row after row of every type of minivan sold in the United States. According to their intel, the average attendance for a Sunday service was six thousand people. Six thousand lambs sequestered under the steel and stained-glass arena of the Church of the Divine and Sacred.

Ripley stood between two Caravans and looked into the faces of the men and women filing into the church. They looked like good, hard-working folks who only wanted to take care of their families and give weekly thanks to a power they found strength and solace in.

What would they do when they discovered they were embroiled in a story as old as time? A story of another charlatan who claimed that his way was the one true path to enlightenment, and used every underhanded technique to ensure their followers depended only on them. Sure, some prophets believed that they were helping mankind, but most were more than willing to take advantage of the purity of others' faith for their own personal gain.

No one wanted to believe that they were being taken by liars and thieves. Some even denied they were wronged even as you stood before them and took the money straight out of their pockets. Would these people refuse to believe they were deceived and go after the messenger who revealed the truth, or would they lose faith in not only mankind but any higher power? When it came to the most zealous, there was rarely an in-between.

A person could be reasoned with, but a congregation the size of Lowell's had the potential to incite a fuck-fest of epic proportions. Ripley wanted Alisia far from the storm when the apocalypse began.

Ripley joined the steady stream of parishioners passing through the ornate double doorway, filling the arena from the front on up to the nosebleed section in the balconies.

The congregation was opened to any who wished to enter, but there was reserved seating for those who lived on the compound itself. Ripley strode with confidence down the aisle to the front as if he belonged there. Seven rows back from the stage he spotted a gentleman with his passel of children spread out along the pew. Plenty of space for one more.

"Excuse me." Ripley flashed his most charming smile at

the girl on the end, and lowered his shoulders to try to appear less intimidating. "May I sit here?"

Her glittering brown eyes blinked up at him as if she were waking from a dream. "Oh, certainly." She scooted across the bench, pushing at her father to create more room.

She wore a simple peach-colored dress with tiny, dark-orange buttons that ran from the base of her throat to where the hem fell near her calves. A little austere, he thought, for a girl who looked no older than twenty, but the way she wore her hair braided and her lack of makeup reminded Ripley of the photo of Gretchen. Apparently, this was the way the women on the compound dressed.

"You're new," the girl burst out. Her gaze raced over his features and down to linger on his shoulders and biceps stretching the fabric of his shirt. "I would have remembered seeing someone as strapping as you before."

He held back his chuckle over her use of the word "strapping" and sat beside her.

"Yeah. I'm from Spokane, actually. I've seen the reverend many times on TV, but I felt the need to experience him in person. I'll be moving out onto the compound in a few weeks. Just need to get my housing all settled."

"Oh, you'll love it here. Reverend Lowell's fantastic. When he speaks, it's as if all is right in the world. And if I close my eyes and reach out, I can touch the face of God himself." She sucked in a breath. "I love church."

Ripley kept his smile in place and fired up all his senses. Her fingers were plucking and twisting the button of her dress near her navel, the thread fraying under the constant worrying. Her knee bounced a frantic rhythm, a movement copied by others in the vicinity. Under layers of Dial soap and Herbal Essence shampoo was the acrid stench of sweat and human, and the air buzzed with anticipation. These people were jonesing for their fix.

"Did you grow up near here?" he asked the girl.

She nodded and dabbed at her nose with a tissue she pulled from inside her sleeve. "I've never left. My husband, Earl, grew up here, too." She patted the knee of the silver-haired man next to her who Ripley had thought was her father.

Shock, surprise, and a wee bit of disgust screwed up his face before he regained his pleasant expression. "Oh. Wow. Hello, sir. That's, that's great. Have you been married long?"

"Six years," Earl answered. "Are you looking for a wife of your own?"

"Not really."

"You won't find a better wife than the girls we have here at the Divine and Sacred."

"Ha. Right." He choked and tried to smile. "You make it sound like you're growing them out in a field."

The man scoffed. "We are. But not in the soil. Our girls are cultivated from an early age to be good wives and mothers for our young. They're trained to be obedient and care for their families. You're too late to get one of the next group of girls who will come of age this summer, but you may be able to get on a list for one of the girls coming out a few years from now. If you pass inspection, of course."

"List?" There was a *list*? "For what?"

"Marriage, of course." He nodded at his wife. "Stephanie's father is about to collect a list of husband-candidates for her sister."

"How old is your sister?"

Stephanie's nails clicked at her buttons. "Twelve."

Bile rose in his throat. "That's a child."

Her giggle raised the hair on his arms. "Don't be silly. You wouldn't get married for another few years."

As if that made it all better. How had Alisia avoided the marriage trap? "Why aren't these lists mentioned on the television?"

"The televised sermons are for part-time Christians. If you really want to be among the blessed, then you make the effort to be here in person, like you did. Those who live and work for the church are the ones who are truly rewarded."

And by reward, he meant with young girls to take advantage of.

Under Ripley's skin the muscles rolled in waves, mimicking the anger boiling inside.

What was wrong with these people? How could the trafficking of young girls be discussed as calmly as a trip to the pet store? The immorality was spreading from the deacons down to the men *and* women, and it was a sickness that had to be stopped.

His animal demanded to be released and annihilate the evil. The compulsion was so insistent, Ripley had to fight the impulse to reach across Stephanie and rip the throat out of the bastard she called husband with his claws and rush at the deacons gathering in front of the stage. Only the knowledge that Alisia might need his assistance kept the man in firm control of the animal's leash. Barely.

The lights dimmed as a spotlight hit the five-piece band and a rather pedestrian version of "Joyful Joy" began on the piano. The crowd of thousands immediately fell silent as the audience's buzz of anticipation tickled the skin along Ripley's neck. These people were Pavlov's dogs, subconsciously aware that their fix was on its way.

A pretty young girl wearing a lime green dress walked

across the stage and took a seat on one of two red velvet chairs that sat off to the side. Ripley rubbed his eyes as he stared at Alisia's doppelganger. Her features were sharper, but she shared the same almond-shaped eyes, full lips, and long blonde braid. That had to be Alisia's little sister.

Mary Beth Lowell sat with her hands folded in her lap and her back ramrod straight. She looked out into the audience with a slight, serene smile on her lips, but her eyes stared blankly, as if in her mind she was a million miles away. Alisia used to wear a similar expression when she would try to ignore his presence.

Deacon Winston joined her and placed a proprietary hand on her shoulder. Fangs threatened to erupt from Ripley's gums and claws burst from his fingertips as he fought the urge to tear apart the man that hurt his woman.

Soon, he told the animal, soon Winston would die by his hand. Just keep the fuck in control until then.

Mary Beth didn't flinch, didn't even blink in response as Ripley saw Winston's grip tighten. Was she even aware what was planned for her? Did she have any idea of the type of man her father promised her to?

Thank God Alisia wasn't there with them now. While he might be fighting the urge to kill, he knew she would have climbed over every man, woman, and child with guns blazing to get to Winston.

Reverend Lowell took center stage to thunderous applause that shook the building and sent tremors under Ripley's seat. His broad smile flashed white against his tan face as he raised his hands. As one, the crowd stood. The sound of six thousand people getting to their feet boomed like a heavy oak door slamming shut.

"What's going on?" Ripley whispered.

"Communion," Stephanie answered. "We partake before the sermon begins."

Weird. He was used to communion being taken in the middle or near the end of a sermon.

"They do communion with all these people?" He gestured to the assembly in the stands. "Wouldn't that take forever?"

"No. Only those on floor level here. We provide the church with the most support, so we are the most worthy."

Most worthy? That remained to be seen. More than likely that meant the most malleable.

Even with only a third of those in attendance receiving their "reward," that was still a few thousand lining up in front of the deacons stationed at the end of each section, waiting for their turn.

Ripley followed the line of sheep before him to where Deacon Winston stood with a silver box clutched in his bony grip.

One person after the other gleefully accepted the wafer placed delicately on their tongue, their eyes closed in ecstasy. There was no way in hell Ripley was letting that rat bastard anywhere near his face.

Winston used a set of small tongs to hold up the quarter-size piece of flour, water, and chemicals. "The body of Christ."

Ripley held out his hand, palm up. He met Winston's questioning gaze with his own steely-eyed stare, waiting patiently. The line behind Ripley grew restless the longer Winston kept the wafer just above his grasp.

Winston took in Ripley's height and breadth of shoulders before placing the wafer in his palm. Oh, did the deacon want to ask questions. He wanted to ask questions bad.

Ripley flashed him a soft smile and nodded, cupping his palm to touch only the edges, and motioned as if he was eating the cracker while slipping it down the cuff of his shirt.

As he moved past the offering of wine, he glanced up at the stage and saw Mary Beth in the same pose as before with her father standing proudly by her side. Was she too drugged, or was she as unaware as Gretchen had been of her father's transgressions?

The remainder of the congregation began to chant and sing songs in a language Ripley didn't recognize, but it sure as hell wasn't a version of hallelujah or fa-la-la-la-las.

As the chorus rose and swelled in time to the rhythmic swaying, their waving arms and bodies made his vision buck and roll like he was standing on a ship on the Baltic Sea. He shuddered to think what those who had taken the drugs might be experiencing at the sight of the undulating mass of bodies.

When the last of the parishioners had taken their seats, the crowd fell silent in a collective intake of air and focused their attention on Lowell, who stood at an obsidian glass podium with his arms raised.

"Welcome, my brothers and sisters, my sons and daughters. It does my heart good to see so many eager, bright faces before me ready to give and receive God's love. As the earth is warmed by the sun, we too are warmed by His power. As the earth blossoms and awakens from the deep sleep of winter, we too are reborn, renewed, rejuvenated, and recommitted in spreading the word of our Lord and Savior to those less fortunate than we. On this glorious Sunday morning I am asking you to open yourself up to the power of the Lord. Come on, raise your hands." Several hands shot into the air. "Higher. Reach out to God for our opening prayer. Heavenly Father, we beseech you to be with us today. Grace us with your presence. Make yourself be known."

"I see him," a woman to Ripley's right shouted. "He's holding me." She wrapped her arms around her waist and swayed in her seat.

"Thank you, my sister," Lowell shouted. "We need His strength in this time of strife and uncertainty. In these desperate hours when down is up and up seems so deep down, you can feel the heat from Hell scorching your face. We are living in a world where those in positions of power will extend their right hand in friendship while the left is ready to stab you in the back. Where every day hundreds are losing their jobs, or their homes, and their faith, we are living in a world, my children, where there are people claiming to have super powers. Can you believe that? They are spitting in the face of God by pretending to *be* gods. We need to be vigilant. We need to stand strong together and give ourselves over to the wisdom of our Lord. That reminds me of a story in the Bible. Let me share it with you."

Ripley wished Max was sitting next to him so that they could marvel together at the cojones the reverend had tucked in his trousers. With each word spewing out of his double-talking, hypocritical mouth, he continued to dig his own grave. Gone was the concerned father who had tearfully asked for the Evolutioneers for help, and in his place was a scared little man spouting dissidence and hate.

"The lesson here is to not believe what you know in your heart to be untrue," the reverend continued. "The only powers granted to man are those God gave for love and compassion. Do not become tainted by those who are dancing with the devil. Now is the time we band together and cleanse your soul to receive His wisdom."

Underneath Ripley's seat, the vibrations of thousands of people bobbing, bouncing, and shuddering, caught under the pull of Lowell's speech tingled his backside.

"Jesus Christ," Ripley cursed out loud. Several sharp glances shot his way. He threw up his hands. "Is my Lord and Savior."

"Hallelujah, brother, hallelujah."

"My people, I am here for you." Lowell stood with his arms in the air, eyes tightly closed and his face turned up to the spotlight, feeding off the energy of his people. "Let me be your conduit to the Lord. At this time of renewal, purge your soul of its worries. Expunge your sins unto me. Speak, speak to me now."

The thunder of drums rolled across the sea of swaying bodies, whipping the waves into a frenzy. A wailing guitar rose and fell with the shouts of sinners.

"I lied to my boss."

"I've sinned in my heart."

As the confessions poured forth, a woman screamed behind Ripley. He turned to see an older woman on her feet. Spasms shook her, ruffling the gray hair escaping her tight braid. She pointed to the ceiling, arms locked straight out as incoherent mumbling spat from her lips.

"My sister has the spirit." Lowell pointed to her. "She's speaking with the Lord."

The woman fell into convulsions, her eyes rolled back into her head as she collapsed into the arms of a deacon standing at her side. All around Ripley, chaos erupted as men and women succumbed to the drugs in their system.

Lowell ran around the stage pointing and shouting, "You are one with God. You are one with God."

Mary Beth was a gentle breeze in the eye of the storm. Back and forth she rocked gracefully in her seat, eyes closed, barricaded in her own world. Ripley's heart ached for the Lowell sisters, and for the rest of the children whose parents were slowly being ripped away.

Stephanie clutched his arm, her knuckles turning white as a strangled cry broke past her lips. Ripley caught her as she collapsed, her eyes fixed dead ahead and her breath stuttering.

"Sir, we'll take her."

Ripley looked up to see Deacon Ryan and another man standing over them. "She's sick."

"She's conversing with the Lord." Ryan reached out and gripped her wrist. "We'll take her."

"She needs a doctor."

"Let her go." Earl tried to slap at him with a weak hand. His drugged stupor made him oblivious to the worry in Ripley's voice. "That's my Stephanie. She's talking to the Lord."

The girl was ripped from his arms and carried through a door near the stage. Anger zipped along Ripley's skin, bunching muscles and lengthening his claws. He swiped a hand over his face, struggling for control when all he wanted was to tear after Ryan and rip his throat out.

How dare they exploit innocent people this way? The way they were using something as pure as faith to corrupt for greed and narcissism sickened him to his soul. This madness needed to end, but he had to be smart about it. Max was the planner. He looked at every angle before he acted, and Ripley had to do the same or risk the success of the mission.

Another cry echoed behind him. His vision fluctuated as his eyes changed shape from man to animal with the need to act.

"Fuck it," he growled and charged through the throng of revelers for the door.

CHAPTER FOURTEEN

J UST AS RIPLEY reached for the door, the lights in the church went out. Spots formed in his vision at the sudden darkness and his ears rang as silence quickly fell across the crowd.

The only light in the giant cathedral was a soft white spotlight shining down on Lowell. Sweat sparkled on his forehead like diamonds, his arms raised in entreaty.

"Dear Heavenly Father. We are blessed to have you grace us with your presence. We bow in the glory of your power, and pray that you watch over us and our children, like my daughter Gretchen, who are out in the world risking their lives spreading your word to those less fortunate. Bring them home to the haven of our arms."

Several shouts of "amen" rang from the crowd.

"We've had a mighty call to action today, my children. Thank you for sharing your spirit with me today. God bless." Lowell clasped his hands to his chest and bowed. After he straightened, he leaned over the edge of the stage to press his palms against the foreheads of those reaching out to him in adoration. To these people he was a rock star.

As the band continued to play, one of the deacons took over the microphone at center stage. "My brothers and sisters, aren't we blessed to have a leader like Reverend Lowell? I can feel the power he has generated for us today. And now we must channel that love. For those of you joining us today for the first time, this is the time when we quietly reflect on the lessons taught to us this morning. Close your eyes, sit back, and fall into the embrace of the Lord as the collections plates are passed around. Give generously, folks. Give generously."

Yeah, more like wait for the worst of the drugs to wear off before getting behind the wheel of your vehicle and maiming someone on your way home from church. Ripley sucked in a growl and strode to the door near the stage.

Winston stepped in his path. "Can I help you, brother?"

He stomped on the impulse to smack the man down and gritted out between his lengthening teeth, "That girl, Stephanie. Is she all right?"

Winston eyed him up and down, noting the tense muscles in his body. He probably realized that a man of Ripley's size could be potentially dangerous if he had consumed the drugs. Unbeknownst to him, a sober Ripley was an even greater danger. Despite Winston's reassuring smile, Ripley noticed, he grounded his stance and kept his arms loose at his sides.

"Your concern is kind, but the girl is doing well. Just a little overwhelmed. Please, take your seat. It is best to rest your mind after one of Reverend Lowell's sermons."

Ripley flexed his fingers. Lowell had disappeared backstage and most of the arena congregants had fallen into a stupor under the soft blue lighting and melodic music. Causing a scene here would not do him any good.

"I need some fresh air."

"There's an exit just over there." Winston gestured.

Ripley nodded and strode toward the set of doors that led out onto another parking lot.

Bright sunlight burned his skin and the cool air did little

to ease the stench of corruption that clung to him like the effects of a fog machine.

After ensuring that no one followed, Ripley ducked behind a group of shrubs and quickly shed his clothing. Tucking the thin communion wafer into a plastic bag then his pocket, Ripley carefully stashed his clothes into the thick foliage. Spreading his arms wide, he hunched over, grimacing as fire raced up his spine and along his bones. Pale flesh turned into brown leather wings as the bat soared into the air.

Metal scraped his back as he flew between the slats of an air vent, and the tips of his wings brushed against the smooth metal tunnel. Fire raced through his veins again as the bat dropped to the floor of the air shaft and in its place a fox slinked deeper into the dark, following his nose to the next shaft of light, searching, seeking Lowell and his men.

The stench of acid and ammonia to his right brought him above a makeshift clinic tucked into the inner recesses of the church. Over twenty parishioners were laid out on thin mattresses supported on flimsy metal cots. Some people were in shock, caught in the grips of the drugs, while others lay comatose, their pale skin shiny with sweat and the stuttered rise and fall of their chest as they treaded a thin line between life and death.

Several deacons followed orders given by an older gentleman who furtively swiped his silver bangs off his sweaty brow. "Keep that woman covered. Deacon Thomas, restrain that man's hands before he tears his skin off. This is, this is not good," he murmured, taking another swipe at his thinning hair.

Deacon Winston strode through the door. "Dr. Petrov, can we release any of them yet?"

"Release them?" Dr. Petrov sputtered and dropped the stethoscope he held pressed to the chest of an elderly woman. "Look around you. These people should be in a hospital. I almost lost Sister Irene here. Deacon Winston, this has been the worst reaction of all. This has to stop before we start killing hundreds of people. End this madness now."

Winston snatched Petrov by the arm and hauled him across the room to stand under the vent Ripley was crouching in. With a small shake, Winston released the frightened doctor, then smoothed the man's lapels while wearing a gentle smile that made the fierce power in his eyes all the more terrifying. "Dr. Petrov, I apologize if this morning has been more stressful than usual. We are fine-tuning a new formula and it obviously has not gone the way we need it to. We shall correct it immediately."

"It's more than just today. It's too much. The human body cannot withstand the stress of such narcotics for a long period of time. I don't want—I can't bury another member because of these actions."

Winston's smile grew warmer as his eyes chilled further. His big scarred hands brushed at imaginary lint on Petrov's shoulders before coming to rest with heavy intent. "Do not worry, Johan. You are doing the work God has meant for you to do."

"Drugging people is not what He meant," the older man choked.

Winston laughed and tightened his grip. "You are helping them back from the journey to enlightenment. Never forget that's what we're paying you to do."

Petrov jerked away and adjusted his jacket with a forlorn and disappointed acceptance in his pale eyes.

"You're right. I will have to trust that God will see the truth in our actions. All of *our* actions," he added boldly as he turned back to his work administering to the sick.

Cold contemplation settled in Winston's eyes as he watched Petrov for several long seconds before he snapped to attention and vacated the sick room.

Ripley sprinted from vent to vent, sticking close to Winston's scent as the man paused to inform those waiting that it would be a bit longer before their friends and relatives returned to their earthly bodies. Ha. They would be lucky if they didn't end up buried six feet under.

Deep under the influence of their own trip, the small crowd swallowed the lie. Envy and disappointment that they hadn't been fortunate enough to reach euphoria like the others clouded their eyes and slackened their cheeks. With the group settled, Winston continued down the hall to a single white door at the end of a long hallway.

Reverend Lowell sat inside a plush office with teak furnishings and hunter-green wallpaper. The ornate Louis XV desk gleamed with a fresh polish in the sunlight from the floor-to-ceiling windows. The schematics Addison had pulled up on the church said the glass was bulletproof. Now Ripley understood why the reverend would take such a precaution.

There wasn't a file folder, piece of paper, or stapler in sight. It was a pristine room straight from the pages of *Better Homes and Gardens* magazine—Old Money edition. It was a space designed for only one type of work. Networking.

The reverend leaned back in his leather seat, his elbows resting on the arms of his chair and his fingers steepled under his chin. Only his eyelids twitched as he stared straight ahead. The slight movement was caused by the cigarette smoke billowing in his face from where Ryan stood on his right, puffing on a Swisher Sweet.

Neither man said a word, each lost in their own thought as Lowell looked like a freeze-framed photo next to the twitchy fast forward of Ryan puffing on the cigarette as if they were made of candy. Both men jerked and glanced expectantly at the door when Winston entered and quietly pushed the oak panel into place.

"How many?" Lowell burst out as he shot to his feet.

Winston drew a deep breath before responding. "Twenty-three."

A grunt was Lowell's solo response as he sat back down. The rapid tap of his thumb on the arm of the chair was the only indication of his agitation. "How bad?"

"They'll live."

"Do not treat this lightly," Lowell snapped. The spark that flared in his eyes burned orange against the deep green iris.

To Ripley's surprise, Winston paled and looked down at the floor. Perhaps Winston wasn't the only muscle in the operation.

"Some have fallen unconscious, but they're stable. Recovery time is taking longer than normal, but all will survive without any permanent damage."

"So we hope." Contemplation tightened Lowell's lips as he re-steepled his fingers. "I'm getting the feeling that there's more you need to report."

"Petrov is questioning his purpose."

"And you set him straight. Correct." That wasn't a question.

"Yes, sir."

Lowell's fingers began a steady tap-tap-tap. Tap-tap-tap. Ring finger, middle finger, forefinger. Ring finger, middle finger, forefinger.

Ryan sucked down another cigarette, burning the paper down beyond the filter, while Winston watched Lowell with wide eyes as if he were watching a bomb about to detonate.

"Damn!" Lowell exploded, his face flushing. "Damn, damn, damn."

Holding his arms straight out, Lowell pressed his fingers deep into the blotter until the tips turned white. Winston, Ryan, and even Ripley, held their breath as they waited.

Lowell's lips moved silently while the red in his cheeks subsided in slow degrees. With a final sigh, he muttered an "amen" then straightened and pulled on his shirt cuffs.

"This is what we'll do. Ryan, contact Dr. Strangelove. Tell him that the shipment will be delayed. The point of the drug is to bring in followers, not kill them. There is too much on the line with the new church opening soon to bring any negative attention about how we're killing the current congregation."

"What if he wants a new date for delivery?"

"Tell him it will be a week at the least for us to adjust the formula. One week." He sighed and his nostrils flared. "Winston, what have we heard from those people about Gretchen?"

The way he spat "those people" had Ripley's hackles rising and his thin black lip curling over a sharp fang.

"Maestro called late last night," Winston answered. "He believes that someone from Sam Connor's family took her in and helped her escape."

Ryan lit another cigarette with the butt of the first. "I still think someone found her and tossed her body in the ditch after raping her to death."

Lowell flinched, his cheeks paling at Ryan's statement. "Did Maestro say who?"

"It was a cousin of Connor's by the name of Michael."

"No. The private investigators said that line went nowhere. That the cousin knew nothing of Gretchen."

"One of the women, Prism, read his mind."

Both Lowell and Ryan hissed. "Unnatural. Only the Devil would grant powers to those so unworthy. We must guard ourselves against having such atrocities being performed against us."

Winston raised a dark eyebrow. "Any idea as to how to do that?"

"Holy water and silver crosses?" Ryan half-joked.

When neither man laughed, or even broke into a grin at the ridiculousness of the suggestion, a heavy stone of unease settled in Ripley's gut. These men definitely had bats in the belfry.

"It wouldn't hurt," Lowell replied in all seriousness. "God is our protector, but we should still err on the side of caution and limit our exposure to those creatures. Once Gretchen is under our control, we can begin to spread to the outside word of the evils of pretending to be a god. And end these people for good."

That ungrateful SOB. White-hot anger shot down Ripley's spine. Red fur morphed to orange with black stripes as his paws grew and his fangs lengthened.

Shit, shit, shit. The instinct to lunge through the grate and tear them apart threatened to override the common sense that an eight-hundred-pound Bengal tiger would not fit in a two-by-two air shaft. As the slick metal surface buckled under his weight, Ripley squeezed his body down the rapidly tightening tunnel.

He had to get his shit together or he was going to become the stuffing in an aluminum sausage. Thick whiskers bent as he shook his head and thought *bat, bat, bat, come on, bat.* Darkness gave way to light as he neared the entrance to the vent.

Come on, you son of a bitch.

Echoing down the air shaft behind him were the shouts and outcries from those inside the building guessing what could be causing all the commotion coming from the ceiling.

Yes, finally.

Meaty paws gave way to thin wings and Ripley flew between the slats of the grating. Well… Most of him did, anyway.

With his body in mid-shift, his back paw caught in the slats, pulling him up short with a sharp jerk. He flopped, bat face first, into the brick siding. The smack to the forehead broke his concentration, allowing him to slip free from the trap and land in the shrubbery with a high, pitiful squeak and a rustle of leaves. Stars flashed in his vision from the combination of bright sunlight and the knock to the head.

What the fuck was wrong with him? Even in the early days of his powers, he never got stuck between forms when shifting. Either he was losing his powers, or something else was wreaking havoc with his control. Neither option was favorable.

Lifting up on his pointy, brown elbows, Ripley dragged his little body deeper into the shadows, hiding from the rapid clip of approaching footfalls.

"Do you think it was a coon?" a deacon asked. His black shoes raced past Ripley's hiding place.

"Possibly. There are so many types of critters out here. God, I hope it doesn't have rabies, or laid a litter in the building."

"Let's get the guns and put it down."

When his sonar detected no movement in the immediate area, Ripley popped out of the rhododendrons on two human legs. Scratches crisscrossed his arms and chest, and his ankle was sore from being pinned.

Yeah, that had been a sexy move.

Thank God no one witnessed his spectacular fall from grace If that had happened to Max or Chase, he'd have been on the ground and pissing his pants from laughing so hard.

"Shit," he bit out and scrambled for his clothes to take the wafer out of his pocket. He bit down on a corner of the baggie before shifting back into a wolf.

His pride had to take a back seat. Now because of him, there were armed men searching the area. And Alisia was a sitting duck.

CHAPTER FIFTEEN

R IPLEY'S SENSE OF smell picked up the scent of Alisia's tears long before he saw her. They were salty like an ocean breeze. Sad, but without the peppery bite of fear. She was upset, but not hurt or in immediate danger. Still, he kept up his break-neck speed until he saw her with his own eyes.

By the time he burst through the woods into their meeting spot in the clearing, she was on her feet, wiping at her cheeks with one the sleeve of her hoodie while the other held her pistol at the ready. When she realized it was him, she holstered her weapon and swung her backpack over her shoulder. "Geez, could you be any louder? I thought your skills lay in being stealthy?"

Without breaking stride, he shifted. "Are you all right?"

She barked a sharp, bitter laugh. "I'm fine."

Right, he recognized that tone. "You're going to tell me everything, but right now we've gotta run. I kind of have a posse chasing me."

"What?"

He pushed the baggie into her backpack. "And they're armed. And they think I might be rabid."

"What did you do?"

"They just don't make air vents like they used to." He dropped down to all fours. "Giddy up."

Snap, crackle, pop. Damn, he was going to be sore tonight.

Once her weight settled onto the stallion's bare back, Ripley's heartbeat slowed, but only a fraction as her arms circled his neck and her cheek nuzzled his skin. She was physically safe, but whatever she had found obviously affected her a great deal. The myriad of emotions he sensed rioting inside her buffeted him like a hurricane. She was lost in a sea of uncertainty and he'd be her anchor, if she let him.

At the truck Alisia kept a cautious eye out for their chasers while he tossed on a T-shirt and pants before jumping behind the wheel and tearing off down the trail.

"What exactly did you do?" she asked him again.

"I was listening in on a conversation and the air vent started to cave. The noise drew some attention."

"What shape were you in, an elephant? And what happened to your face?"

"Huh?" A glance in the rearview mirror revealed dark pink scratches running down his forehead and nose from where his face got cozy with the brick wall. He ran his finger over the marks and frowned. "Must have hit the grate flying out. Anyway, I found out why your father is still looking for you."

He risked taking his eyes off the road to check her expression. She wasn't hanging onto his every word. Instead she slumped against the door and looked out at the scenery flying by.

Plowing on, he continued. "It sounds as if your pops is opening another church soon. You're a loose end they want tied before they open."

"Cut off altogether sounds more like it," she muttered.

"They're planning on drugging the new followers, the same as they do on the compound, but there's a problem.

The drug they're using is too strong. Lowell doesn't want to risk suspicion if people start dying. He told Ryan to contact a 'Dr. Strangelove' and delay an exchange." His acute hearing picked up on her soft gasp. "Who is that? A church member?"

She snorted. "Not that I know of."

"But you recognized the name." A mile passed with her remaining silent as she traced the grooves in her denim jeans with her fingernail, becoming entranced by the pattern. "Alisia," he barked.

She glared at him, lips tightening before she answered. "I've heard his name when I lived on the streets. He's a middleman. Puts dealers and suppliers together so that the suppliers can remain anonymous."

Ripley shot her a long, considering glance from the corner of his eye, weighing the words she didn't say. "How dangerous is he?"

"Hard to say. He gives the impression of being a talker more than a fighter, like he couldn't care less as long as he gets your money, but you don't get the cred he has without busting a few heads. I wouldn't underestimate him."

The hair on the back of his neck stood on end. "Sounds like you know him personally."

She turned back to the window. "We've crossed paths. I tried to remain as invisible as possible." She shrugged. "Sometimes you're in the wrong place at the wrong time. Seems to be the pattern of my life."

"Do you know where to find him?"

"I have an idea where to start." She rubbed the heels of her hands against her closed eyes. "Guess we're going into the city. Gah. I just need a nap and then I can think straight."

"Don't worry, sweetheart. We wouldn't even hit the city until early evening. I know a place along the way we can stay for the night since the cabin isn't an option." Even if the cabin was vacant, he didn't need the temptation of them alone for a repeat of the fire they blazed the night before. A cuddle, maybe. But even that was pushing it. He needed to remain focused to keep them safe. "We can make a plan and tackle it first thing in the morning. What did you find in the house?"

Her fingers tightened on her pack. "I found a ledger. It has dates, numbers, letters. Hopefully it's everything we need." She pinched the bridge of her nose then rubbed her finger over her eyebrows. "I'm starting to get overwhelmed."

Ripley had to keep her talking. Alisia was a master at tuning out the world. The fact she let him know what she was feeling, even just a little, was a good thing. She was trusting him.

To touch or not to touch? His hand flexed, burning with the need to absorb all her pain, as if a simple caress would make her whole. "What else, baby?"

The fact that she didn't balk at the endearment told him how deep in thought she was. He gave in to the need and reached out. Under his palm her thigh tensed then relaxed.

"There were contracts, correspondence, sermons." She licked her lips. "The women in the church are nothing but property. I found a contract between my father and Winston. When I turned eighteen, I was to be given to him as payment for services performed for the church.

"When I left, my sister was put in my place. It's not just my father. All the families barter their daughters like livestock. Most of them at a younger age. The only reason my sister and I were given more time was to prolong

Winston's service." She pulled at her hair with both fists. "How could I have not known? I thought everything was perfect. Happy families that honored and respected each other as human beings. I was so wrong."

Ripley kept the fact that he was offered a spot on one of those lists to himself. "Sweetie, you were a child. Your world consisted within a little tiny bubble in a sea of suds. You were sheltered from that on purpose."

"I still should have known."

"And done what?"

"Something. Anything. That man is deranged. He wrote letters to me, blaming me for disrupting his utopian dream, praying for God to have mercy on my soul for not following His will and letting my weak mind be led astray by my evil feminine desires. Who the hell thinks that way, let alone write it down on paper? He never saw me as a person. All my accomplishments that I thought he was proud of wasn't because I was his daughter, it was because it made me a more valuable commodity."

Ripley swallowed against the tightness in his throat. His concentration was torn between the freeway, the lack of distance between them and the compound, and the pain he could hear in her voice.

"Do you know why he really wants me back alive?" She turned toward him with eyes bright with the glitter of tears clinging to her lashes. "So that I can be made an example for the church. I'm to be brought back and made to confess all of my sins before the core of the congregation. Then used as a teaching tool to the rest of the men as to how to control their women."

"That will never happen," he argued in a guttural voice. "I will kill them all before they touch you."

She didn't hear him, lamenting to the road stretching before them. "What did I do? I've asked myself that so many times. What did I do? Why are fathers so horrible to their children? Max's dad, Crystal's dad, my father? Why can't they just love their children for the people they are and not as a reflection of their own grandeur?"

He squeezed her leg again. "Not all fathers are assholes. Mine is pretty great. Both my parents are. They always encouraged me to do whatever I wanted. If I was happy, they were happy, and I liked making them happy."

"That's easy to do when you're Mr. Golden Boy All-American."

He ignored the sneer in her tone, knowing she was hurting. "Not always. I wrestled in school, but the only medal I won was for the math Olympiad, and a science fair or two. I was a pretty geeky kid. All of this—" he gestured to his tightly packed muscles—"was after my change."

"You, a geek? I don't believe you."

"No, really. My parents taught me that I could do anything I want as long as I wanted it bad enough. They picked me up when I fell, and knocked me down when I got too full of myself. I never wanted for anything, well, except a motorcycle or tattoo. My leash was only allowed to go so far."

"You're lucky." She sniffed. "It's sad how it seems so few children live with happy, supportive families."

"Alisia, I can't feel bad about having a great childhood."

"I didn't say you had to." Indignation snapped in her tone like a rubber band and she pushed his hand off her thigh.

Ripley shifted in his seat as his ears burned hot. No, she said nothing of the sort, but in their little family of the

Evolutioneers, only he and Chase came from what was considered a "normal" family. And it definitely made him feel like the golden boy, as if he was somehow lacking toughness because he never had to fight for his life. A shrink might say that he tried to make up for his lack of street cred by driving a battered truck, gambling too much, and never giving his full hundred percent. While he would never wish to live the nightmares some of his colleagues had, the guilt burned his throat at being fortunate to have the life he had led.

He rubbed the back of his neck. "I'm sorry. I know you didn't. I guess I do feel bad sometimes, because I didn't appreciate how good I had it."

"It sounds to me like you did."

Her husky whisper brought his gaze around to hers. Those big green eyes of hers seared him right to the soul, and his heart swelled when she let him rest his hand back on her thigh.

"What did your parents say when they found out about your powers?" she asked.

"They don't know."

She looked at him in surprise. "But you're so close to them. How can they not know?"

"I don't want them to worry. Even if I wasn't an Evolutioneer, they'd be concerned about my safety, or become targets because of who I am. Plus, my dad would turn me into a workhorse if he knew I could literally turn into one."

"I'm sure they would be proud of you, Ripley." She patted his hand. "They sound really nice."

"They're going to love you."

She blinked at him in confusion. "Why do you say that?"

"Besides being smart and beautiful, you never hesitate to put me in my place. But you don't have to take my word, they'll tell you themselves."

"Like that will ever happen."

"Oh, I wouldn't say that. We're almost there."

"Almost where?" She leaned forward to look out the windshield. "Ripley, where are we?"

Tall pines had given way to the green rolling hills of Skagit Valley. With the winter having lasted for so long, the tulips were still in full bloom late into the season. Bright pinks, yellows, reds, and purples painted the ground like a dancing rainbow.

Ripley turned down a beautifully manicured street lined with custom Craftsman homes in soft blues and grays. Pulling into the third driveway on the right, he turned off the truck and waved to the woman kneeling in the flower bed.

Red tulips glowed in the setting sun like melting popsicles and complemented the yellow apron she wore over her lime green sweater set, but it was her smile that glittered more brilliantly than the flora.

Alisia's nails bit into his hand, drawing blood. "Ripley. Where. Are. We?"

He smiled a toothy grin. "We're at my parents' house."

CHAPTER SIXTEEN

A LISIA STARED OUT the grimy windshield of Ripley's truck in horror as a diminutive woman wearing a wide-brim sunhat ran to them with her hands waving in the air.

"Why are we at your parents'?" she forced out through frozen lips.

"We need a place to rest. And between gas and that trip to the thrift store, we're short on funds. Nothing will touch you here. Even me." He flashed her a wink.

She barely heard that last part because her entire focus was on Ripley's mother, who was jumping outside his door, clapping her hands in delight. The pearls around her neck glinted in the sunlight with each bounce.

Alisia clasped her throat as she began to hyperventilate and the layers of dust and grit covering her skin itched. How could Ripley bring her here? She was too dirty to be anywhere near such loveliness. What could he be thinking, bringing a thieving, murdering—

"Alisia." His sharp commanding tone broke through her rising hysteria. He flashed her a smile. "It's going to be all right. Get out of the truck, sweetheart."

Get out of the truck? Ha ha. Ha ha. Right.

Okay. What were her options? Refuse and stay in the isolation of the cab in a completely immature act of rebellion and look like a fool, or meet his parents and potentially embarrass both herself and Ripley with the effort to hide the facts about…well, everything, and still look like a fool.

"Alisia." Ripley looked at her with those big blue eyes as if he were a puppy.

Damn it. Option two it was.

Her sweaty hand slipped off the door release twice before she managed to pop open the door and slowly slide out.

Ripley's mother squealed and stood on tip toe to throw her arms around his shoulders. "Oh, my baby boy. What a surprise."

Baby boy?

"Georg," she shouted, startling Alisia. "Come here. Our boy's home."

"Hey, hey." A giant the size of a Viking statue she once saw in a museum display stepped out from the interior of the dark garage. But instead of leather and a fur vest the man wore a gray cardigan sweater and black slacks that he tucked a handkerchief in the back pocket of after wiping his hands free from garage dust.

And Ripley had led her to believe that his size was a by-product of his super powers. Sure. Whatever.

Mr. Jorgensen's wide smile showed pearly teeth that matched the white streaking through his wheat-colored hair. "There's my boy."

He gripped Ripley in a huge bear hug that should have crushed his ribs, but Ripley returned the enthusiastic hug with a huge belly laugh while his mother watched her men. Her smile was blinding as she clasped her hands under her chin and swayed back and forth with joy, the hem of her cotton apron twirling to and fro.

Alisia had to look away as tears pooled in her eyes. The Jorgensens were such a fucking beautiful family, it hurt to look at them. She rubbed her palm against her leg, as if the denim and friction would scrub the filth off her.

Jealousy was a bitter pill to swallow and only slightly more palatable than the slug of guilt that stuck in her throat, because at that moment she hated Ripley with a passion that stunned her. Fine cracks spread across her composure like a spider's web, and were just as delicate.

"Alisia."

She snapped to attention and she barked, "What?"

Fuck. All she needed was to collapse into tears for her humiliation to be complete.

"Sorry. You caught me off guard." Her smile felt as fake as her name as she forced her feet to stand at Ripley's side. He placed both hands on her shoulders, as if sensing she'd bolt if given a smidgen of a chance.

"Mom, Dad, this is my girlfriend, Alisia."

A squawk of surprise eked out before she snapped her mouth closed and clenched her fists to resist reaching for the dagger she kept tucked into her pouch.

"It's so nice to finally meet you. I'm Helene." Ripley's mother reached for her tense hand and gave it a soft squeeze. "We've heard so much about you."

"You have?" Good God, like what?

"Oh yes, and you're just as beautiful as Ripley said. And this is my husband, Georg. He may look like a grizzly, but he's as soft as a teddy bear."

"Ah, Mother." The giant actually blushed. "Welcome to our home, Alisia. It's such a pleasant surprise to see you two."

"Yeah, sorry about that." Ripley rubbed at his chin. "We

were doing some research over in Concrete. I wasn't sure if we would have enough time for a visit, and I didn't want to get your hopes up."

"If this is a bad time, we can go." Alisia seized the opportunity to escape. "I don't want to impose."

"Oh, no." Helene latched onto her forearm and pulled her toward the wide covered porch. "This is a fabulous surprise. Father brought home some trout he caught this morning. There's plenty for everyone. Will you be able to stay long?"

"Actually, Mom, I was hoping we could stay the night. It's been a long day and the drive back to the city can be such a chore. I can take the guest bedroom and Alisia can have my room."

"And frighten the poor girl? Don't be silly. I'll just move my crafts from the guest room and tidy up, lickety-split."

"Let me put my fishing gear away and I'll be right in." Ripley's father disappeared back into the garage.

With Helene tugging her from the front and the bulldozer that was Ripley behind her, Alisia was dragged across the threshold and deposited in the entry way, where Helene left her to run up the maple staircase.

Alisia whirled to yell at Ripley in her quietest voice. "Your girlfriend?"

"What?" He shrugged.

"Just because we had an encounter does not make me your girlfriend."

"You are my girlfriend." He stepped closer, backing her against the wall until the wainscoting pressed into her back. "You're my girlfriend because I like you and you like me. You're my girlfriend because we're like thunder and lightning. Together we're explosive. I'm yours and you're mine. If you weren't so stubborn, you'd realize that."

Her mouth fell open to launch a blistery retort, but only rough panting worked past her closed throat. No matter how lightly she may have treated their relationship, they were well past the teasing stage. Ripley was marking his territory and the first person he was notifying was her.

"Why did you bring me here?" she asked on a wisp of air.

"You need to rest." He leaned back far enough to run his finger over her cheek. "Tomorrow is going to be a big day, and you've been running hard. You'll be safe here. You can relax."

Relax? Was he nuts? He had delivered her into the land of Ozzie and Harriett.

Over his shoulder was the living room, which looked like a set from a 1950's sitcom right down to the flower paintings on the wall and overstuffed couches. Under her feet crinkled a vinyl runner that ran like a roadmap across the carpet.

The house was pristine, conservative. In her third-hand clothes and covered in travel dirt, she was like a dust bunny hiding under the china cabinet, waiting to be swept up and tossed out with the rest of the trash.

"It's too clean here. And I'm…not."

"Why don't you go wash up? There's a bathroom just down the hall. Oh, yeah." He caught her by the belt loop when she turned away. The pulse of muscles along his jaw and the hard press of his lips dared her to defy him. "There aren't any windows in there, and if you do find a way to run, I'll track you down and pull you back by your hair. I protect what's mine. Even if it's you from yourself."

"What's yours?" she echoed, rolling her eyes as a shiver

skated down her back. She bent to remove her boots before padding over the vinyl, muttering all the way. "What does that even mean? Like you'll keep me on a keychain to fondle whenever you wish? Or I'll do whatever you say because I'll suddenly lose all capacity to take care of myself? Well, think again, buster."

Knock that off, she admonished that tiny part of her that twittered like a pre-teen about having someone, and not just any someone, claim her with such possessiveness.

Damn it. Why didn't she admit to herself what irked her the most? The bastard was right. She wanted him. Forever. She wanted to lie beside him just to bask in his heat every night. She wanted to bake him his favorite pie and take long hikes in the woods until they found a place to create their own slice of heaven. She wanted to give herself into his keeping, to trust him, more than she wanted anything ever before.

But that was in a perfect world. In a world where her past didn't color her future. Ripley thought he knew her. There was still a lot he didn't.

"Holy geez." She winced as she caught her reflection in the mirror.

The dust bunny comparison changed to a tumbleweed as she tried to finger comb the wayward strands of hair. Static made the mess grow to Medusa-like proportions until she gave up and twisted the sides into an intricate braid and secured them to the base of her neck with a rubber band. Dirt streaked her chin and forehead, and her red eyes matched the extra sun on her nose.

Her gaze turned to the marble sink with gold faucets and little fleur-de-lis soaps in a wicker basket. *Oh God.* She cringed. She could strip down and climb into the sink for a full bath and still not feel clean enough to be in the Jorgensens' home. With the water turned to scalding, she soaped up every inch of bare skin she could reach.

After one last attempt at knocking the dust off her jeans, she cracked open the door and peeped through the slit. She opened the door a little more and found the hall empty. A vinyl runner led the way to freedom. She took one step toward the front door, then another.

"Alisia," Mrs. Jorgensen called from the top of the stairs. "My, doesn't your hair look pretty. You look so much better than when you arrived."

"Um, thank you, Mrs. Jorgensen?" She forced the fake smile on her face.

"Please, call me Helene."

"Okaaay."

Helene looped their arms together at the elbows and patted the back of her hand. "Now, the boys are in the den watching the game, so that gives us a chance for some girl time while we make dinner."

Alisia's smile faltered. "That's...great."

The kitchen was a sea of beige tiles and cream-colored cabinets broken up by navy dish towels and several vases filled with flowers in bright red, yellows, and pinks. There was a massive double-door refrigerator and double ovens in stainless steel that Alisia imagined in heavy use during Ripley's teen years.

Over the island hung a profusion of copper pots in a variety of sizes. Alisia wondered if the men smacked their heads into them often, but she had a strong suspicion they rarely set foot in the kitchen.

"The flowers are beautiful," Alisia said, desperate to find a topic of conversation other than about herself. "Are they from your garden?"

"Why, thank you, and yes, they are." Helene tapped her forefinger on her lip. "Let's see. Father prepped the trout, how are you with vegetables?"

"As in chopping? Fair enough."

"Excellent."

Mrs. Jorgensen set up a station on the island for Alisia to work. Vegetables fresh from the garden outside were handled with care as Alisia washed and set out to dry every leaf of lettuce with a towel. This was going to be the most perfect salad ever assembled.

"Ripley told us that you're a researcher with his firm, but in a different department," Mrs. Jorgensen said.

Alisia froze with a handful of pea pods. What? Oh, right. If she remembered correctly, he had told his parents that he had left the zoo to work for an environmental company. "Yes, I do."

"What do you study?" She dredged the filets in a mixture of flour and herbs, then set them on a tray.

"I...uh, I study the effects of the environment on the human body." Which was true. Mostly. "I'm actually a registered nurse."

"Oh, nursing." Helene placed her flour-covered palm on her chest, leaving a white handprint on her apron. "I had planned on going to nursing school. My mother was a nurse. But during my first year at college, I met Georg. We were married during the summer and Ripley was born nine months after that."

She turned to test the temperature of the oil, leaving Alisia waiting for the rest of the story. What, she had a baby and that was the end of her dream? Seriously?

"So where is your family from, Alisia?"

Ack, more questions. This was what she hated most about leading a double life. The more you answered, the more details you had to keep track of until you severely screwed yourself. She kept her focus on cutting the carrots matchstick-thin. "I was born in Spokane."

"Any brothers or sisters?"

"I have a sister. She's quite a bit younger."

"And your parents live in Spokane still?"

She barely moved her lips as she replied in a low tone. "My mother died a while ago. I'm not close to my father."

"Oh, you poor thing," Helene gasped. "How horrible. It's a shame how some families can't recover from tragedy. I've seen it at my church all the time."

Alisia nodded and turned the conversation away from potential land mines. "Why didn't you go back to nursing school after Ripley got older?"

Mrs. Jorgensen waved a spatula in the air as she thought. "Life happened. There was PTA, Boy Scouts, basketball, wrestling, science fairs. I was kept quite busy. Plus, Father liked me at home to greet him when he got home from work."

Alisia started to snicker until she glanced up and realized Helene did not mean that as a joke.

Whoa.

"So, what are your plans for when the children come?" Helene asked.

Alisia blinked in confusion, lost in the quagmire of *what the fuck?* "What children?"

"Yours and Ripley's, of course."

The knife twisted in her grip, chopping off the tip of her fingernail and sent it flying into the salad bowl. Shit. "What? We—no. We're barely dating. We—children—no."

"Well, not until after the wedding of course, but it's not too early to start planning for the future. I know, Ripley said that you like to take things slow. Playing a little hard to get with a man is not a bad thing." She winked. "But I know my boy has no patience when it comes to getting what he wants."

"We're. Not. Even. Dating."

"You call it shacking up, I call it dating." She laughed in a trill that rang like wind chimes. "Don't look so surprised. I was young once, too. I understand the draw of young love." She clapped her hands. "Oh, I do hope you have a summer wedding and a spring baby. That would be wonderful. You know, I should get a bottle of wine from the cellar to go with dinner. What do you think, chardonnay or a Riesling?"

Alisia stared at her, her mouth open wide.

"Chardonnay it is. I'll be right back. The oven is ready for those potatoes."

She left a stunned Alisia in a cloud of White Shoulders as the kitchen fell into an eerie silence broken only by the bubbling of frying oil.

What the hell.

"Hey." Ripley poked his head around the doorframe. "How's it going?"

She turned toward the door, her hand reaching for the butcher knife as her eyes narrowed with murderous intent.

His gaze jumped from her face to the knife and back to her face. "Okay." He slapped the door jamb once with his palm then disappeared.

Helene emerged from the cellar with a green bottle in hand, and Alisia almost asked her to go back for two more. "Did I hear Ripley?"

"He poked his head in." Speaking of heads, the tip of the

green beans popped off with a satisfying snap.

Alisia smiled with the beginnings of a plan. "Helene, what was Ripley like as a child? And please, don't leave out a single detail."

CHAPTER SEVENTEEN

"**C**AN WE GO home *now*?"

"Max," his beautiful wife admonished and pinched his biceps where she had her arm linked with his. "This is your family's fundraiser, and as the last Madden, it's bad form to leave after ten minutes."

"I'm not the only family member here." He worked his finger under the bow tie strangling him, desperate for some room for his Adam's apple. "My uncle the senator and his wife are over there, and my aunt is here somewhere. Probably trying to keep my grandmother from offending someone."

"You know what I mean."

Unfortunately, he did. They were his family by blood, but on his mother's side. With his father and mother both now dead, it fell onto Max's shoulders to be the face of all Madden holdings. Despite his father's attempt at a military coup, the Madden name still carried power. The financial institutions were going strong and people continued to want the Madden brand.

It was only because the gala was the children's hospital's biggest fundraiser that he made an appearance at all. Although the idea of sending one of the board of directors in his place next year along with a big fat check held considerable merit.

Max slipped his hand under the long fall of his wife's

hair and skimmed his palm down the warm length of her bare back. "If you wanted me to spend my time with this stuffy crowd, then you shouldn't have worn this dress. I want to sneak you into a dark corner and inject some life into this party."

Her husky chuckle sent heat racing through his veins. "You've already injected me with life."

Yeah, he did, he thought with pride.

Crystal wore a strapless gown in crimson velvet that clung to a body made firm by daily workouts. Her skin glowed with an inner radiance and the pale expanse of cleavage drew more than one admiring glance. Max imagined what she would look like as her pregnancy advanced and smiled at the image of her round and lush. He loved his wife, no matter what her size, but he missed the curves she had had when they first met.

"Excuse me, Mr. Madden. May I have a moment of your time?"

Max turned and immediately tensed as he recognized the man standing to his right. Despite the gala being a black-tie affair, the man still looked sharp going against dress code in a charcoal gray worsted wool suit and burgundy silk tie. His dark brown hair was swept back in a pompadour that always amazed Max in its ability to remain in place without appearing greasy.

"I can spare *a* moment," he replied.

"Excellent. I'm Clancy Carrigan, Associated Press. I just have a few questions for you. May I call you Matthew?" he asked, referring to Max's actual given name.

Max shook the offered hand. "Matthew was my father. You may call me Mr. Madden."

Carrigan paused for a moment before he chuckled with

a nod of respect. "Very well."

The reporter's hands were empty, but Max would bet his net worth that he had a recording devise on him somewhere. "Mr. Carrigan, this is my wife, Mrs. Madden."

"Ah, yes. Very nice to meet you." He dropped a kiss onto the back of her hand, oozing charm. "You're more beautiful in person. The pictures on social media do not do you justice."

Max shared an eye roll with Crystal as she batted her lashes. "I'm quite familiar with your work, Mr. Carrigan. Especially your more recent series on the Evolutioneers. But they do seem to be more opinion pieces instead of news stories. Where does all the anger come from that make you hate them so?"

Carrigan stepped back, his eyes wide at being questioned. "I don't hate them."

"Then why are you so unfavorable then? You don't think they're trying to help?"

"Help who? Mrs. Madden, believe what you will, but I have no personal opinion of them, one way or the other as long as they bring me readers. My job is to uncover their story, and right now, they're a big unknown. They could be like drug pushers where the first one's free, but the second will cost you. Let's say they are acting with the best of intentions. We know how that can turn out. Take the Middle East, for example. The US government continues to storm in with the best of intentions." His sneer conveyed exactly how he felt on that matter, and he widened his stance, really getting into the topic. "They screw up big time and the public allows it. Why? Because they're the government, they must know best. But the Evolutioneers—now, they're private citizens. All they need to do is slip up once, and there will be a manhunt for anyone with special abilities we haven't seen since the Salem witch trials. It'll put the ICE raids to shame."

Max didn't like his anticipatory smile one bit. "And you'll be the one to lead the charge, Mr. Carrigan?"

"Nope. But I will be there to report on every detail." He grinned. "However, I'm not the one the Evolutioneers should be worried about. There are plenty of groups who want to know more about them. From the military on down to the medical community. Even churches are expressing interest. There's that reverend from up north, Lowell. I saw a video where he's preaching about how the devil is making an appearance in the form of people who claim to have powers only God can possess. He's calling for all those 'tainted by the devil' to be rounded up and destroyed. He's just one ripple in a wave that's going to grow and grow. The longer these people contain their secrets, the deeper the ocean they'll drown in."

A waiter came by with a tray of hors d'oeuvres that Max refused as his stomach roiled. Carrigan wasn't saying anything that Max didn't already suspect. And yes, Carrigan's writing bordered on the lurid and sensationalistic, but his sources were sound. To have his worries confirmed by someone who researched all the angles and was dialed in to the public didn't make him feel better about the precautions he was taking to protect his family.

Crystal burrowed closer to his side and Max stroked a comforting hand down her spine. She was as much aware of the dangers they faced, perhaps even more so. All day long she had been quietly alert, focused on every phone call and communication that came to the mountain. Trouble was brewing, but he knew better than to press her for details.

There was the very real possibility that if she told them the future, the outcome would be worse than if she let events occur as they were meant to be. Unless there was an immediate danger, he knew she would not reveal one detail.

"Well, Mr. Carrigan," Max said with a dry throat. "That is certainly an interesting theory, but I don't think you approached me to talk about the Evolutioneers."

"No, sir. I wanted to ask how you felt about the direction Madden Financial is taking, and if you regret not taking over as CEO and president when your father died while staging his coup?"

Ah, fantastic. There was nothing he liked more than talking about his rat-bastard father. He was almost tempted to steer the conversation back to the Evolutioneers.

Almost.

CHAPTER EIGHTEEN

ALISIA HAD NEVER seen anyone talk with such joy and passion about a subject as Helene Jorgensen did about her son. Her blue eyes shone like the sky on a bright sunny day, and the more stories she regaled her with, the faster she spoke and the wilder her hand gestures became. Her trilling laugh punctuated every anecdote, and bounced off the copper pots like rain on a tin roof.

And Alisia absorbed every word. Every naked baby, awkward adolescent, therapy-inducing story she hugged to her heart as if she held a winning lottery ticket. Oh, the goods she had on Ripley, aka Mr. Snuggle Bear, were worth the price of gold to the right person.

"Alisia, why don't you tell our men to wash up for supper while I finish in here?"

Oooh. Alisia hid her cringe as she walked away. That right there she would gladly forget. It shouldn't bother her that Helene was stuck in the 1950s, but it did. Man, did it ever.

Not once did Helene speak of doing something because it was what *she* wanted, it was only about Father liking this and her boy liking that. Alisia wanted to seize the woman by her thin shoulders and shake her until her pearls hit the floor and her helmet hair cracked. But she seemed so damn happy living with the sole purpose of pleasing "her men." How was that possible?

The den was a man cave in dark paneling broken up by wildlife portraits and a petrified bass stuck to the wall on metal mountings. The two male primates sat in oversized La-Z-Boys, each holding a sweaty can of beer with their gazes transfixed on the flickering television displaying images of manly behavior. The room's only concession to femininity was the dainty Queen Anne chair upholstered in "the little woman" pinks and blues set between the recliners.

"Excuse me," Alisia said from the doorway, afraid to step one toe into the testosterone pool. "Dinner is ready."

"Excellent." Georg righted his lounge chair and patted his sweater vest–covered stomach. "What was your contribution to the meal, little lady?"

The question made her brow furrow. "The vegetables."

"Hmmm." He scratched his cheek. "Not the best indicator of your culinary skills, but it's a decent start on testing your wifely potential."

She tried not to show any reaction to such a stupid statement, really she did, but she felt shock slacken her face as if she had walked into a sliding glass door.

"Come along, son." Georg slapped Ripley on the back and gave her a pleasant smile as he passed her on the way to the dining room with nary a concern.

"So." The Neanderthal's spawn jammed his hands into his back pockets and took a few hesitant steps toward her. "How are you and my mother getting along?"

She stared at him. And stared. And stared until sweat broke out on his forehead and he swayed on his feet.

"That good, huh?" he asked.

She held up her finger and waved it in his face before turning on her heel and forcing her feet toward the dining room as if she were heading to detention.

The Jorgensens took their places at the ends of the table, leaving her and Ripley to take the center chairs. The table was set with creamy bone china, a delicate complement to the sturdy silverware and thick glass wine goblets. Anything daintier and the glassware would probably be crushed in the men's beefy grip.

Fresh tulips and daffodils graced the center, adding brightness to the earthy golden-brown trout and the green of the sautéed beans.

Alisia perched on the edge of her chair. Every family had their own protocol when it came to mealtime. Her father had demanded complete stillness until after he said grace and gave the go-ahead nod to eat, while Jameson's house had been a free-for-all as soon as it was announced that supper was ready. Uncertain as to which way the Jorgensens swayed, she sat with her back straight and her hands folded in her lap until given the cue that she was allowed to move.

"This looks delicious." Ripley took an appreciative sniff. "Smells good, too."

"Thank you." Helene patted her son's cheek. "As our guest, I think Alisia should say grace."

"Grace?" She looked at Ripley in a panic. She hadn't prayed in seven years, not unless one counted the brief "Thank you, sweet Jesus" when a dumpster dive proved successful, but she bet the Jorgensens didn't roll that way.

"Mom." Ripley shook his head. "Don't put her on the spot like that."

"Why not?" his father asked. "Does she have a problem with thanking the Lord for providing her sustenance?"

Alisia barely restrained the urge to grit her teeth and roll her eyes. "No. I do not."

"Then let's hear it, missy."

Boy howdy did she want to give him an earful, but she bent her head and closed her eyes, focusing on slowing her pounding heart and racing thoughts.

It had always been her father who had said the grace before every meal. The reverend had used that time to reinforce how humble they should be and the importance of obeying their superiors. The consumption of a simple flapjack was an opportunity to remind her of how grateful she should feel to be blessed as a member of the Lowell family. Confessing your sins before being allowed to take a bite had been a very effective diet plan, and even now her stomach curdled at the thought of giving the blessing.

With every intention of laying down a quick thank-you-Jesus for this food, amen, she was surprised to hear herself say, "Dear Heavenly Father. We ask that you bless this bounty that we are about to receive, and as it nourishes our bodies, we will not forget about those who are going without. We also thank you for the tiny gifts you give us each day that we sometimes take for granted, such as the sun that helped to grow the flowers that grace this beautiful table, and the family that provided refuge to two weary travelers. I ask that you keep them safe and secure in your arms and that they shall never have to burden more than they can bear. Amen."

"Oh, Alisia." Helene dabbed at the corner of her eye with a linen napkin. "That was so eloquent. You could teach the people at my church a thing or two about offering a blessing."

Alisia murmured a soft thank-you, then passed the salad to her right.

Ripley winked at her from across the table. The corner

of his mouth twitched with a smile and the light in his eyes darkened with silent praise. Oh, how she wished his approval didn't send a warm rush down her body. It shouldn't matter, but it did.

"Ripley said that you are a researcher, too," Georg said as he piled five filets on his plate. "What exactly do you research? The best brand of coffee for the break room?"

Her fork hovered so close to her face, the steam warmed her lips as she searched his expression. Was he being serious or making a tasteless joke?

He stared back at her with clear blue eyes and his square jaw working on his food without a trace of snark or malice on his face.

Oh ho. Game on.

And just like that, tension made her spine snap like a weak fishing line dragging a two-hundred-pound marlin. Either Mr. Jorgensen saw nothing wrong with his chauvinistic self, or he never met a woman ready to challenge him about his idea of the modern female. It would be a delight to set him straight.

"I study the effects of pollutants on the human body and the change to our molecular structure," she replied.

"Well, good thing we don't have to worry about that out here in the countryside. We've got a good, clean environment out here."

She heard Ripley choke on a carrot stick as she said, "Actually, pollution has pervaded everything on Earth. Take this trout, for example. I bet there's more caffeine in this fish than in a cup of coffee."

"Why is that?"

"The people in Western Washington drink massive quantities of coffee. All of that goes into the sewer system, through the treatment plants, then into the rivers and streams where it's absorbed by the plants and fish, which humans, in turn, consume. There's no escaping pollution, Mr. Jorgensen."

"Are you telling me that my piss is contaminating the trout population?"

Helene's fork hit the china plate with a clang. "Father! Watch your language."

Alisia answered his teasing grin with one of her own. "Yes."

"Hmmm." He nodded once in contemplation. "So, son, what do you think of the Ducks' chances next year?"

With a turn of his head, Alisia was dismissed. A familiar and icy shiver of unworthiness constricted around her like a straitjacket.

Would there ever come a time when she didn't seek approval? She was smart. She pulled herself from the gutter and became a productive member of society. She did not need validation from anyone.

So why did Mr. Jorgensen's rejection sting so badly?

"If they can keep Chambers as running back, they'll definitely be in the top ten," Ripley replied around a mouth full of fish. Both men shoveled their dinner into their mouths in such a way Alisia didn't think they tasted a single bite.

"No way. No way." His father waved his fork. "Chambers will be in the draft, mark my words. Buffalo will snap him up."

What happened next must have been the Devil that made her interject.

"Buffalo doesn't need a running back," she said. "Their weakness is defense. Besides, Chambers is not going to enter the draft this year because there are too many running backs graduating. He'll be better off waiting another year and racking up more accolades. Then he'd be in a prime position to be drafted by Green Bay or Dallas when their 'backs retire."

Ripley and his father stared at her with their mouths wide open. Helene's brow was furrowed and her lip curled as if Alisia had passed gas in her presence.

She froze, not even daring to blink lest it too was a wrong move.

"How the hell do you know that?" Ripley asked in disbelief.

Her brow arched. Seriously? "I do know how to read, and occasionally it's the sports page."

Between checking slides under a microscope and monitoring the team's activities from the comm room, a whole lot of nothing happened on the mountain. She had become very resourceful in finding ways to occupy her time that didn't include mooning over a particular shape-shifter.

"Really?" Georg rocked back in his seat as if settling in for a good match. "And what does the newspaper say about who Buffalo will take instead?"

"Well, according to the *Times* and *Sports Illustrated*, it's speculated they'll court Tauopa from UCLA, or search for a tailback. But I think they'll trade their first-round pick for Stanswick and a fourth-round pick."

Georg's chuckle started slow, like a simmer, then thundered loudly. "Ah, little girl, that is the cutest thing I've ever heard." He slapped the table once and all the plates jumped. "This one is a live wire, boy. Hey, did I tell you about the new rod and reel I got? It's a birch wood beauty."

Poof, she again ceased to exist.

Talk of the benefits of feather flies over hand lures drift-ed on air that blew through her like a frigid wind. Light, buttery trout turned to mush in her mouth, tasting as flavorful as a ball of wax. To her left, Helene began a running dialogue on her knitting group and their battles over sheep's wool versus synthetic wool. She appeared to be talking to Alisia, but her face was turned up toward the chandelier and she answered her own questions. Neither man responded, or even glanced in their direction.

Alisia stacked her green beans, with the perfectly cut lengths, one on top of the other to form a cube. All that hard work to be perfect. She shook her head. Another desperate attempt for approval.

"Ladies, that was delicious." Georg tossed his napkin on his plate and pushed away from the table to stand.

"Yeah, Mom, that was great." Ripley got up and leaned down to give Helene a kiss on the cheek. He circled around the table and dropped a quick peck on Alisia's as well. "You too, honey."

The men walked out of the room without a backward glance.

Alisia surveyed the remains of the once-elegant dinner. Rumpled linen, stained with grease, lay like sheets over the picked-over carcasses of the fish, creating a little aquatic crime scene. A stray green bean peeked out from under-neath a plate as if trying to escape the massacre. Tulips once proud had wilted, their petals dropped on the table like tears for the fallen.

Helene stood as well and began to scrape the dishes and stack them for transport.

"Are they really not going to take their dishes into the kitchen?" Alisia asked, unable to believe that Ripley would leave his mother to pick up after him at his age.

"I don't like to bother them with women's work."

She said what?

Georg's bellow rippled down the hall. "Mother, can you bring me a sherry?"

Ripley's shout followed right behind. "Honey, can you bring me a beer?"

Alisia shot to her feet and laid her hand on Helene's arm. "Please. Allow me."

"Oh, thank you dear. The sherry is on the side table right over there in the corner."

The rose-colored crystal sparked in the light as Alisia filled it two-thirds full of amber liquid. The dainty glass appeared ill equipped to withstand the meaty paws of Georg Jorgensen. She paused in the kitchen to retrieve Ripley's beer then shook the can in a syncopated rhythm to her footfalls down the hall.

This time it was a shooting competition on the History Channel that held their attention.

"Your sherry," she said to Georg.

"Thank you, darling." He accepted the glass, his gaze fixed on the screen.

Great restraint kept her from tossing the can at Ripley's head and making it a true silver bullet.

"Thanks, honey." He blew her a kiss. "You're the best."

She batted her lashes and flashed her sweetest smile as she left.

One. Two. Three.

Crack. Fizz, "Ahh! Holy shit!"

Her smile turned real and she returned to the dining room, whistling a merry tune as she picked up a platter and took it into the kitchen.

CHAPTER NINETEEN

ALISIA TOSSED THE paper towel she used to wipe down the kitchen counter into the trash and considered following it right into the bin.

"Mrs. Jorgensen, if you don't mind, could you please show me to my room? I'm really tired."

Helene hung up her apron then stepped closer. "Those circles under your eyes have gotten darker. You poor thing. I'll take you right up."

Alisia followed Helene's sprightly steps at a much slower pace. She was too tired to muster any indignation at the comment.

Thirteen steps never seemed so steep, and she had to lean heavily on the banister to haul her suddenly heavy body up.

"I know what will perk you right up," Helene chattered. "A nice, hot shower. Let me get you some towels."

While Alisia waited in the hallway, her attention was captured by the row of photos hanging in redwood frames on the wall. Wow, Ripley had been kinda nerdy. Tall and thin, he wore his hair in a side spike and dressed in an array of polo shirts in every color of the rainbow, primary and pastel. His Adam's apple was so huge, it looked as if he had swallowed an actual apple, and his jeans were hiked up to near armpit territory. But he still had those brilliant blue eyes that hinted at great adventure and that smile that made you want to be a part of whatever secret he was hiding. Ripley was one hundred percent different from Sam, so how could she be in love with him?

Love? She fell against the wall at the realization. What the hell?

Well, that was a kick to the head to wake a girl up.

No, no, no, no. She was not in love with Ripley. Lust, oh yeah, but never love. Love was complicated, every day, hopeful. And she didn't believe in hope anymore. She couldn't.

You mean you don't want to.

"Here you go, dear." Helene interrupted her internal freakout and handed her a stack of fluffy cotton towels before leading her into a small room decorated in blues and greens. "Bathroom is right in there, and don't forget to use the squeegee on the glass when you're done in the shower."

"Thank you, Mrs. Jorgensen. And please tell the boys good night for me."

Helene looked her in the eye, her gaze hard and searching. For what, Alisia didn't know, but she didn't dare move as she froze like a gazelle caught on a lioness' hunting grounds.

"I'll do that," she said after a moment. She reached out and laid a delicate hand on Alisia's shoulder. "Rest now. Nothing will trouble you here."

Unexpected tears stung her eyes. "Thank you," she whispered.

With a smile and a nod, Helene left her to her solitude. She stripped down, then carefully folded her clothes and placed them in her pack, careful not to let the dust fly haphazardly and mar the pretty decor. The cleanest outfit she possessed was a sports bra and workout pants, and those she took with her into the bathroom.

She let the glass cubicle fill with steam before she stepped under the spray. Bracing her palms against the tile, she watched the sweat, dust, and the last dregs of her energy swirl down the drain. It was peaceful, so quiet. The drone of the water created a cocoon that made the world completely disappear. If only she could stay in there forever.

A sigh escaped from her lips, long and slow. If she stayed much longer, then she would take up all of the hot water, and what kind of guest would that make her?

Her arms cut through the steam like a rubber knife through Jell-O. Despite her exhaustion, she made sure to use the provided squeegee and that the stall was dry and free from water spots before using the fabric softened–fluffy towel to attend to herself. With every second that passed, the pillows on the bed looked fluffier and fluffier. *Soon, babies, soon,* she promised and squeezed the towel around her hair.

A soft knock at the door brought her head out of the shroud of cotton.

"Alisia? It's me. Ripley."

She rolled her eyes. As if she'd mistake that husky drawl for anyone else. She almost told him to go away, but recognized the childishness of the impulse, and cracked open the door.

Ripley filled the doorway, blocking out almost all of the light from the hall. Lines bracketed his mouth and his hair stood up in sticky spikes. It was odd seeing genuine contrition on his usually confident face.

"You going to bed?" he asked.

"Yes."

When she didn't say more his lips tightened. "You

didn't say good night to me."

She folded her arms. "Sorry. I'm just really tired."

"I'm guessing by the booby-trapped beer that you're mad at me. Why?"

"Maybe because you didn't tell me that you were bringing me to your parents' house, which is the land of chauvinist oinkers, and that you were the spawn of a pig."

His eyes rounded. "We're not chauvinists."

"Excuse me? Excuse me. You didn't offer to help with dinner, you didn't clean up, and you spent most of the night sitting on your ass drinking beer. Did you once ask your mother how she was doing? Oh, and don't get me started on your mother."

"I thought you two were getting along."

"She's a lovely woman who must have lost staggering amounts of oxygen when she gave birth to you. She's almost as bad as your father."

He sputtered and placed both of his hands on his hips. "Come on. You're being ridiculous."

She cocked her head to the side. "She asked me if I was prepared to give up my career when we got married, and that my existence as I know it would be set aside to fulfill *your* wishes and desires."

Shocked blue eyes snapped to hers. "That's not true. She did not say that."

"She also said that I would have to get up extra early because your favorite pancakes take time to ferment." She scowled. "And when I asked why you weren't helping with the cleanup, she said that you shouldn't be bothered with women's work."

Ripley jerked back as if she slapped him. His golden tan turned yellow as he paled.

"The girl who ends up with you will have to have zero self-confidence and no decision-making skills in order to be happy living with you."

"No," he barked, then glanced around to make sure they were truly alone. In a lowered voice he said, "You're wrong. My mother's wrong. I'm sorry. I—" He rubbed the back of his neck. "I'm sorry I spaced and I didn't offer to help. That's just the way things have always been around here. I don't want a woman who will blindly follow. I want a mate who's strong and passionate. I want a woman who can carry a conversation and booby-trap my beers to remind me when I've stepped out of line. What I want is you, Alisia."

Her arms tightened around her chest. When his voice lowered to a purr that way, he was completely irresistible and impossible to stay mad at. The bastard.

"I brought you here to rest, and I'm sorry if it only stressed you out. Please, lie down. Sleep in as long as you want. I'll take care of everything." The tip of his finger trailed over her cheek and his lips followed, soft and sweet. "Good night."

Cold pebbled her skin at the loss of his heat. This was crazy. She wanted to grasp those shoulders and spend all night tasting those lips. Perhaps staying with his parents was for the best. She'd have at least until the morning before she did something stupid.

"Good night," she said. Ripley licked his lips and nodded. She waited until he turned before adding, "Captain Polka Dot."

Red raced up his neck and scorched the tips of his ears. He looked back at her with a sheepish grin. "She told you about that?"

"Oh yeah. Even showed me the photos." It was the

cutest thing she'd ever seen. A five-year-old Ripley jumping off the couch wearing nothing but swim goggles, tighty-whities and a blue and white polka dot sheet tied around his neck. "Took a picture of it with my phone. And the ones of you rolling in the mud in just your diaper. For posterity."

He tapped at his heart. "You're ruthless, Caldwell. It's one of the many things I love about you."

And there she was. Back in the muck of emotions and feelings.

Like the coward she was, she ducked into the room and closed the door on his smiling face. Sleep. She needed sleep and lots of it. Alone.

She had barely pulled the comforter up to her chin when the dreams began. Running, she was always running. Through the woods or across wheat fields. The scratchy stalks slapped her bare legs as her boots slipped in the soil. Down dark alleys, as she dodged piles of garbage and filthy people.

And *they* followed.

Every time she risked a glance over her shoulder, it was someone new. First it was her father and Winston. Their polished black wing tips clipped on the asphalt like gunfire. When the clicking ceased she looked back and found Max at her heels. Only he wasn't Max, this was Maestro, the leader of the Evolutioneers, with his dark sunglasses covering his laser-like stare and the tails of his black leather coat flapping behind him. He was a man intent on capturing the guilty.

Pavement gave way to hard-packed dirt covered with pine needles. Trees gathered in tight clusters, their branches snagging her hair as she wove between the gnarled trunks. A snarl snapped in the air like a whip, announcing his arrival. Tall and wide, he was a true therianthrope, caught between man and animal.

She quickened her pace, jumping over tree roots and shredding blackberry vines that wrapped around her ankles as he crashed through the brush behind her. Her lungs burned. Puffs of white billowed from her mouth with each harsh breath.

A clearing of grass opened before her, a sea of gray-green under the light of the huge full moon hanging in the night sky. She kicked harder, increasing her speed.

The hot breath on her back was her only warning before the tackle came. He curled his body around her to cushion the fall.

From flat on her back, she gazed up at her attacker and froze in terror and fascination. Silver light glinted off his curved fangs and the sweat covering his sinewy muscles. Every inch of him was tense, pulsating with restrained energy. Between his legs his cock jutted out, thick like iron, the swollen head wet with cum. His knees pushed her thighs wide open and he threw back his head with a triumphant roar. Gold hair streaked with white fell to his shoulders and framed glittering eyes that were black with the slightest ring of Ripley blue.

"Shhh, sweetie. It's okay."

Cold air hit her throat as she jerked awake with a cry. Heat burned along her back and coiled around her waist. She blinked hard, her eyes peering into the dark and the small amount of light coming through the curtains.

"Ripley? What are you doing here?"

He took up almost of the space on the full-size mattress as he cradled her in his arms.

"I couldn't stay away. I tried, but I need you."

Dream and reality collided. The image of the aroused

beast flashed behind her eyelids as Ripley slid his hands over her body. His right hand palmed her breast, pulling at her nipple through the thin cotton of her top, while the left hand smoothed up underneath the material against her belly. Against her backside, he ground the hot, hard length of his cock.

"Ripley." She slapped at his roving hands. "We can't have sex in your parents' house."

"I know. God, do I know. I was banking on that, but I can't stay away. I need you." He pressed his face into her neck, his evening beard scratching her skin. Her name came out in a rumble that rippled down her back, causing her to arch and push her breasts deeper into his hands.

"You smell so good." His gravelly whisper kept her in the dreamlike state of being. "So ripe. I need that scent on me. I need my scent on you."

His fingers delved beneath the waistband of her pants and parted the flesh of her pussy. "So hot and wet."

Remaining still was impossible, and she didn't have the energy to push his heavy body away. His touch was good, so good, and the more she moved, the better the sensations. The desire grew to engulf her, and her blood raced like lava through her veins. She dug her nails into his arm when two thick fingers pushed deep into her channel and set a thrust and retreat rhythm that matched the bump and grind of his hips.

His palm rubbed her clit. "Melt for me. I love that. I love the way you go liquid in my arms. Come for me. Come for me."

His teeth scraped along her shoulder, snapping the string holding her control. She bit into her pillow and grabbed a fistful of sheet as she broke into pieces.

"Ripley," she panted. "Ripley," she moaned at the loss of his fingers. Hungry, she was hungry for more. The emptiness he left must be filled.

She turned to face him and gasped at the sight of him palming his hard flesh. She wanted more light. She wanted to see his cock, see how much he wanted her.

She reached out, her fingers tangled with his as she grasped his shaft. A whimper escaped from both of them as her palm rubbed over the crown weeping with pre-cum. Her mouth watered and her tongue wet her lips. She had to taste.

Jerking his hand away, she fell on him, sucking the velvet length into her mouth. He tasted like a man should. Warm, salty, and rich.

Sharp nails scrapped her scalp and his hips bucked wildly. "Alisia, baby, you have to stop," he panted in a lust-deepened voice. His words slurred. "I'm gonna come."

"Do it. I want to taste you."

"Dammit," he sobbed. "I wanna see it."

He yanked her off him by her hair and tossed her back on the bed, stripping her of her yoga pants and spreading her legs wide.

"Show me your tits. I want to come on your tits." She offered him her breasts, tugging at her nipples. Holy shit, was he sexy. She loved his dirty talk. The rasp of his voice alone could make her come again. "Turn on the light. I want to see you."

He worked three claw-tipped fingers carefully into her pussy, stretching and filling her to bursting. In the dim light she could barely make out his hulking form. His biceps bulged and flexed as he worked his cock, and his cheeks hollowed with each gasping breath. Was that a glimpse of fang?

This was her dream come to life, but she wasn't frightened. Oh no. She was far from frightened. With shameless abandon she rode his hand, her gaze fixed on the wet head of his cock, aching for both of their release. She wanted, hungered to be claimed, to be consumed in the pleasure only Ripley could give her. She wanted to be devoured by him in all ways. No, it wasn't his fangs or claws that scared her. It was her want.

His back arched and his mouth fell open on a silent howl. The first hot stream of cum splashed across her breasts, the second her belly, tossing her over the edge into oblivion.

Gritting her teeth, she swallowed her screams as she shook and writhed, clamping down on the fingers stuffed deep inside. Under her hands, his semen was sticky and still warm from his body.

"Yes, rub it into your skin. I need you covered in me."

Need you. Yes, she needed too.

A tear slipped down her check, then another. Shivers raced through her until her teeth chattered. Weakness of the body and of the mind left her limp and out of control.

"Alisia?" His voice was hushed, but clear and strong. "Alisia, baby, what's wrong?" The fangs and claws receded as he shifted into the Ripley she knew.

He scooped her into his arms and arranged them side by side. His hands stroked over her as if he couldn't get enough, and she clung to him like wet rag.

"It's not enough," she wept and pressed closer. "It's not enough."

"I know. I promise, after all of this is settled, I'm taking you away and doing this right."

Alisia bit her lip. There was no "after" for them. Tomorrow they were stepping back into her past and he was going to find out the truth about her. Once he did, he was going to walk away without a backward glance and leave her alone.

Being on her own had never bothered her before. Another shudder shook her. But this time she didn't think she'd survive.

CHAPTER TWENTY

A LISIA SLIPPED OUT of Ripley's warm embrace the moment the night sky turned a periwinkle-purple dawn.

The morning before, she had escaped the bed while Ripley was still asleep because she had feared she would never want to leave. Now she escaped because she was absolutely certain of it.

A small smile softened her frown as she dared to look back. Wow. The man really knew how to sleep. He had one arm thrown over his head with the blanket pulled low, leaving his body splayed out like a buffet for the eyes. How could a woman not appreciate the magnificence of all that strength and power? All of her femininity wanted to match all of his masculinity, fitting them together to create the perfect union.

The tips of his fingers were blunt, his lips soft with sleep. He was not nearly as ferocious as she remembered from the night before.

Had she imagined the fangs and claws? Had her dream muddled fantasy and reality? How depraved did it make her to have been turned on by the beast?

Had been? You still are. Get back on that bed and lick that man from head to toe.

Down, girl. Down.

Was that her heart or her head issuing demands? Ha.

More than likely it was her sex organs. The fact that she couldn't tell the difference propelled her out of the room after throwing on some clothes. If he woke and looked in her direction, she wouldn't let him leave the bed for a very long time.

The quiet of the house was both peaceful and unsettling. If this had been another Sunday in an idyllic life, she would be looking forward to spending a lazy morning followed by an even more sedate afternoon with the man she loved zoning out in front of the television, and indulging in a lot of hot sex. But on this day, she was facing the end of life as she knew it. There was very little to look forward to.

Please, please, please let me remember where they keep the coffee.

The sun was taking its sweet time rising, leaving the kitchen in shadows. A light over the stove welcomed her and illuminated the coffee pot like the lost idol.

"Thank you, powers that be," she whispered and reached for the magical wonder.

"Good morning, Alisia."

"Ah!" The plastic filter flew out of her hand and clattered on the tile. "Oh, Mrs. Jorgensen…Helene. You startled me. Obviously."

"I'm sorry." The older woman sat at the kitchen table, a cup of tea in one hand and the newspaper laid out before her.

Her sweater set was in tangerine, warmly complementing her pearls. Her blonde waves were in their perfect helmet shape and her makeup applied to perfection. Helene was so clean and pressed, and there Alisia stood with sleep in her eyes, pillow head, and covered in semen. Criminy, could she be any filthier?

"You're, uh, up early." Alisia rinsed out the filter and searched for the coffee. She didn't want to look like the coward she was by asking for location of the nearest coffee stand.

Helene took a sip of tea. "I wasn't sure what time you two would be up and about, so I thought I would wake up early to make sure Ripley got his favorite pancakes."

Alisia smiled as the Mr. Coffee bubbled and hissed. "Ah, yes. The pancakes."

"I thought you'd sleep until noon."

"That was the plan. I have a lot on my mind."

Helene hummed and nodded to the chair across the table. "Would you like to join me?"

"Okay." Oh please let the Jorgensens be heavy sleepers. Alisia stalled for time, preparing her coffee with cream and sugar before stepping across the tile to the kitchen table.

"I have to tell you," Helene said. "Georg was very impressed with you last night."

"Uh, what?" Was she still asleep?

Helene laughed. "Georg. He thinks you're just wonderful."

"Oh." She took a healthy gulp of the dark brew and enjoyed the rush of liquid caffeine hitting her system. Nope, Mrs. Jorgensen still wasn't making sense. "Really?"

Helene's smile held a touch of knowing. "Oh, I know. He forgets that the women of today have different priorities. And I know that Georg and mine's relationship is a throwback to another time. My own sister says I'm an affront to the women's movement. But I'm happy with my life as it is." She fingered the pearls around her neck with a trembling hand. "Georg knows I don't handle stress well. He takes care of everything so I can concentrate on the things that I love, like family and my garden. Our relationship works. For us. We know it's not for everyone. We know it's not for our son, but sometimes we forget. I get so caught up in mothering and the possibility of grandmothering that I tend to get a little overboard. Ripley needs a woman like you. He thrives on challenge and you can give him that. You're not afraid to shake his beer if need be."

Alisia ducked behind her cup. It had been a childish move, but one that had felt fitting at the time. Still did, if she was honest.

Helene continued, "I want to apologize if I made you uncomfortable with talk of marriage and such. I just want Ripley to be happy and you make him smile in a way I've never seen. And I can't wait to spoil some grandbabies, but no pressure. Take your time." Her blue eyes danced with mischief and Alisia knew she was bursting with the prospect of doting on her son's children.

Despite, or maybe because of, her exuberance and devotion, Alisia knew Helene would make a wonderful grandmother. This wasn't the first time Alisia had thrown up the preservation wall when confronted with people who appeared to be perfect—people who reminded her of her father and stepmother. Obviously, Helene adored her family and lived a life that suited her. Sure, it was a lifestyle that would make Alisia pull her hair out if submerged in it for a long period of time, but Helene was happy. Genuinely happy.

The only person who had to worry about combating potential misogynistic ideologies was the mother of Helene's future grandkids. And that was not her. Right?

Right.

Unless…

Grrrr. This was getting complicated.

"Helene." Alisia paused to clear her throat of the longings only women who were not being hunted were allowed to possess. "Ripley is, well, one of a kind. He and I being together is really, really, really new, and I've learned not to count on tomorrow. I can't make any promises about Ripley and me, but you should know that you have an amazing son." A sly grin stole across her lips. "Most of the time."

Helene slapped playfully at her hand. "You are Ripley's match." She stood and dumped the dregs of her tea in the sink. "What would you like for breakfast, Alisia?"

"Actually, I would like to learn how to make those pancakes I keep hearing so much about."

Helene turned to her with eyes wide with surprise. She blinked several times and smoothed down the hem of her sweater as her smile trembled at the corners. "That would be wonderful."

✧   ✧   ✧

MOTHERFUCKER. SHE DID it again.

Ripley groaned into the pillow. For a man who possessed heightened senses, he was clueless when it came to keeping track of his mate.

The trill of his phone added to the headache gathering at the base of his neck. He was so not in the mood to talk to anyone, but the slumberous beat of "Teardrop" by Massive Attack was like the drip, drip, drip of a leaky faucet in a sink full of dishes. The incessant pulse of Doc's ringtone was not going to leave him be.

"What? What?" he grumbled into the phone.

"Where are you?" Doc asked.

"Somewhere safe." He wiped the sleep from his eyes.

"What's up?"

"Are you alone?"

"Right now, yes."

If Doc's heavy sigh didn't cut through the last of his sleep, her next question was as effective as a bucket of ice water poured over his head. "Have you had sex with Alisia?"

"Doc, that's not really—"

"Yes or no, Ripley," she all but shouted. "It's vital that I know."

"All right! Yes, we did."

"Errr!" She sucked in a scream. "No. No. No. I told you to keep your dick in your pants."

"I know. But things happened. We're getting along. You know, aside from the entire thing with her dad, I think it's going well."

"No. No, it's not." The hair on the back of his neck stood up at the foreboding note in her voice. "Okay. Look. While you've been gone, I've been running more tests, especially after you said you were losing control of your shifts. Well, I think I found the answer."

That got his undivided attention. If he could control his shifts, he could control the beast. "I'm listening."

"Your intense reaction to Alisia gave me an idea. Since Alisia is non-super, we've been using her bodily fluid and tissue samples as one of our controls in our research. I've discovered that if you were to mix samples from you and Alisia together, your hormones level out to normal."

"Mix samples? What do you mean? Like a transfusion?"

"No…" The way she trailed off made his eye twitch. "Mix as in if you are to mate her, introduce your semen and saliva into her system through sex and biting, you may be able to gain control of your shifts."

"What?" He had *not* heard what he just heard. Had he? She made it sound so matter of fact.

"If your animal claims his mate, marks her, he will be satisfied, leaving you in control."

At Doc's words, all the synapses in his brain fired in a million different directions. Blood rushed to his cock as his nostrils flared, instinctively searching for his mate.

"That's great then, right?" He searched the floor for his pants. Where in the hell were his pants? "Since we've had sex, we're mated and all cool now. My animal, Alisia. We're all synced together in harmony."

"That depends on several counts. How much did you intermingle?"

"What?"

"Sexually." She huffed out a breath. "God, this is so much easier to discuss with patients who are not my friends. Did you use a condom? Did you bite her?"

"Oh." He scratched his head. "Well, yes, we used a condom. But I haven't bitten her." *I think.*

"Good." Doc's sigh was palpable. "Good. Maybe this isn't so bad yet."

There went the hairs on his arms again, shocked straight. "Doc, why am I sensing that there's a great, big, jiggly *but* about to squeeze through the door?"

She released a long slow breath. "If you mate her, she is yours. Only yours. All other men will reject her."

While his animal howled in approval, the man knew that this could be a really bad thing. "Explain that, please."

"Alisia's biological makeup will change so that her scent and taste will ground your animal, and in doing so, all other men will instinctively recognize that she belongs to you. Since animals rely so heavily on sense of smell, I used the changed hormones to create a spray and ran some tests. The male sample cells wouldn't go near them. It was as if they were repelled. I even sprayed a bit on myself and walked around the compound. You know how Chase is always flirty? Not this time. He just smiled, nodded hello, then practically ran out of the room. After I took a shower, I tried again, and he was back to his normal flirty self."

"Doc, what exactly are you saying?"

"Until I do more testing, I can't be certain, but it appears that once you mate, no other man will desire her, because instinctually they will know that she belongs to you. And it won't matter if she later changes her mind. Meaning, if you two break up down the line, no man will have her in that way."

The area under his nose where his whiskers would be twitched while he digested the information.

"Are you listening, Ripley?" Doc asked, clearly not content with his silence. "You cannot touch her again unless you tell her exactly what will happen. You have to let her choose. And I know you, Rip—sometimes you just jump in without thinking things through, relying on your powers to save you. But you can't do that to Alisia, thinking you can sweet-talk her after the deed is done. That's why you have to bring her home before you do something you'll regret—"

"Doc. Doc! Yes, I understand." Just because he carried the Y chromosome didn't mean he was stupid. Alisia bound to him forever whether or not she wanted to be was a double-edged sword. Question was, what side was he on? Moral correctness or his animal instinct?

As he breathed in deep he knew she was close. Her citrus scent hovered in the air, richer than the day before, with hints of vanilla and a heady layer of patchouli. The scent of his mark.

Had he passed the point of no return and claimed her forever?

Fuck. He turned to pace left in the room, then right, then left again. Which way was up, which way was down? He didn't know. But one thing was certain. If they had burned that bridge and they were mated, Alisia had every right to kill him.

"Look, Doc," he eked out from his tight throat. "I got it. No more sex, no biting. Don't worry. I'm not going to touch her. We've got one more stop to make, then we'll come home. I'll—I'll worry about the rest later."

He hung up with Doc and streaked down the hall with a sheet wrapped around his torso. There was no way he could face his family with little pink scratches running down his abdomen.

Back in his room he jerked on a T-shirt, popping a few seams, and pulled on a pair of loose track pants, hoping to God that the extra material covered the erection that sprouted at the thought of gaining more of those pink scratches.

He took the stairs three at a time. Alisia's citrus scent mixed with sweet maple syrup and rich coffee made his stomach rumble for food and woman. Dammit, that thought was not helping his erection.

His bare feet squeaked against the kitchen floor as he skidded to a stop. Wait. What was going on?

His parents sat side by side at the breakfast table with the daily crossword puzzle between them. The morning sun shone through the windows behind them, making them sparkle in the light.

"Eight letters. Islands off the mainland," his father said.

"The Hebrides," Alisia replied as she stood in front of the stove with a spatula in hand, flipping a golden pancake on the griddle.

"Naw, that can't be right."

"Father, I think she's correct. How do you spell that, dear?"

"H-E-B-R-I-D-E-S. Chain of islands off the coast of the mainland of Britain."

"H-E-B—well, damn. That fits. Good job, girlie."

Alisia did a double take when she heard Ripley's gasp of surprise that she hadn't tossed a pancake at his father's head. She smiled at him and returned to the griddle. "Good morning, Ripley."

His father peered at him from over his glasses. "It's about time you dragged your carcass out of bed."

His mother swept up from the table, crossing to his side to stand on her tiptoes and plant a kiss on his cheek. "Good morning, baby boy. Would you like some coffee? Alisia made a fresh pot."

"Yeah. Sure." A hot mug was pressed into his hand, and a gentle touch guided him to a chair, but all he saw was Alisia.

Something was different about her, something from within. There was an assuredness to her movements, a serenity on her face as she worked. Resting his elbow on the table, he leaned his cheek against his closed fist and watched her, melting a little more with each gentle smile she gifted him.

Breathtaking. She was absolutely breathtaking.

"Here you go, Georg." She placed a plate stacked high with fluffy cakes in front of his father, then squeezed Ripley's shoulder as she passed.

"Thank you, girlie." His father drizzled syrup over his stack.

A beam of warm sunshine flashed from his mother's huge smile. She was so giddy, she vibrated in her chair.

"What are you waiting for?" Alisia asked after setting a huge stack of hotcakes before him then took a seat by his side. "Dig in."

Oh no. It was too late. They must have mated. What else could explain this display of domestic bliss?

She licked a drop of syrup from her thumb and froze as she noticed him staring. Again. "What?"

"Are you all—How are you feeling?" he asked instead.

"Good." Her smile struck him as bittersweet. "I'm good."

What did that smile mean? It was so warm, yet a touch of sadness darkened her eyes.

She knew. She must. But how? Fuck. This was getting complicated.

"Ripley, your pancakes are getting cold," Alisia pointed out.

What? He started. Oh shit. He was still staring at her like a lost puppy. "Right."

The fork quivered in his hand as he lifted a steamy morsel to his lips.

"How are they?" she asked after he took a few bites.

Sweet and light, the pancake melted on his tongue. With the amount of acid churning in his gut, they should have tasted like sawdust, but they were perfect.

"Good," he mumbled. "They're great."

A blush touched her cheek and a giggle escaped. "You're welcome."

Oh, he was so fucked.

For the other three in the room, breakfast passed in comforting normality, as he watched with horror and amusement while they finished the crossword puzzle as if it were a morning tradition.

"What is going on here?" he whispered to Alisia when his mother got up to fetch his father another cup of coffee. "You're all getting along now?"

"We never *not* got along," she whispered back. "Well, you know what I mean. But your father and I have come to an understanding."

"Why does that terrify me?"

"Don't worry." She patted his thigh and shared a wink with his father. "He is well aware that I will not hesitate to call out his BS if I think he's crossing a line. So far, so good."

"If you say so." He leaned closer, and inhaled, searching for any sign that they may have become mated. Since he had no idea what he was looking for, the task was difficult, to say the least. "And you're sure you feel fine?"

"Yes." The furrow in her brow deepened. "Are *you* okay?"

"Yeah. Maybe. Doc called. We… We have things we need to discuss." He pulled away as his mother returned. "Later. But we do need to get going soon."

"Must you?" his mother asked with a pout. "I'm having such a good time. And today's a glorious day for a picnic."

"We have lots of work to get back to. But I'll come back for a proper visit. I promise."

"And Alisia will come too, right?"

She sputtered into her cup of coffee. "I'll see what I can do. They keep us pretty busy in the lab."

"Ripley, make her come with you."

"Ma, I'll try. That's all I can do."

It pained him to dim his mother's pleasure, but he couldn't promise that Alisia would even be willing to be in the same country as him, let alone take a trip back to his parents.

Packing their bags took less time than cleaning the kitchen, and within minutes they were ready to depart. Alisia tossed her backpack in the truck while his father checked the air pressure in the tires.

"Here are some sandwiches." His mother handed him a vinyl cooler. "And a few oranges, apples, oh, and a bag of chocolate chip cookies."

"Thanks, Mom." He hugged her extra tight with his free arm. "You really are the best. I don't think I tell you enough that I love you and appreciate everything you do."

"Oh, honey." She wiped the tear from the corner of her eye. "I love you, too. I'm so proud of you." She hugged him again, trembling in his arms, and brushed her hand over his hair. "Call me when you get home. Even if it's just a quick hello to say you made it safe and sound."

"I will. Bye, Dad."

"Take care, son." The air whooshed out of his lungs as his dad slapped him on the back. His father leaned forward and winked. "And don't let that girl go. She adds the vim to your vigor."

"I don't plan to."

As they drove down the road, Alisia turned to look back at the rapidly shrinking house and the couple waving good-bye. "You have a nice family, Ripley."

"Thank you." The affection in her voice tightened his throat. Now would be the time to bring up the whole mating thing. Yep. It was definitely the time to discuss the possibility they were tied together forever.

Alisia leaned over and rested her head on his shoulder with a soft sigh.

Maybe it could wait until later.

"I checked in with Max and Addison while you were packing," he said as his face heated and sweat broke out on his lip. God, he was such a coward. "We're going to meet up with them after we track down this Strangelove fella. Max told your father that you've been found and contained. He's on his way to meet with the team. That's where we'll round them up and wait for the authorities."

"I hope there's more to the plan than that," she remarked and readjusted her seatbelt.

"They're consulting with Sheriff Lancaster as well, and hope to have local law enforcement nearby to make the arrest."

"I know, I know. I'm just anxious."

He reached out and placed his hand on her thigh, finding the muscle tight. If she worried her lower lip any more with her teeth, she was going to pierce the skin.

"Addison tried to dig up some information on Dr. Strangelove. A few drug pushers mention him on various social media, but it doesn't appear like he's ever been arrested. He's a ghost, and a good one."

Her thigh bunched under his hand. "I have an idea where to find him."

"Then let's tell Max. Let the team bring him in."

"No. They'll never get near him. It has to be me."

Ripley didn't like the faraway look in her eyes and the way she sat stiff in her seat. His animal sensed her anxiety as if she were shouting at him with a bullhorn. If he opened the window the breeze would shatter her into tiny pieces.

While he understood her need to see the job done herself, she had friends ready to back her up. She wasn't alone.

As much as he didn't like it, he'd follow her lead. For one, he needed her to see that he believed in her. And two, he'd rather haul their asses to safety if required than spend time arguing.

"Where are we going?" he asked as they entered the city limits.

"Marian Heights." Her lips barely moved in reply.

"Seriously?" Marian Heights was the poshest neighborhood in the city. "Should we change vehicles? The truck will stick out. We'll be profiled in a nanosecond."

"We won't be stopping. Just keep to the speed limit and obey the traffic signs."

Following her directions, Ripley turned the beat-up Chevy down a beautifully manicured street where green leafy alder trees lined the road like sentries. Their leaves rustled in the spring breeze sounding like pennies falling from the sky. It appeared as if the neighborhood was experiencing its own lazy Sunday, leaving the street empty of cars and people. He examined every shadow and scanned every shrub with his sharp gaze.

"Don't slow down or a housekeeper will think we're casing a house," she said.

"What are we looking for?"

"Nothing. I want to check something out first."

They rolled past a three-story Tudor that sat right on the edge of the lake. The iron gate of the ten-foot high wall surrounding the property provided a clear view of the garage and empty driveway. It looked similar in style to all the other houses on the block, but for some reason held Alisia's complete attention. She craned her neck, maintaining eye contact with the structure as they drove by.

"Is that our guy?" he asked.

"Maybe. It's been a while. Head to King Street, near the train station."

"Are you sure?"

"Yeah."

"Alisia—"

"Don't." She raised her hand. "Just drive."

A growl lodged in his throat. Damn it. How could he help if he didn't know the details?

"Park on Occidental," she instructed.

The clock tower on the top of King Street Station cast the side street in shadow. Midday in downtown was a hive of activity, but the area closest to the stadiums on a non-game day was fairly empty.

The lack of bystanders didn't lessen his tension, but at least his truck fit in better with the atmosphere.

"Look. This is how it's gonna go down," Alisia said in a tone meant to put him in his place when all it did was raise his hackles. "I know this world. The less that's said, the better. Do not call me by name. *Any* name. In fact, just stand there with that scowl you're wearing right now and that will be enough."

Alisia drew a purple satin drawstring bag from her backpack then pushed the pack through the open window to the flatbed. From inside the bag she took out a stick of black eyeliner and rimmed her eyes. A coat of mascara darkened the effect and brought out the brilliant green of her irises. Next came a thick layer of gloss on her pouty lips, making them look luscious enough to sample, despite the chance of getting covered in goop. She removed the band from her hair and shook the waves loose, scrunching the tresses in her hand, then leaned forward to arrange the view of her cleavage for maximum impact.

When she was finished primping, she looked like a woman who had recently rolled out of bed after a long night of sex and was ready for more. While his cock appreciated the effect, his big head reasoned that he wasn't going to like what was about to happen. Not one bit.

"Let's go," she said, all cool and no-nonsense as she tucked her Glock into the waistband of her pants at the back and tucked the makeup bag out of sight in the dashboard.

Ripley followed her as she wound her way through the outskirts of the square. For-rent signs covered the windows of every other building of the once-bustling corner that had been the hub of interior decorators, art galleries, and assorted pubs. With the economy still in the toilet, many of the buildings sat empty with only ghosts occupying the brick structures.

They took a left at the corner and ducked into the third doorway on the right. For a woman who claimed to only know this man in passing, she seemed incredibly sure of where she was going. She didn't even need to read the directory before selecting a button. The label read "Dr. Marcel LeStrange GP."

The intercom screeched and a garbled voice asked, "Yes?"

"Bonjour," Alisia replied.

A buzz signaled the door unlocking.

Ripley rubbed the back of his neck. "What is this place? I don't like it."

"Dr. Strangelove," she whispered, tapping the label.

Behind the door was a short hallway, which led to an ordinary clinic waiting room. Two rows of three chairs sat back to back. A rack of tattered magazines stood to one side.

In the corner grew a potted ficus that had withered from the lack of sunlight. Plants did that if they were forced to live in a room with no windows and the only light came from flickering incandescent bulbs hanging from the drop ceiling.

Yup, just a typical waiting room, except it was devoid of patients and the receptionist behind the counter was smoking a cigarette as she stared at them through two-inch-thick bulletproof glass.

A stream of smoke puffed out between wrinkled lips covered in faded pink lipstick. "Do you have an appointment?"

Alisia leaned against the counter. "No. We're walk-ins."

"The doctor is busy." A long red nail flicked the ash off the end of her cigarette.

"Really," Alisia drawled and pointed up at the camera mounted in the corner of the receptionist's area. She plumped up her cleavage until her breasts touched her chin.

The phone rang and the woman sighed. "What?" she barked into the receiver. "Fine. He's with a patient. Wait over there."

"Thank you."

Alisia sat but Ripley stood, arms crossed as he leaned against the wall. This was the second time on a mission in his human skin. The experience was unsettling, to say the least. He was used to following his animal instinct, which worked at maximum capacity when in animal form. As it was, his human instincts were screaming to get the hell out of there.

As Alisia had said, she knew this world. They had agreed she would take the lead. However…

Would it make him less of a badass if he fell to his knees and begged her to let him take care of everything? Better yet, just get them out of there and form a new plan that involved her staying a hundred miles out of the fray.

Just as he was about to snatch her up and toss her over his shoulder, the door opened and a man limped out. The left side of his face was swollen and purple, the right arm hung in a cast. He didn't glance their way as he hobbled out the door.

"You can go in now," the receptionist rasped through the slats in the glass.

Ripley followed right on Alisia's ass, anticipating danger at any moment. They passed by one dank exam room, then another. There wasn't a bio-waste container or sanitizer in sight. These rooms he wouldn't treat any animal in, let alone a human being.

Alisia paused by a closed door and held up her hand. She was calm. Calm in that lull before the storm way that made the hairs on his arms stand on end. "Stop. Stand over there to the side."

"Like hell."

"Two steps. That way. Please." She implored him with her eyes to trust her.

"One step."

A hint of a smile curled her lips. "Fine."

He held his breath as she knocked.

One thousand one. One thousand two. One thousand three.

The stench of Aramis and herbicidal soap tickled Ripley's nose as the door opened. Dr. LeStrange was younger than Ripley expected. Approximately mid- to late forties at a guess, he had an unlined face under his tan skin with gray streaking his black hair. The gold chain and cross around his neck looked as if it weighed five pounds, and dark chest hair curled over the top of his scrubs.

His ultra-white smile widened. "Well, well, well. Long time no see. You're looking good, Sam."

Ripley started. *Sam?*

Alisia propped a hand on her hip and batted her lashes. "You do remember me."

"How could I forget a luscious piece of ass like you?" the doctor all but purred.

Two thoughts slammed into Ripley at the same time. Obviously Alisia knew the man more than she had let on, and two, if the man felt comfortable enough to flirt, then he and Alisia weren't mated. That was a good thing, right?

A wolf's warning growl erupted from his chest.

Nope. Apparently not for his animal.

The doctor jumped back. "What was that?"

Through her wavy bangs, Alisia flashed a warning of her own at Ripley with her green eyes. "My protection. May I come in? He won't bite."

LeStrange chuckled, yet his brow puckered with worry. He stepped back to let them in, then swallowed when he took a good look at Ripley. "You've traded up, I see. Business must be good. Where have you been hiding?"

She shrugged. "Around."

Ripley stepped into LeStrange's private office. To the left was the desk, with a computer and files stacked on the surface. Along the wall were monitors displaying footage of the entrances and the waiting room with the receptionist puffing away at her cigarettes while she watched television on a tablet. But it was the full-size bed to the right that made Ripley's stomach roil. The rumpled sheets did not appear to be from a restless night's sleep. The musk of sex and human assaulting his nostrils confirmed it.

The roiling stomach turned into a full volcano of disgust when LeStrange pulled Alisia close to his body. He went in for a kiss, then thought better as he eyed the slick lip gloss.

"You look better than I remember. You've rounded out." He nodded at Ripley. "Your man can stand in the corner. I don't like to perform for others." He bit his lip and grabbed Alisia by the ass. "How about I pay you double to take your mouth and pussy?"

Ripley's vision turned red and he leapt the few feet to grab LeStrange around the throat and slam him into the wall.

"Rip-T," Alisia shouted and pulled at his arm. "Put him down."

"Don't you fucking talk to her that way." Spit flew from his mouth and his fangs lengthened as the animal fought to protect its mate. "She's not a whore."

"Yes, I am." Alisia ducked under his arm and slapped at his chest. "T, he's right. No joke. That's how he knows me. I am a whore."

CHAPTER TWENTY-ONE

I AM A *whore.*

The words were out and there was no taking them back.

Alisia let out a long stuttering breath through her nose. She couldn't look Ripley in the eye, couldn't bear to see the disgust, so she stared at the pulse in his neck. The vein throbbed in a frantic beat as if it were about to burst. Under her hands, his meaty arm felt ready to snap with the tension as he held LeStrange against the wall.

The doctor fought to pull the manacle-like fist off his throat while his legs kicked fruitlessly for release.

Deep, painful, growls rumbled in Ripley's chest before he uttered a heartbreaking, "No."

"What do you think happens to young girls who end up on the streets all alone?"

"Not you." He shook his head. "Not you."

The pain in his guttural whisper raked like claws down her chest. She swallowed against the lump choking her and slapped at his arm. *Later,* she mouthed. "Put him down."

Ripley released his hold, and LeStrange slipped to the floor, gasping for breath. She watched as he floundered, red faced, on the ground as the heated laser of Ripley's gaze bore a hole right into her heart.

"What the fuck is going on?" LeStrange choked out.

"We're here for information," she answered. "Not

games. Tell me what I want to know then we'll be on our way. And be careful with the, uh, compliments. My friend here is very possessive and offends easily."

"What are you talking about?" He rolled to his knees.

"Deacon Winston and the Church of the Divine and Sacred."

The flopping ceased and a contemplative look narrowed his eyes. "I don't know what you're talking about."

She tsked. "Well, I'll tell you what I know. I know that Reverend Lowell and his deacons have been manufacturing a form of meth and drugging their parishioners. I also know that you are somehow involved. What I don't know is *how* you're involved and what the deal is that Ryan called you about yesterday to postpone."

A chuckled started low from his belly. He climbed to his feet, adjusting the waistband of his scrubs. "I always knew there was more to you than big tits and the need to fuck to get paid." Ripley snarled in warning, but LeStrange paid him no heed. "Whatever I have to say is going to cost you. Pussy and ass. Have you had her ass?" he asked Ripley. "She milks your cock so tight."

The lion's roar raised the hair on her neck. A second later Ripley swung his giant fist, deliberately missing LeStrange's head by millimeters and punching a hole the size of a bowling ball in the plaster.

Alisia cringed on the inside, but she deliberately placed herself between the savage and the terrified dumbass. Ripley could bitch all he wanted, but they needed this information. "He will tear you apart. I know that a few people will miss you, but no one would ever admit that publicly. Talk."

"Answer her," Ripley roared.

The doctor fell back against the wall, gaping in horror as

he lost his arrogance. "They need a distributor. With multiple locations they'll need a runner, someone from the outside who wouldn't care what happened inside. I'm making that happen."

"How?"

"I know some people."

She strode to the desk and grabbed a prescription pad and a pen. A framed portrait of a young man in a Marine uniform gazed at her with resigned eyes. Poor kid. "Names. What else?"

"That's all."

LeStrange's lucrative practice was built on patching up those who lacked proper identification to go to a legit clinic. With his location near both stadiums, thousands of people from a variety of social classes passed through his doors, allowing his operatives to come and go with ease. Arranging a few drivers would be hardly worth the effort for someone like LeStrange.

"There has to be more."

He eyed Ripley, who took a step closer. "They're taking the drug public. A stronger version than what they've been giving at the church. They need that info hushed, so I'm taking care of it." He shrugged. "The economy's bad. Everyone needs to diversify."

That didn't make sense. Her father manipulating and scheming for the church, yes. Willfully endangering people's lives for money? No. Impossible. Money wasn't a grand-enough aspiration for Creed Lowell. There had to be another player pulling the strings.

"When is the first delivery?"

"In the near future." He smirked. The man just couldn't resist playing with his life.

"I want specifics."

"I want to come all over you."

A blur of tan streaked from the corner of her vision and before she could blink, LeStrange was on the floor with three deep grooves cut into his cheek.

"T," she cautioned and pulled the Glock from the back of her waistband. She aimed the barrel at LeStrange's chest and motioned for Ripley to search the room.

LeStrange touched his cheek, eyes widening at the blood on his fingers, then wider at the gun trained on his heart.

Behind her she heard Ripley circling the room. The air whistled as he breathed in and out. With a small grunt, he was off to the desk, climbing on top and lifting a panel in the ceiling. Bound in thick rubber bands were several bundles of cash and sheaves of paper. It could be the evidence they needed, or something else to put LeStrange away for life.

Ripley pulled a flash drive from his pocket and inserted it into the computer. A few key strokes later and the signal was sent to Addison's computer back at headquarters that began the program to download the entire contents of the hard drive and off the network.

"This warrior woman routine is a turn-on." LeStrange spat blood near her feet.

"You really want to die, don't you?" She risked a quick glance at Ripley. "I think the good doctor could use a nap. Don't you?"

"I think he could use a permanent vacation," Ripley grumbled. He rifled through the cabinet and came up triumphantly with a bottle and a syringe. "How about some good ole special K?"

He plunged the needle into the bottle and pulled a deep

draw.

"No fucking way." LeStrange lunged at Alisia, who knocked him back with a kick to the stomach.

"Lie down and take your medicine."

Ripley didn't bother with disinfectant and yanked LeStrange's limp arm out straight and injected the narcotic into his throbbing vein. "Nighty-night."

"I will kill you, Sam Hill," he slurred.

She smiled grimly. "Didn't you hear? I'm already dead."

Once LeStrange had passed out, Ripley picked him up and tossed him like a sack of dog food on the bed.

Ripley was pissed. The muscles in his arms and face twisted and rolled, a sure sign he was fighting the urge to shift. And he was too quiet. No snappy comebacks or one-liners about lying down on the job. He was C-4 wired to blow.

"Let's go out the back. There's an escape route in case law enforcement comes knocking. The receptionist won't come down until the end of her shift for her pay."

Down the hall and through the door marked supplies, Alisia pushed aside a rolling shelf of bandages and opened a secret door to a dark tunnel. The rough brick walls with motion sensor lights reminded her of the rock hallways back home in the mountain.

"How do you know about this exit?" Ripley asked in a voice caught between his normal bass and an animal's growl.

"I've been brought through here before."

"Why?"

"You don't want to know."

His hot breath ruffled her hair as he stuck right on her tail. Bright sunlight blinded her when she exited out the end of the tunnel. Ripley loomed over her so their shadow looked as if they were one person.

Once they reached the truck, he gripped the handle of the door and he whipped it open with a gruff, "Slide over."

To the driver's side? "Why?"

"Get in and slide over," he commanded. His chest rose and fell with his quickening breath.

Unease exploded in her chest and rippled down her torso to clench around her upset stomach. For the first time his size and strength snapped her spine straight with the awareness that he had the potential to cause her harm.

Twenty minutes earlier she had believed with all her soul that Ripley would not hurt her, but this was a side of him she'd never seen. Mad, disgruntled, angry, yes. Furious, never.

Around them, the few people out on the street paid them no heed. The truck was in the shadows, and they were in a rougher part of town. Perhaps it was desperation on her part, but she wanted to believe he still cared for her, wanted to believe he would understand. And it was that hope that propelled her into the truck. Her jeans snagged against the torn vinyl as she slid across the bench seat and behind the wheel.

Ripley and his attitude climbed in behind her, sucking all of the space in the incredibly shrinking cab. A gauzy blanket dropped over her mind. She drew her arms in tight to her sides and faced the windshield. Her gaze focused inward to that place where no one could touch her.

"How? How could you sell yourself to slime balls like him?" Ripley lashed out.

"You go three days without eating, or spending the night under a tree while it's raining, not in your animal form, and then ask me that question." She spoke the words, but didn't hear herself say them.

"There must have been some other way. Something, anything else."

"I could have just died instead."

"No!" He smacked the dash so hard it cracked. "You don't. You don't give up. You don't let anyone use you. No one touches you."

A claw-tipped hand grabbed her arm around the bicep and hauled her across his lap. "No one touches you."

His lips crushed against hers, his tongue thrusting into her mouth to steal her breath. Under her hands, his muscles pulsated and pulled as if his skin was an ill-fitting suit that would tear itself loose.

And just like that, past and present collided and she was in another front seat with another john who thought that for twenty bucks, she belonged solely to him.

Ripley was frantic, his hands and lips never settling in one place for longer than a second. His pupils dilated, shifting from circles to slits and back again as the skin over his cheeks tightened. She had to slow him down, had to calm him or he would hurt her.

Stroking her fingers through his hair, she let her head fall back and automatically cooed, "Oooh, baby, that's so good. Make it last. I'm all yours."

Sharp teeth scraped over the rise of her breast, leaving long red grooves over the pale flesh. Seams popped, fabric tore, and cool air hit her bare backside as her jeans were ripped to shreds.

She closed her eyes and made the appropriate sounds to convey pleasure while inside she died a little more with each moan and groan.

"Alisia." He growled in a voice that rasped like skin over broken glass. "Look at me."

She forced her eyes open and gasped at the monster before her, pinning her with his hands. Fangs protruded from his lips pressed tight together and his skin was mottled with orange and black fur. His muscles rippled and twitched as if he were fighting himself.

"Ripley. Ripley come back to me." She brushed her fingers over his cheek.

"Alisia," Ripley whimpered. Then he roared so loud the windows rattled and the vibrations jolted down to her bones.

He shoved her off his lap and tossed her aside. Her hip hit the steering wheel and her back crashed against the door. He scrambled out of the truck and slammed the door shut. "Lock the door. Stay in here."

Claws turned into paws and silver fur erupted over his skin as a great wolf replaced the man and loped off down the street.

Alisia lay sprawled across the seat, clothes in shreds and her muscles aching. He said to lock the door, but she needed air. Her hand slipped off the latch twice before she cracked the door open enough to stick her head out. Her stomach revolted, spewing the contents all over the asphalt.

Well, that went about as well as she expected. She knew better. She should have known better. Just when she thought he had accepted the darkest parts of her past, he crudely shoved it down her throat at how worthless she was.

She allowed him to shout at her, let him hurt her. Why? Because she believed in him. Believed that once he got over his shock, he'd understand. Believed that he loved her. What a fucking idiot. When would she learn that she wasn't worth loving?

She needed to leave, needed to disappear for good to a place where it was guaranteed no one knew who, or what, she was. She searched the seat for the keys, then the floor of the truck and her bags, growing more frantic with each passing second. Where the hell were they?

Her breath caught as she remembered Ripley had had them in his pocket. She looked out the window and spotted the heap of shredded cloth on the sidewalk several yards away.

Please, please, please, she prayed that the keys were in the scraps of cloth and opened the door. A breeze kicked up and skipped across her bare skin. Pulling back in alarm, she looked down and realized she was all but naked and covered in a pattern of fine, pink scratches. Crap, she couldn't go out in public looking like this.

The window to the tailgate was open halfway. She pushed against the glass to widen the opening, cursing when it wouldn't budge. She reached into the back, her shoulder wedging into the hole until the metal cut into her skin. Her hand was a good foot away from her bag, yet she continued to stretch until her hand went numb.

A slow stream of tears turned into gasping sobs as hopelessness set in. She was trapped, mentally and physically. And so damn exhausted.

All the neurons in her mind shut down, leaving her a wailing, pathetic creature. Somehow, she found the energy to curl into a ball before giving up altogether. Who gave a shit if someone saw her in this condition? Certainly not her.

CHAPTER TWENTY-TWO

MOTHERFUCKING IDIOT.

Ripley dashed from shadow to shadow, mentally kicking his ass at having lost control. He hurt her. He frightened her and almost tore her apart, and for what? A past she couldn't change.

Then there was his animal to deal with. A very pissed-off and territorial animal. Apparently, he and Alisia had not mated, otherwise LeStrange wouldn't have had the cinnamon heat of lust pouring off him. While the man inside him was ecstatic that they had dodged that bullet, the animal was outraged. Nothing was going to stop him from claiming what was his. It had taken everything within him to keep the beast from taking her right there in the truck. It horrified him to know that it was a battle he was losing. He had been one heartbeat away from tearing her to shreds when he gazed into her eyes.

She looked like a living corpse staring right through him. Alisia had left and in her place was a shell to protect her from the monsters of the world. Monsters like him.

He had to make things right between them. Take any punishment she dished out. When it came to beg her for forgiveness, he had no shame.

But not yet. He was too close to the edge. The animal was fighting for control and the man had to find him a release or risk harming her further. He shifted from his preferred wolf form into the German shepherd. In the city the wolf was going to draw too much attention, but something as cute as a kitten was not enough to take the edge off.

Prey rustled in the dark corner of the alley. A raccoon, digging deep into a pile of trash bags. As if sensing that the only thing between life and death was a thin plastic bag filled with half-eaten burgers and steak fries, the raccoon dashed for the safety of a garbage can.

The coon was no match for the dog, and had become a mass of fur and bones in three quick bites. While the veterinarian in him was disgusted, the beast hungered for more.

The scent of wet dirt and ammonia drew him around the corner and deeper into the shadows of the warehouse district, where three men argued over the price of a small pouch of white chemicals.

Ripley charged the trio with a guttural howl, the raccoon's blood still dripping down his jaw. The men stared at him in terror as he tackled the one with the bag to the ground. He tore the plastic baggie apart with a swipe of his claws, gouging deep scratches in the skin of the pusher's hand. The other two men scrambled out of the alley, trailing the stench of fear and piss behind them. The dog didn't stop his attack until all the inventory the drug dealer carried on him was a white stain on the cement. Only when he pleaded for his life did Ripley let go.

It served no purpose other than personal satisfaction, but he howled directly in the face of the pusher before he stepped back with a constant growl rumbling from his chest, and allowed the man to scramble to his feet and stagger away.

Ripley's lungs heaved and his legs trembled as his adrenaline ebbed. With his aggression leashed, he returned to Alisia ready to face his fate. The truck was where he left it, and although it appeared empty, he sensed her inside. Regret soured his stomach as the acrid scent of her vomit on the concrete filled his nose.

The shepherd shrank away as he shifted into a Labrador puppy, his golden fur turning into a downy-soft fluff. Slap a red bow around his neck, and he'd be the perfect Christmas present.

Was he playing dirty? Maybe. If he managed to pull at her heartstrings as well, all the better.

He called out with a high-pitched *arf!* that sounded sad and pitiful to his own ears. Sitting on his haunches, he barked again and waited by the passenger door. With each passing second his tail grew straighter and his ears drooped. He barked again and whimpered. *Please look at me.*

The top of Alisia's head appeared as she slowly rose to peer out the window. Black tears streaked her face and that dead expression clouded her eyes. He barked again, and she frowned at him in confusion until he rolled over onto his back, exposing his belly. The confusion melted into a glacier-cold expression that screamed *fuck off* through the glass. Oh, yeah, she recognized him now.

He ran around the truck several times, then rolled onto his back again, whimpering.

The pop of the lock sounded, then a metallic creak as the door cracked open just wide enough for the tiny puppy to squeeze through. His relief that she was allowing him to climb up front with her obliterated abruptly when she gripped him about the waist and shoved him through the back window onto the flatbed. He fell flat on his face and shifted once the stars cleared from his vision.

"Okay. I deserved that. And more." He climbed to his knees and peered through the opening. A howl ripped from his throat as he saw the rags he created that covered her. Shame and horror sliced through him like a knife to the stomach. "Alisia. My God. I'm so—"

She grunted and held her hand up, huddling behind the wheel with the other hand ready on the door release. "Hand me my bag," she whispered in a raw voice.

He fumbled for her pack and squeezed it through the window. The ache in his chest was so painful, he thought his heart would crack his ribs.

"I'm sorry. I am so sorry, Alisia." His throat closed and his eyes watered with the fear that he wouldn't be able to make her understand. "I didn't mean to hurt you. I'm just so fucking mad. At LeStrange and those like him. Mad that I wasn't there for you years ago, that I didn't protect you, which is crazy, I know. God, I feel like such a failure." He smacked his head twice against the metal frame. "Life has given you shit, and I have been trying so hard to make it up to you. You deserve so much better. You—you are amazing. You are so strong, so brave. So much braver than I am."

The danger he placed himself in was with the full knowledge of what was at stake and with an eager anticipation to prove himself as a supreme male. It was all about ego, and never once had he felt apologetic for it. But Alisia had been repeatedly tossed into the deep end of the cesspool time and time again, each time dragging herself out of the mire in triumph.

Before the manifestation of his powers, the toughest challenge he had faced was choosing which college to go to. Compared to her, he was nothing but a tough-talking wuss.

"When you're hurt I can't control my rage. I want to rip apart every fucker that's hurt you. It kills me. But to be the one that caused you pain—I can't begin to describe how sorry I am. I love you so much and I'm scared shitless that I've blown it with you. Please don't push me away. I know I don't deserve your forgiveness, but I'd give anything for another chance."

Nothing. She was like a porcelain statue, clutching her pack to herself like she was ready to bolt, clothed or not. The weight of her gaze pressed against him like the g-force in a jet plane, judging, measuring, valuing his worth. It was agony holding still for her inspection. Every muscle drew tight until he began to shake and his lungs burned with the need to explode.

Dark spots began to float in his vision when she finally blinked. Once. Slow. Then she blinked again. Her fingers, white with tension, slipped from the door release. She lowered her head and opened her pack to dig through the contents. He continued to hold still while she pushed her arms into the sleeves of her hoodie and pulled the zipper to her throat.

"Turn around, please," she requested. Softly. Her voice raspy, as she held her pants across her lap.

The breath he held released in a shaky rush. It wasn't much, but it was progress.

"I'm gonna get dressed. Okay?" he asked. "Take us someplace safe to talk. That's all, just talk. Is that all right with you?"

At her imperceptible nod, he moved like lightning, digging through his pack to find something to cover his nakedness.

The few people milling down the street paid no heed to

the man climbing out of the back of a beat-up truck, nor did they pay any attention to the woman in the cab struggling to maintain her dignity and modesty. He stood in front of the window, facing away to grant her what little privacy was available. When the rocking ceased, he walked back to the driver's side and opened the door.

Blonde curls spilled across the seat as she lay curled on her side in the corner of the cab. He reached to skim the back of his fingers over the tresses then pulled back as if he'd be bit. She didn't ask for his touch, and he had no right to take any more from her. Liquid gold, that's what she was. Inside and out. A precious treasure he had to protect. Even from himself.

He collected the keys then started the truck and set off. The freeway ran along the waterfront area like the city's spine. A mix of hoity-toity, artsy, and salt of the earth cohabitated along the vertebra that was crumbling with age. Ripley parked in the shade at the far north end of the docks, and the moment he set the brake she was on the move, all light and grace as she slipped out of the truck.

He followed as she glided across the street and over to the railing of an empty pier. During the summer a grand-stand was erected for live music, but in the spring, it was nothing but wide-open space and an unobstructed view of the bay.

The wind picked up the ends of her hair, blowing the strands across her face, but she didn't lift a hand to smooth them into place. She didn't do anything but stand against the rail and track the comings and goings of container ships and ferries.

If he was going to regain her trust, he had to get her to open up. Really open up. And he was going to have to listen.

Not comment. Not "fix." Listen.

No matter how much he'd want to maim anyone who harmed her in her past, she needed his support more than his vengeance. After his earlier behavior, he'd be lucky if she gave him the time of day, but he wasn't going to give up hope.

They had so much to talk about, so many layers to uncover, but he hadn't a clue where to begin.

He drew in a breath and jumped off the proverbial ledge, hoping to start off with something easy. "Why did he call you 'Sam'?"

She flinched as if poked with a stick. He heard her draw in a few breaths of her own before she answered, "That was the name I went by for a while."

A response. Yes! Yet the defeated tone of her voice chilled him more than the breeze. "Why?"

She shook her head and shrugged. "Gretchen was dead and I—I was so lost. I needed Sam with me somehow."

"Then how did you get to be Alisia?"

Another sigh, then she looked up as if the sun would provide her strength. "She was another hooker."

The word nicked him like a blade. "What happened to her?"

"She died."

An answer that lead to a million more questions. "How?"

"I don't know."

When she fell silent and continued to stare out at the water, he took a step closer. "You knew her, though?"

She nodded.

"Were you friends?'

A shrug, nothing more.

Come on, baby. Talk to me. "How did you know her?"

"She was a party girl. She liked the drugs and sex, and she was a real bitch. She lived with her grandmother, who was elderly and needed care. Alisia wanted to live life on the edge and was always mining the streets for the next high, however that came. One morning I found her body, that had been dumped with some trash behind one of the hotels on 99. Could have been a trick gone bad, or she could have ODed. Didn't matter. She was dead."

He filled in the blanks. "So you took her identity."

"We looked alike, so I switched our IDs." She licked her dry lips. "People thought we were related, and sometimes we would take jobs, pretending to be twins when someone wanted to satisfy a kink. When I saw her body, I saw my future. That could have been me in a month, or a week, or even the next time I climbed into a car. Part of me was envious that she no longer had to care. That scared the shit out of me."

He shoved his hands in his pockets to keep from reaching for her. "Weren't you afraid you'd get caught?"

The bitterness that coated her laughter raked down his back like jagged claws. "She was a dead whore. Half of her face was purple and swollen. They had identification that looked enough like her and I knew that with no one looking for Sam Hill, they would write her off as just another dead whore."

The truth of her words was another stab to the solar plexus. A reality made even more painful with the knowledge that the poor girl was someone's daughter. Someone's grandchild. And she had died alone.

"What did you do next?" he asked, barely getting the words out.

"I went to her house."

"Seriously?" he sputtered.

A tiny smile broke through her frown. "It was Jameson's idea. Alisia's grandmother was sick and her eyesight was failing, so I pretended to be Alisia. I apologized for not being there for her and said I wanted to get clean, go back to school, and be a better granddaughter. And that was that."

"If you knew Jameson then, why were you on the streets?" He couldn't imagine her fierce friend would stand by as she placed herself in danger.

She licked her lips and stared down at the railing, picking off chunks of peeling paint with her fingernails. "Jameson's mom ran the shelter back then. I went there when the weather turned bad, or if I hadn't eaten in days. But I couldn't stay there too long. At some point you're expected to try to better your situation. Get a job, apply for housing, especially when the government comes to check on how the home uses its charitable donations. If I tried to find legit work, hell, even get an apartment, I'd take a risk on being found out. Jameson hated when I went back to hooking, but she understood. And she was only a phone call away if I needed it."

He and Jameson might have not met under the best of circumstances, but he had to admit, she was a good friend to Alisia. "Do you think the grandmother knew you weren't Alisia?"

"I think so, but she never said anything." Tears gathered on her lashes. "We were only together for a few months when she passed away. When she was on her deathbed, she told me she was grateful that God had sent her an angel in her time of need."

Fuck. He swallowed hard. "Perhaps she was sent to

you."

The statement finally pulled her gaze away from the horizon as she turned to him with a frown. "What?"

"Perhaps God knew that you needed help, so he gave you an opportunity."

"By having a young girl die? That doesn't make sense."

"Look, Alisia, there are a lot of influences in this world. Good, bad, and indifferent. Alisia, the real Alisia, chose to go with the bad, and she paid for it with her life. You didn't choose your circumstances. You were surviving, and that's different." He let out a frustrated sigh. "You keep thinking that you're unworthy of good things, that you're being punished for some unimaginable reason. But did you ever consider that you were matched with those who needed your help?"

"And then they all died," she exclaimed. "No one deserves that. Sam didn't deserve that."

"He deserved you, and I'm thankful that you had him. Baby, you're a smart girl and you would have caught on to your father sooner or later. You made Sam happy, and without your memory of his love for you, you might not have had the incentive to keep going. You've helped so many people because of your capacity to love. Don't be afraid of it." His fingers flexed, dying to touch her, hold her, shake some sense into her. "This is your time to shine. Your time to embrace life, *your* life, and not let anything stop you. The past can't be undone, sweetheart. No matter how much either of us wishes it. But I want to be part of your future. A good part, if you'll let me. Please."

"I killed my stepmother. I've had sex with men for money."

A tick started near his right eye. "Not anymore. Right?"

The spark of anger that flashed in her eyes and the tightening of her lips was a welcome break from the blank expression of despair and loss.

He held up both hands. "See, exactly. That's not who you are. You are a good person, Alisia Caldwell, formerly Gretchen Lowell. You are a fighter and a survivor. I believe in you."

She crossed her arms, her palms rubbing the bare skin marred with purple bruises in the shape of his fingers. The lines around her mouth deepened, but she couldn't keep the softness of hope out of her eyes. She wanted to trust so badly, the scent washed over him with the breeze; sweet like a peach, but tinged with fear.

"I want to hug you." He rested back against the railing and braced his palms along the top, curling his fingers over the worn wood railing. "I need your touch. Please."

She looked out to the water then back at him, biting her lip while he watched her mind turn behind those wary green eyes. The suspense was painful, as if he were on trial and awaiting sentencing. He closed his eyes and breathed, focusing on the simple action to keep from launching into a dissertation as to why she needed to accept him. It had to be her choice.

The scrape of rubber sole against wood quickened his heartbeat. The closeness of her body radiated more heat than the sun's rays as she hesitated by his side. Holding firm to his resolve, Ripley waited her out as her breath warmed his skin though his cotton T-shirt right over his heart.

He jolted at the brush of her finger over his lips.

"In the truck you were turning into...something. You had fangs. Something different than what I've seen from you."

"Yes," he admitted, his lips barely moving.

"Why?"

His hands tightened around the railing and he closed his eyes tighter. Fuck. What was he going to say? *"I'm one overly passionate kiss from tying us together for eternity. Neat, huh?"* Yeah. No. As his father would say, that conversation would go over as well as a turd in a punch bowl.

Also, it had not escaped his notice that not more than thirty minutes prior he had told her that he loved her and she hadn't even flinched. While she hadn't outright refused his declaration, she hadn't reciprocated either. After the way he treated her, who would blame her for not wanting the love of a monster?

Yet she was still there, standing no more than an inch away. That had to mean something, didn't it? Why would she still stay after he dropped this bombshell?

He swayed as if he were balancing on a high wire over a pit filled with shards of glass. One misstep and he'd be shredded to ribbons.

"Why, Ripley?" she asked again with more force in her tone.

He cleared his throat. "The line between my animal and human sides is getting thin. Blurring. Doc is looking into it, but when I'm stressed, it's a struggle. Back there, my animal was afraid for you. He wanted to protect you and remind you of his ability to do that. He's a little possessive."

"So I don't belong to *you* anymore. I belong to the animal."

"He's willing to share, but only with me."

"Why are your eyes closed?"

"Because." His breath shuddered. *I'm a fucking coward.*

"Because I don't want to push you and it hurts to see that fear in your eyes. To see you afraid of me."

The weight of her hands landed on his hips and her cheek rested on his chest. He wilted at the contact, his grip on the railing holding them both up.

"I'm going to put my arms around you," he warned.

"Okay," she said in a small voice.

His arms overlapped around her back and he gritted his teeth to keep from crushing her. "I know I haven't earned it, but will you trust me?"

She stiffened in his hold. "With what?"

"With you. To stand beside you."

Her hands stayed on his hips, but strands of her hair rose on the wind to wrap around his neck. "I'll think about it."

"That's all I ask." It was going to take a lot of work, but at least she was giving him a chance. He laughed and gave into the urge to squeeze her tight.

"So, what happens next?" she asked.

"We call Max. We stop the threat against you, then you can begin the next chapter of your life." *With me.*

"You make it sound so easy."

"Because it will be. By eight o'clock, this will all be over and then you and I will go out to celebrate. Trust me."

CHAPTER TWENTY-THREE

"T HEY'RE COMING."

Alisia looked over at Ripley. Behind him the setting sun covered his face in shadow, but the relaxed set of his shoulders told her whoever was approaching was a friend. At least to him.

Underneath her leather jacket she wore her hoodie zipped up to her throat and a long-sleeve tee, and still she was chilled in the last of the sun's rays. Tall grass scraped against her jeans as she paced in a circle that was much like her life. Constantly moving, but never going anywhere.

The field they waited in was five miles away from the church's retreat house near Lacey where Ripley and Max had first met her father. Tall evergreens and blue spruce surrounded them, and with each blink of the eye she imagined the thick trunks crowding closer and closer, ready to imprison her in their limbs as the rough bark scraped her to the bone. Her gaze wandered to the trail leading to the main road. How far away would she be able to run?

"Don't even think about it." Ripley slid his fingers along her palm to grasp her hand. "Relax. I'm not going to let anything happen to you."

Crazy, but she believed him.

Never before had Ripley lied to her. Omitted, yes, but never outright lied. When it came to his feelings for her, they were always right there on his sleeve. Persistent, yes, but never pushy. He bared all, leaving her to do with his feelings as she wished.

His affection for her scared her witless. Bad things happened to people who loved her, and although Ripley wasn't like other people, he was still mortal. Whether he acknowledged it or not.

That had been real regret and tears in his eyes when he apologized earlier. It was a vulnerability she had never seen from him before and it was the final blow that knocked down the flimsy wall she had built between them. Her heart belonged to him.

A tornado of thoughts picked up speed in her mind, shredding her confidence and flinging her concentration to the far corners of Oz. Past, present, and future. Love, fear, and uncertainty whipped up a destructive storm that squeezed like a tourniquet around her chest. She tightened her hand around Ripley's, siphoning his strength and steadfastness to calm her rising hysteria. Was securing her future going to be as easy as he believed? Hell no, but it was that optimism that made Ripley who he was.

The crunch of tires coming up the trail snatched her attention away from his calming touch. At the moment life didn't exist beyond the next five minutes, then the five minutes after that. Once her father was disposed of, and Winston became nothing but an ugly memory, she would ask Ripley to hold her forever. Until then she was going to stand strong on her own two feet and make him proud.

No. Make herself proud.

One Range Rover, then another emerged into the clearing.

Her throat worked hard to swallow the lump of surprise that stuck in her windpipe. "Did the entire team have to come? Does Max think Lowell is going to cause that much trouble?"

"They're here for you." He brushed his thumb over her hand when she stiffened. "To support you."

"Oh."

The assurance did nothing to calm her. For years she had lied to people she called friend. Would she give herself a second chance if she were them? She would like to think so, but probably not. Once bitten, twice as likely to bite back first. So why should she expect them to afford her the same courtesy?

Doc was the first to jump out from the driver's seat. She was dressed for battle in black leather from head to toe. Her dark hair was pulled into a low bun, emphasizing her large brown eyes that sparked with relief and fury.

Alisia took a step back, but Ripley was right behind her and absorbed most of the impact as the taller woman slammed into them and engulfed her in a huge hug.

"Alisia Caldwell, I could kick your ass. I understand why you kept your secrets, but you're my best friend. I could have helped you."

"You two look like shit," Max said, shutting his car door.

Doc pulled back and brushed Alisia's hair off her face. "Are you all right? You look fine, but how are you really? Any sensitivity, unusual reactions to anything?"

"Doc." Ripley placed a hand on her shoulder and pushed her back. "Easy. We're okay."

She narrowed her eyes. "I'll be the judge of that."

"Hey, sexy lady." Chase opened his arms for a hug. "You missed a workout."

"Believe me," Alisia said as she accepted Chase's hug.

"I've been getting a workout the last few days."

"Well, now you have us to keep you going." He laughed and stepped aside.

Crystal came forward and held out her hand. "Alisia, I'm so glad you're okay."

"Thank you," she replied but refused to take her hand. Crystal's powers could easily see the images of her past, which was why Alisia had avoided physical contact with her whenever possible.

But Crystal wouldn't have any of that. She rolled her eyes and enveloped her in a warm embrace. "You are my friend. Don't be afraid to be around me. Your memories belong to you, and I would never intrude."

Alisia hugged her back, overwhelmed by the show of affection. She had been expecting scorn, disappointment, and a deep-seated mistrust etched across her forehead.

Much like the expression worn by her husband. Black sunglasses hid his glacier blue eyes, but that laser-like stare managed to cut through the lenses to make her feel two inches tall. Max had taken her into his home, let her in on some of his most valuable secrets, and she threatened what he worked so hard to create.

In comparison, facing her father was going to be a thousand times easier than approaching Max, and he did not appear as if he was going to make it any easier. His handsome, stone-cold features were as welcoming as a rabid dog.

"Max." She cleared her throat and tried again. "I'm sorry for causing so much trouble."

He didn't melt a drop, but his voice held concern when he asked, "How are you holding up?"

"Um, as well as can be expected, I guess."

He nodded once. "We'll talk later."

The implied threat hung in the air as he slid his arm around his wife. "If anyone else has a ne'er–do-well parent plotting an evil plan, let me know now so I can mentally prepare."

Alisia turned back to Ripley to see him involved in a heated conversation with Doc. Unintelligible words were spoken, and there was a lot of grunting, finger-pointing, and furious facial gestures. Ripley made a motion across his neck and Doc followed up with a punch to his shoulder.

He issued a low growl and a glare before turning away from the infuriated doctor and returning to Alisia's side. "Thanks for coming, guys."

"Of course we'd come." Crystal threw her arms around his neck in a hug. "You're family. Both of you."

"You're the best." His smile faded as he drew in a deep breath. "And you smell like cookies. Like you *are* the cookie." He stared down at her, his brows rising higher and higher with each passing second. "Your hormones have changed."

Crystal gasped and her cheeks turned pink as she glanced at Max. "I'm—*we* are going to have a baby."

"What? That's great. Congratulations." Ripley hugged Crystal again and held up his hand to give Max a high five.

Okay. Alisia scratched her head. What was going on?

Something in the universe was off. The team seemed happy to see her, Max hadn't yelled at her yet, and even more stunning, he allowed a pregnant Crystal to step foot off the mountain. This did not compute.

However, judging by the strain that bracketed Max's tight-lipped grin, perhaps he was given very little choice on the matter of Crystal's involvement. When his wife was passionate about something, she didn't let up, which meant she was there either to support Alisia, and/or she had a vision that revealed that whatever was going to happen was mild enough for her to risk her safety to be present.

For all their sakes, Alisia hoped to hell it was the latter. If any of them were hurt because of her, the guilt would be the breaking point that would finally send her to the mental hospital.

"Come on, Alisia." Doc looped their arms together. "Let's get you some clean clothes and have a chat."

"Hold on a second, Doc." Max stopped them. "Not yet. Let's allow Lowell to think we just picked her up off the street. Unless you're in any sort of discomfort, Alisia?"

"No. I'm fine, only anxious to get this over with. Is there a plan?"

Max smiled. "Of course there is. But first, let's get you geared up."

He withdrew an amulet from the pocket of his duster and handed it to Ripley. "This is coming out of your paycheck."

Ripley accepted it with a hardy-har-har and fit the camera around his neck. Next, Max handed him an inner ear implant, which adjusted to remain in place no matter what form Ripley took.

"And for you, Alisia." Max held out another implant.

"Really?" She cupped her hand and examined the little plug. This was the first time she was given a piece of tech to wear in the field. The technology in the device was amazing, made even more so because Max had constructed the piece in a literal cave.

"Here, sweetheart, I'll put it in for you." Ripley plucked the earpiece and brushed her hair behind her ear. "Just talk normally, and if you want to adjust the sound, or who you want to listen to, let Addison know."

The plug felt like she had water trapped in her ear, annoying, but not too distracting. "Addison?"

"Hey, girl." Addison's voice echoed in her ear. "How's the volume?"

"Good."

"I miss having my shadow near me."

Alisia blinked away sudden tears. "I miss you, too. How's your allergy?"

"Better. A little congested, but I'm ready to get you home."

Home. It had been so long since that word had brought her comfort. So long since home meant more than a place to store her clothes and have a meal. That cold, isolated mountain was home, and these people her family. She wrapped her arms around her middle and squeezed tight. Yeah, she was ready to go home too.

"Did you find anything in the information we sent you?" Alisia asked Addison.

"Oh yeah. Maestro, if you please?"

Max led them to the back of Rover One and popped the lift gate. The dark gray interior looked normal but like everything with the team, the SUV was anything but. Under the floorboards lay an assortment of guns, knives, and clubs. There were ropes, hooks, and other restraining devices, as well as a laptop and several cameras.

Max took out a small black globe, about the size of his fist, and turned the switch on the bottom before setting it flat on the ground. In the growing twilight a lime green light shot from the top and a holographic image of the pages from her father's journal projected in front of them.

"After looking at Lowell's journal and Dr. LeStrange's computer, I found the code they used to communicate." As Addison spoke in their ears, more photos and charts appeared from the globe. "What appears to be a series of sermons are actually coded messages. A reference to a Bible verse would indicate the meeting place, and the date on top is not the date of when the letter was written but the date of the meeting. For example, this one here. On the surface it looks like a sermon he intended to read on February 5, but in actuality the meeting was on February 5. And this verse that reads, 'In the hallow of sin and vice, the revelers come,' matches a notation in LeStrange's records of a meeting at a club called The Pulpit."

"But the sermon is about giving thanks to the Lord," Chase pointed out. "What does that have to do with the Bible verse? Won't people who know that verse think it's weird that it doesn't fit?"

"Do you know all of your Bible verses?" Doc asked.

He shrugged. "No. But someone must."

"These weren't meant to be read out loud," Max explained. "Only to look innocent enough on paper in case they were found, but if you didn't know what to look for, you wouldn't think anything was strange. But knowing the code isn't enough. We need to tie Lowell to the drugs."

"Which is where the information from LeStrange's computer and notes come in. Lowell may not have kept records on a hard drive, but LeStrange did. He had a chart of patient accounts that are actually all of his drug transactions. And he was the one supplying Lowell with the massive quantities of decongestants."

"Looks like LeStrange is branching out from being the middleman," Ripley said.

"An economy when only the top one percent is doing well makes people try all sorts of things." Addison continued, "There's enough evidence here for the police to launch an investigation and put LeStrange away for the rest of his life, plus twenty years."

"What about my father?"

"Him too. Doc, what did you find in those samples?"

Doc Kelly looked up from the little lab she had set up in the trunk and was testing the samples collected at the church. She lifted a vial filled with a purple liquid. "We have ketamine. Now we all we need is to tie this to the wafers still on the compound."

"Right." Max clapped his hands together once. "Here's the plan. Lowell and his crew are meeting us at the retreat house. We'll start the discussion of completing the transaction when Alisia makes a break for it. Ripley will give chase, but alas won't catch her. In the chaos we'll detain them long enough for the local sheriff, who is supposed to arrive five minutes after us. Gretchen will fade away forever, and Alisia Caldwell will take her place back in society."

While that sounded as nice and easy as L'Oréal, too much was left to chance. Plus, there was more than her future at stake. "What about my sister? What about the church?"

"We'll find your sister, baby." Ripley wrapped his arm around her waist.

"But there's still the church. Those are decent people—well, most of them. But they rely on the church for everything. If we leave them leaderless, it could cause more damage than leaving my father be."

"What are you saying? We don't take Lowell in?" Chase asked.

"No." She rubbed at the ache growing between her eyes. "We can't destroy their world then walk away. They'll need time to recover."

Max swiped his hand over his face. "I get what you're saying. Something will be worked out, but not in the next ten minutes. Let's get through the night first. All right?"

Max was right. One drama at a time. And if he said he'd help the church, then he would. The man had the money and resources to make it happen.

"Do not let your guard down for one second," Max instructed while stowing the equipment. "Stay in control. We don't want Lowell or any of the deacons using our actions against us later. The specifics of our part in all this needs to be kept out of the media as much as possible. Stick to the plan. I'll be the one to take Lowell."

"And I'll take Winston," Ripley declared with lethal intent.

"No way." Max slashed his hand in the air. "We want them alive, not turned into puppy chow. Chase will take Winston. You handle everyone else."

"I want Winston."

"Ripley." Alisia placed her hand on his chest. "You're no good to me in jail. Whatever you are planning, I appreciate the thought. That's enough for me."

His pupils dilated and his upper lip curled with a twist. "You are worthy of more than a thought. You deserve action."

"And that's what's happening. Please, Ripley." She brushed her thumb over his lip and gave him a seductive smile. "You can make it up to me later."

A shudder tore through Ripley as he closed his eyes and cupped her hand in his, pressing a kiss to the center of her palm before he swept her up in a kiss that was as passionate and as strong as his arms holding her, supporting her, comforting her.

"When you're done sucking face," Max drawled, "let's roll. Rip, why don't you scout the area and make sure we're not walking into a trap?"

Ripley pulled away and she almost whimpered. The heat in his gaze conveyed that whatever was between them was far from finished.

"I won't be long, and you'll be safe with Max."

"I know. I can live without you for five minutes, Jorgensen." But it wouldn't be as much fun.

He nodded with a secret smile, then leaned in close to whisper in her ear. "That's why you're stronger than me. Because I couldn't."

She didn't know how to react when he dropped little bombshells like that. And he knew it, judging by the smile in his eyes. He was so confident that they were meant to be, so sure. While he thought she was stronger, it was he who was the brave one.

Ripley ducked behind the cars before shucking his clothes and shifting into a wolf. The great beast trotted out for a quick lick of her hand then he was off into the woods.

Alisia turned to see a beaming Crystal, a smirking Max and Chase, and a frowning Doc.

"Did you two have sex?" Doc demanded. "Did he bite you?"

"Doc!" Heat flamed across Alisia's cheeks. "For Pete's sake."

"Please tell me that he wore a condom."

"No, no. I'm not discussing this. Here. Like this. Like, ever." She flashed an open palm and pulled open the door to

Rover Two. "Get in your car, Megan Marie Kelly."

Chase let loose with a belly laugh. "Oooh, she called you by your full name. You're in trouble now, Doc."

"Bite me, Junior. And this is not over," she warned Alisia as she stomped to the car and climbed into the driver's seat.

Alisia took her seat in the back of the second car and buried her face in her hands, taking a deep breath to temper the burn of embarrassment as Max and Crystal joined her at a more leisurely pace.

Crystal turned in her seat. "Sorry to have to do this, but we need this to look good." She held out a set of handcuffs. "Don't worry. Max can release them with a thought."

In the rearview mirror she caught Max's inscrutable gaze over the rim of his glasses. He never confirmed where exactly she stood with the team. So far, he was acting as if it were business as usual with them, but it wouldn't surprise her if he left the cuffs on and marched her right into the sheriff's office behind her father. Could she blame him? Hell no.

Funny how it was only a few hours earlier that she must have looked at Ripley much the same way Max was looking at her now. Which made her all the more aware of how complicated a concept forgiveness was. Was it more difficult to give than to receive? Any yokel could say or show they were sorry and mean it. But it was the person who was trespassed against who was the only one with the right to accept that apology. And even then, they might accept just to drop the subject while the truth festered deep within.

Max wasn't one who allowed things to fester. Simmer, yes. Stew, occasionally. But it never took him long to make up his mind. Sooner rather than later, he'd let her know how he felt about her.

As if Max was the one who could read minds, he used his powers to open the cuffs with a small squeak. "I can have you out in a second."

Their gazes met again in the rearview mirror and held steady for several heartbeats. Alisia let go with a long sigh then held out her wrists and allowed Crystal to cuff her.

"All right, everyone. From here on out we're in game mode," Max ordered.

And just like that, the team snapped into place like the power switch being flipped on an appliance. The silence hummed in her ear and earpiece like a vibrating tuning fork. Crystal tucked her red-brown hair into a black knit cap and settled the black Jackie-O sunglasses on her nose. The stern line of her lips matched her husband's.

Usually Alisia watched this part of the mission on a thirty-two-inch monitor in the cozy confines of the mountain. In person the colors were more vivid, her sense of smell stronger. She swore she could separate the difference in scents between the trees, car exhaust, and Crystal's floral shampoo. Anticipation of the upcoming mission zipped up her spine and sent goose bumps over her skin.

Ripley's voice came over the earpiece. "I've circled the area a few times. There doesn't appear to be anything newly added or changed. We'll be the first ones to arrive."

"Thanks, Therian. Where can we pick you up?'

"I'll be at the turn down the lane."

"10-4."

Max turned off the main road and onto the dirt lane leading to the farmhouse.

Alisia scanned the side of the road and pointed to a

shuddering bush. "There he is."

Leaning across the seat, she opened the passenger door with her cuffed hands. The wolf shot from the foliage and shifted into an eight-hundred-pound Bengal tiger mid-leap. She shrieked as the back seat was filled with furry animal and the back end of the Rover scraped bottom on the uneven gravel road under the extra weight.

Max shouted, "Too big, too big. I can't bottom out with explosives under the car." The tiger melted into a sleek black panther. Just as lethal, but at a slimmer three hundred pounds. "Better."

Max used his powers to shut the door and then they were off as Ripley sniffed at her cuffs, looking up at her with a questioning snarl.

"For appearances. I'm okay."

He chuffed out a hot breath and laid his head on her lap. His black velvet fur was flecked with gold, plush and luxurious. So soft and tempting, she couldn't resist stroking his pelt. Ripley's eyes rolled back in pleasure and he let loose with a deep hum that vibrated through her body down to the bone.

"What are you doing to him?" Max asked in a low suspicious tone.

She jumped as if caught with her hand in the cookie jar. "Nothing."

"What is that sound?" Chase asked from the car behind them.

Laughter rang in Crystal's response. "Alisia's stroking Ripley's ears."

"You know, a German shepherd makes more sense here, plus I don't want to blow all of our tricks yet. And keep it above the collar, please," Max insisted.

Alisia shut her eyes tight and bit her lip to hold back her chuckle. This wasn't the time for comedy, but it was a nice break in the tension. Once Ripley completed his shift, she resumed the rhythmic stroking of his fur. The motion settled the flip-flop in her stomach and probably soothed her more than it did him.

The car rounded the bend and entered a clearing. Sunshine hit her right in the eyes, blinding her until she blinked the spots away and the retreat house appeared. Her fingers gripped Ripley's fur and her body tightened and burned as if her every molecule had been dipped in liquid nitrogen.

The last time she had been to the house was when she was sixteen and on a Bible study trip with her school friends. The weekend had been about reading Scripture and recanting all of her sins. Even those she hadn't made. It hadn't been nicknamed the House of Penance for nothing.

She remembered the house as being much larger, charming in a quaint country-cottage way. Now the house seemed tiny, dilapidated, and sad, like in those old cartoons when the house fell into disrepair and stared out at the viewer with their big, weepy, window-eyes, begging you to tear it down.

Max parked the Rover with its nose pointed down the trail. "Doc, hang back and park near the main road and meet us here. I want a vehicle clear, and out of sight, just in case."

He helped Alisia climb out of the back seat and situated her on his left. Crystal stood to his right, with Chase joining her as he raced in from the trees.

Ripley sat on his haunches by her side. His heat seeped through her jeans but the chills continued to make her shudder until her teeth chattered.

A thud, thud, thud of a V12 and the crunch of tires over pine needles sharpened her focus. In a synchronized move, she and Ripley lifted their heads and looked down the trail.

"I hear a van, multiple vans," she said. "Or something big."

Max looked to Crystal with a frown as he addressed Addison back at base. "Network, does satellite photos pick up anything?"

"I'm zooming in right now, boss. It is a van. And an SUV. Looks like they've got a bunch of people with them, but I can't make out who's inside."

Crystal gasped, her brow puckered above her glasses. "They've brought girls from the church with them. Teenagers." She swayed and turned to Alisia in shock. "They want to make an example out of Gretchen. Show them what happens when you disobey the will of God."

"An example?" Max asked.

"They're going to crucify her."

Alisia choked on sharp breath. "Are you kidding me? You mean figuratively, right?"

Her features pinched tight as she shook her head. "No."

CHAPTER TWENTY-FOUR

AN SUV FOLLOWED by a big blue shuttle van, like the airport transportation vehicles, emerged from down the lane. Behind the windows, several heads bobbed and weaved as the tires rolled over the uneven terrain. Trailing behind was a white station wagon. Strapped to the top was a large, wooden crucifix that ran most of the length of the vehicle.

Holy shit. They really were planning on crucifying her.

There came a time in a person's life when you believed nothing could shock you. You had done and seen it all. Then fate laughed with delightful maliciousness and smacked you upside the head with their well-manicured and bejeweled hand.

She knew her father loved the Old Testament, but this was...he couldn't...possibly...

Numbness washed over her, buckling her knees. To see his hatred for her run so deep was too much to comprehend.

Ripley butted her thigh with his head, keeping her upright while Chase rolled his shoulders and shook each leg, limbering up for the upcoming conflict.

"Don't worry, Alisia," Chase said. "There's no way you'll be crucified. We stop it from happening, right, Prism? Prism?"

When Crystal didn't respond, everyone turned to her

with a sharp, "Prism."

She pressed her fingers to her temple. "I don't know."

"What do you mean, you don't know?" Alisia asked with a high-pitched wail.

"This is why I can't talk about the future. All of you are making plans, and they have consequences, and the future keeps shifting. Stop plotting. I can't focus."

"What are we supposed to do?" Chase asked.

Max cracked the knuckles in his fingers. "We stick to the plan, and if things go awry, we go to plan B."

"What's that?"

"We improvise."

A collective groan rose. Improvise? He might as well have said, *Let the royal rumpus begin.*

Panic bubbled from her belly up her throat and straight into her brain, leaving her dizzy. She blinked hard and forced her mind to concentrate on the basics like breathing and not pissing her pants.

A face in one of the van windows was another kick to her heart. "That's my sister. In the front seat."

"Do you recognize anyone else?" Max asked.

"A few. They were in my sister's class. God, they all seem so young. They're probably the next set of girls my father's selling as prospective brides."

Deacon Winston was the first out of the van. Ripley snarled and moved forward, only to be hauled back by an invisible leash.

"Therian," Max warned. "Don't be stupid. With those girls present we have hostages or witnesses. I know it's hard, man, but stay steady."

The German shepherd fought against the hold then slumped against her leg. Alisia wanted to stroke his head, but knew the show of affection would blow the illusion that she was a trapped fugitive, no matter how desperate she needed that physical contact as she laid eyes on her father for the first time in seven years.

It struck her odd that looking at Creed Lowell invoked the same feeling she had when she had been back at her childhood home—dead inside with a touch of nostalgia. He appeared to be as charming as she remembered, but now not so grand. He had always been a trim man, but now his thinness struck her as more sickly than healthy. On television his hair looked like a thick blond helmet, but up close it appeared fine and shot through with white streaks, and his complexion was pale and less than robust without stage makeup and flattering lighting.

In his hard, blue eyes, she searched for something, anything that gave away his thoughts. What did he see when he looked at her? The girl in the photo from her yearbook, or the inconvenience to his plans whom he planned on crucifying? Yep. Still hard to recover from that one.

"Gretchen," he sighed and shook his head in wonder. "You look like your mother."

The comment was a stinging slap to the face and loosened her tongue. There was the fire of hatred she expected. "Don't you speak of her. You're not worthy to talk about my mother."

Max laid a steady hand on her arm. "What's with the field trip, Reverend?"

The reverend glanced over his shoulder at his entourage. Along with Winston and Ryan, four other deacons stood surrounding the van carrying the young women. "These are Gretchen's equals. They have come to welcome her back into the fold and remind her how a proper lady behaves."

"And that cross?"

He didn't miss a beat to answer, "It's a new part of the landscaping, to remember our Lord."

Max scratched his nose. "Now, Reverend, you remember that Prism can see the future? She foresees you making a mockery of the cross by harming this young lady and trying to scare those girls into submission."

Ice coated Lowell's glare. "Thank you, Maestro, for bringing my daughter home. Your efforts are very much appreciated. We never came to an agreement on payment, but I brought a hundred thousand dollars with me. Cash. I hope that is acceptable."

"A hundred grand?" Alisia smirked. "Is that all I'm worth to you? No wonder it took you so long to find me."

"You have no idea how much I've spent in time and resources looking for you."

"Oh, I know. Those investigators you hired were well worth the money. I even met one. Paid me fifty dollars for sex. A business expense he charged you for, I hope. He even had the file folder with my picture on the seat next to him while he looked me right in the eye as he fucked me in his car. Do you know what I did with that money?"

He flinched, his mouth pursing as if he threw had thrown up a little. "Snort it up your nose?"

"It paid for a night in a shitty motel room so I had a safe place to stay away from monsters like you."

"You're the monster," a high-pitched female voice called out.

Mary Beth pushed her way through the wall of black suits. A cream knit sweater hung down to her knees, covering the rose-colored dress that matched the angry flush on her cheeks. Wisps of blonde hair escaped the thick braid that draped down her back.

The fury and accusation in her eyes cut Alisia to the quick. "Mary Beth, you don't know the truth."

"You killed my mother."

"It was an accident. I was trying to defend myself. She tried to drug me after she told me she killed my mother," she shouted.

Mary Beth stepped back in shock as Lowell roared, "Liar."

"Jillian told me herself. She poisoned my mother so that it looked like she had cancer."

"So you killed her for it?" Mary Beth cried.

"No. I promise, Mary Beth. I didn't mean to kill her. Our father has been lying to you for years. Years. You're in danger."

"Stop lying, you Jezebel." Lowell took a step forward.

Ripley tensed to lunge, but Max stepped in the middle with his hand held up. "This family reunion is touching, but we're getting off track. Reverend Lowell, you seem to have forgotten just who we are and what we're capable of. We never discussed price because we're not your hired mercenaries. Ms. Lowell's hands aren't the only ones that are dirty. You and your men have committed a long list of crimes."

"*My* crimes?" Lowell laughed with a touch of madness. "You, sir, by breathing are committing a crime. A crime against nature and a crime against God. Satan has marked you, desperate in his bid to win the war over mankind, and as a servant of God, I have been charged to send you back to your master in hell."

The slide of metal against leather brought her attention

to Winston and the other deacons, who all drew pistols on them. From inside the van the girls shrieked and covered their heads.

Max grunted as if unimpressed. "I'm sure these theatrics are very impressive on TV, but I'm on the side of right, no matter what side you think that is." He waved his hand and Winston's gun was ripped from his hand into Max's gloved one.

The reverend backed away toward the farmhouse with hurried steps. "A display of satanic powers. Kill them. Kill them all."

The words barely left his lips before Prism shouted, "Down! Down!"

Ripley's fangs snapped at Alisia's jacket, tugging on the ends and pulling her to safety around the side of the house as the deacons opened fire. Bullets, deflected by Max's power, ricocheted off the ground in bursts of dirt. The team scattered in all directions as the girls screamed and spilled out of the van like a container of beads hitting a tile floor.

"Intrepid," Max called out.

"I'm on it." Chase was a black blur as he shot toward the gunmen, disabling one after the other. Those who managed to land a punch quickly found themselves facedown in the dirt.

"Is anyone hit?" Doc called from her position in the Rover.

Negatives came back to her question.

"Prism, Doc, go after the girls," Max directed as the wail of approaching law enforcement drew closer. "We don't want anyone lost or injured."

"Maestro. Cuffs," Alisia shouted as he ran into the melee. "Cuffs."

But he was off, racing to meet with the police, her cries lost in the screech of sirens.

A woman's scream ripped through the air. Alisia peeked from her hiding spot to see Winston holding Mary Beth in front of him as a shield. A wicked-looking switchblade hovered at her throat.

"No," Alisia gasped, then pushed at Ripley's side with her still-cuffed hands. "Save her. Please."

He pressed his muzzle to her middle, which she took to mean for her to stay put.

"I'll be fine, just go."

His whiskered cheek brushed her face then he was gone, streaking the long way around the house to creep up on Winston's backside. Near him men rolled in the mud, their moans of pain echoed against the trees, proof of Chase's efficiency.

Going toe-to-toe with a bad guy was nothing new to Alisia, but Mary Beth had no concept of true danger or evil. The terror and confusion her sister had to be feeling made Alisia's heart crawl up her sternum to lodge in her throat.

Mary Beth stood in her fiancé's grip, pale as hospital linen and trembling like a twig during a windstorm. A fine trickle of blood ran from where the tip of the blade pressed into her skin in a deep-crimson trail down her neck. Behind them a dark shadow waited low in the bushes. Ripley was ready to strike.

"Back away now," Winston shouted, spittle flying from his lips. "I will kill her."

A half-dozen officers raised their weapons, ready to open fire.

"I have a shot, sir," said one of the officers.

"No," Max replied. "You could hit the girl. Let me try."

Max waved his hand to telekinetically remove the knife, but Winston held tight. His arm shook as his white-knuckled grip was moved ever so slowly away from Mary Beth's neck, but his other arm tightened across her torso to keep her trapped.

The knife quivered mere inches away from Mary Beth's flesh when Ripley struck from behind, leaping onto Winston's back as Chase raced in to pull her to safety.

Winston's sharp cry was cut short as the dog wrapped his jaws around the deacon's throat, holding tight as the man thrashed on the ground. His face slackened as he slowly lost consciousness in a pool of dirt and blood.

Alisia pressed the back of her hand against her mouth, holding back a command to make Ripley kill. They had no right to be executioner. The police were there. Sam's murderer was going to be brought to justice in court. That was going to have to be satisfaction enough.

Her celebration was cut short as she was pulled to her feet by her hair. Tears of pain filled her eyes, momentarily obscuring her vision, but she recognized her father's cologne. The cloying scent churned her stomach, making her want to retch.

He pulled her deeper into the shadows behind the house, shaking her head by the hair as he spat, "You filthy whore. You've confirmed your place in hell by conspiring with those heathens."

"You'll be right beside me, old man," she panted, wincing as he gripped her hair tighter.

He turned her to face him, slapping her across the cheek with the back of his hand as he did. She stumbled back, pain and rage making it impossible to see clearly.

Lowell's lack of decorum broke the glass plate that

separated the civility of bringing him to justice and the deep rolling hunger for his annihilation. Like a cork exploding under the pressure, a battle cry burst from her lips to echo through the trees as she charged at the preacher. Her momentum drove them to the hard dirt where they rolled head over tail across the dry grass in a jumble of clawing fingers and kicking legs.

The clouds and sky swirled in a nauseating blue and white pattern as she landed hard on her back. Her lungs struggled under Lowell's weight and her cuffed hands were pinned to her abdomen. The metal cut into her wrists, drawing blood.

Lowell struggled to his knees, trapping her beneath him. "May God grant you the mercy you don't deserve," he bellowed, wrapping both hands around her neck and squeezing. His eyes were glassy, maniacal, as if the act of killing her was a great high.

It was *not* going to end his way, her mind screamed, combating the fear that choked her more than the hands at her throat. She bucked and kicked, fighting with everything she possessed. Blackness crept into the edges of her vision, nevertheless she continued to fight.

Ripley. Ripley.

Was it only a thought, or had she been able to cry out to the man she loved one final time?

Suddenly the crushing pressure was gone. Cool air burned her windpipe at the first big gulp of breath. *Get up. Get up*, her mind shouted, but the signal took a while to reach her shaking arms. A thick cloud of dust billowed near her side.

Peering in to the haze, she gasped and tried to scramble backward away from the snarling beast batting her father around like a chew toy. It had the body of a man, only covered all over in honeyed fur. Its head was shaped like a big cat, with its pointed ears lying flat to its head and long fangs protruding from its mouth like a sabre tooth tiger's.

When the dust settled, the beast had his powerful jaws locked around Lowell's throat. The reverend's arms and legs twitched not in defense like Winston's had earlier, but in the final throes of death.

"No," she pushed past bruised vocal chords. "Therian, no."

At that moment nothing would have made her happier than seeing Lowell torn to bloody bits, but that moment would pass. Lowell was so quick to judge others, it was his turn to be judged.

"Ripley," she pleaded when his blazing eyes narrowed in her direction and her father's blood trickled from around his mouth.

Was this what Ripley was talking about earlier? How the line between beast and man was blurring? Was the line now obliterated?

Crystal appeared at her side and latched onto her arm to help her stand. "Maestro. Her cuffs. Her cuffs."

Ripley dropped Lowell like a ragdoll. The snap of bones shifting sent chills down her spine as he morphed into the shape of an oversized panther. The sharp blades of his shoulders moved up and down before he lowered his head and charged, barreling into Crystal and knocking her to the ground.

"What the fuck are you doing?" Max roared at the cat, racing to his wife.

The great monster was lifted, suspended in the air. He jerked and quaked while his jaws snapped, struggling against the invisible bonds.

"His mate is in danger," Doc answered, kneeling near Lowell and covering his torn throat with her bare hands. "Release Gretchen's hands and step away. Once he sees that she's safe, he'll calm down."

"No fuckin' way," Max gritted from between clenched teeth.

"Maestro, I can only deal with one trauma at a time. Do it! And you need to lie still," she ordered Lowell, who batted wildly at her hands. "I know, I'm Satan, but I will save your life."

Max risked a quick glance at Crystal. "Sweetheart, are you okay?"

"I'm fine."

"Don't hold back on me." He tried to maintain his focus on controlling the animal. "Are you all right?"

"Yes. A little shaken, but I'm good."

He nodded. "Get in the car."

"I want to help."

"Get. In. The. Car." The snap in his voice brokered no argument.

The three women shared a look. Max's allegiance to the team as a whole was wearing thin and everyone knew his wife would win. As long as Crystal was out in the open, Ripley's fate was in her hands. If she continued to push, Max would end Ripley's life.

Crystal ducked her head and stomped to the car. Once she was secured behind metal and glass, Max released the cuffs binding Alisia's hands.

"Alisia," he said. "Stand about twenty yards down there. Toward the trees. And be ready."

"Ready for what?"

"Intrepid, be ready to intercept, if needed."

Chase nodded and braced his legs to run.

"Needed for what?" she shouted as best she could.

Max was going to, what, let Ripley go? And then what? Fear tightened her chest and made her step back, once, then again.

"On my mark," Max said. "Alisia, you might want to start running."

Holy shit. That was his plan? Use her as bait and let the hissing, snarling man-beast run wild?

"Are you serious?" she croaked.

"Three…two…one."

The panther hit the ground and charged after her, leaping in the air. Black fur gave way to smooth golden muscle as Ripley scooped her up in his arms and ran, never breaking stride. Her stomach bounced on his shoulders, knocking her breath away. There was nothing to hold onto except the slick, rippling muscles of his backside. She had to rely on his claws digging into her hips to keep her from falling.

"Ripley," she choked out. "Put me down."

"Safe." His voice was so low, it vibrated against her belly. "Safe first."

"Ripley. I mean it. Put me down." She dug her fingernails into his thighs.

The world spun as he dropped her to her feet and she looked up at his face. The pupils of his eyes were dark slashes in the bright blue of his irises. Fangs protruded over his lip and the skin was stretched tight over his cheekbones. Blood streaked his chin and chest in red splashes. He lightly scratched her with his claws as he ran his hands over her arms and down her side.

He leaned close and inhaled. "Where are you hurt?"

"Ripley, what's going on?"

"Mate. Danger," he rasped. He blinked his eyes hard and shook his head as if to clear it. "Mate. Mine."

He pushed her back against a tree and reached for the buttons of her jeans. He opened his mouth wide against the base of her throat, the sharp teeth grazing her neck. She tensed, preparing to shove him away, when he jerked back with a sharp yowl.

Several yards away stood Chase with a rifle in his hands. Ripley turned with a roar that made her flesh crawl. Stuck in his back was a red flumed dart. Before her eyes Ripley grew another two inches in height as if he were hulking out. Every muscle seemed to pulse independently of each other, threatening to burst through the skin.

Another bellow reverberated through the forest, rattling the leaves on the trees. The electricity of his rage made the hair on her arms stand on end. Under her feet, the ground shook as he barreled over the terrain at this new foe. Only Chase's lightning-fast reflexes kept him out of Ripley's wicked sharp grasp as the two dodged and weaved around fallen trees and rock.

"Criminy, man. Go down already," Chase panted as he ducked another meaty swing.

He raced in circles around Ripley, churning up the ferns that grew at their feet. The fronds twisted around Ripley's legs like a rope, bringing him to the ground with a painful sounding thud. He struggled to sit up, his arms trembled, and a weak howl fell from his lips. His menacing gaze promised retribution before his eyes rolled back and he sank into the cushion of the forest vegetation. The defeat in his wail as he cried out her name broke her heart.

"Ripley," she gasped and ran to him, falling to her knees at his side.

He lay so still and pale. And cold. He was so damn cold to the touch, he could have been made from stone. His face relaxed as he passed out, regaining his normal, human features.

"What did you shoot him with?" she asked.

"Ketamine. Seems to be the drug of choice around here. Son of a bitch." Chase shook his head and looked at Ripley in amazement. "Doc said a dose that high can drop an elephant in five seconds. Guess it's different with a horny shape-shifter. Here, take this, darling." He handed her the dart gun then scooped up the two-hundred-and-fifty-pound man as if he were a baby. "Let's get your boy home."

CHAPTER TWENTY-FIVE

A LISIA PULLED THE zipper on her suitcase closed. The soft whirl of the teeth catching sounded so final in her ears.

The last time she had packed in preparation of leaving the mountain had been rushed and frantic. Then there had been no doubt in her mind that she was never coming back. Now she was packing at her leisure and she intended to be gone for only a short hiatus, though the parting didn't feel any less traumatic.

Roadkill probably felt more alive than she did at that moment. For the last forty-eight hours she had been sucked through a cyclone of interviews, interrogations, and examinations. Until the various law enforcement agencies determined which division had, or wanted, jurisdiction over the case, they all wanted to question her. Telling her story over and over again to strangers had been horrendous enough, but it was the hour spent with Doc in the exam room that was truly the stuff of nightmares.

Doc Kelly's examination had gone far beyond checking her out for bruises and dehydration. With each pass of Doc's pale hands over Alisia's body, the crease between her brows had deepened. Her friend had been frustratingly obtuse and kept reassuring her that there was nothing wrong. The first cold lick of trouble sent her senses into overdrive when Doc pulled out the needles and speculum.

"Uh, Doc. What are those for?" A lock of hair and a vial of blood was one thing, but the swabs of her most intimate areas? Oh no.

"You've spent a lot of time with Ripley, and I need to know why he lost control the way he did. It may be hormonal in nature."

"Then why are you checking *my* hormones? Does this have anything to do with him calling me his mate?"

"I don't know."

Oh, but she did. Alisia didn't need mind reading powers to know that. "What exactly does it mean when Ripley says I'm his mate?"

"Ripley can explain animal nature better than I."

"Megan—"

"I can't, Alisia," she bit out, voice quivering. She glanced away with frustration and worry in her eyes. "I can't because I don't know. I have a theory that you and he are somehow connected, but that's all it is, a theory. This is animal behavior and that's not my specialty. All I can do is gather evidence. Test everything, and hopefully Ripley and I can figure this out together."

Unfortunately, Ripley was still unconscious from the ketamine and unable to do jack squat.

Intuition told her that being his mate was much more complex than being bestowed with the title of girlfriend or lover, and the searing curiosity was eating her up inside. She wanted answers, but there was too much going on in her world for her to wait for sleeping beauty to rouse his mangy hide. Her sister needed her, and that had to take priority.

She tossed her hairbrush into her duffle bag, then froze. Goose bumps dotted her skin and a ripple of awareness rolled down her spine.

"You're awake," she said without turning around.

"Barely," came the rough reply.

A blistering tirade rushed to the tip of her tongue, but those word were all forgotten when she turned around, sucking in a gasp.

Dear Lord, he looked like shit. His blond hair fell in twisted clumps to his shoulders, appearing as drab as the gray cotton track suit hanging loosely on his muscular frame. The whites of his eyes were bloodshot and the rough stubble on his cheeks filled in the hollows.

"How's your father?" he rasped.

"Alive." She tucked her hands in her back pockets to restrain the urge to touch him. "He'll be in the hospital for a few more days. He lost a lot of blood and his vocal chords were ruined. His voice will never be the same again."

Part of her wondered if Doc had purposely left Reverend Lowell permanently damaged to curb him from spreading his prejudice. Not that Alisia would fault her for the action, but Doc had brought Crystal back from the dead. Surely her powers extended to repairing damaged vocal chords.

"What are you doing?" he asked.

She raised her brows in surprise and returned to her bags. "Packing, obviously. My sister needs me. The Daniels twins offered to help Chase and Crystal at the compound, but there's still a lot to do. Those people will need leadership and reassurance."

"Why didn't you wake me? Give me a minute to grab a few things and I'll go with you."

"No."

Now it was his blond brow that rose in surprise. "No?"

"No. You seem to have issues of your own going on."

"Nothing is more important than you."

"Really?" She turned and planted her hands on her hips. "Then explain to me about what happened with my father. More specifically, what happened afterward."

He winced and looked away. "I really can't remember."

"Is that normal? Blacking out about your actions while in animal form? Because that hadn't been the case before. You were out of control. You charged Crystal."

He swallowed hard and looked away. "I'm sorry about that. I didn't mean for any of that to happen. My mate was in danger. Your safety was paramount."

"You keep saying that. 'Your mate.' What does that mean?"

He drew in a deep breath and crossed his arms over his chest, still not meeting her gaze. "It means that my animal recognizes you as his."

This cryptic shit made her want to pull her hair out. "Which means *what*?"

He closed his eyes on another hard swallow. His voice rasped as he replied, "There are some species that mate for life. Like wolves, or penguins, or geese."

Geese? "Are you seriously comparing your beast to a goose?"

He chuffed, his lip curling over his teeth. "It was only an example. The animal part of me recognizes you as his mate. Your touch, your voice, your scent calms him."

"You weren't calm earlier."

"That's because you haven't been fully claimed. The animal won't be happy until you're his."

The animal. *His.* Always a reference to the animal being a separate entity that was not a part of Ripley, the human.

A heavy weight gathered in her stomach as she waited

for him to say anything about how *he* felt, not his beast. Was talking in the third person Ripley's way of not accepting responsibility for his actions? What about his feelings about her? Did the man care anything for her, or had he been driven this entire time by the wishes of the animal?

"How does he claim his mate? What happens after that?" A tremble shook her as she asked.

Ripley's lips pinched tight and his pallor turned green under the stubble. "He marks you."

"How?" When he looked away, she snatched the closest item at hand, a candleholder, and threw it at the wall to the left of his head. The crash of glass covered her cry, "Mother-fucker. Stop being such an asshole and tell me the truth already."

"I'm trying," he shouted back. "This isn't easy for me." He stepped into the doorway and braced a hand on either side. To trap her in or make his escape, she wasn't sure. "I mark you, but it takes more than a cat rubbing its whiskers over its property. I have to mix our DNA. Through saliva and semen."

"With sex, you mean."

"Yes. Mostly. Sex and biting."

"We've had sex and you've bitten me." Her pulse raced as her mind recalled the last few days. Her entire world had changed, but did she feel any different?

"I haven't broken skin, and I wore a condom."

"What will happen if you break the skin?"

"Your DNA would combine with mine, reassuring my animal that you are his."

"And that helps you control your shifts?"

"…Yeah."

That pause did little to comfort her. "And…"

Another deep breath. "You'll be my anchor. Solely mine. With you carrying my DNA, it will provide balance between my animal and human sides, because no other male will be attracted to you."

Wait. What?

"No animal or no human man?" she asked.

"Every male mammal will recognize that you belong to me. With men, my dominance over you prevents them from feeling any sexual attraction toward you. At least in theory. We still need to run more tests."

"That's insane. It's not even possible. How could you say such a thing?"

"Doc ran tests when I started showing symptoms of turning feral. She cross-referenced blood, hormone, and pheromone samples between you and me and other species. Human and non."

"Well, she can run them again. It doesn't make sense that because we mix—" she waved her hands—"stuff, that we repel the opposite sex. It's not biologically possible."

His color went from green to stark white and her stomach sank further with the bobbing of his Adam's apple.

"Just say it," she growled.

"You repel the opposite sex. Not me. Once you're claimed, my hormone levels return to normal."

Unbelievable. Someone must have dropped her in a pool of unfucking believable without a life jacket because she was drowning.

"Fantastic. How perfectly male," she spat. "I become a sexual pariah and you become a chick magnet because you proved you have a dick."

What type of fucked-up twist of nature was this? And the real kicker was she didn't know what ripped her heart out more, the biology or that he had known all along. He never wanted her because he had any deep feelings for her. His animal was running amok and he needed her to keep him on a leash.

God, and she almost gave him everything. When would she learn to never trust her heart?

She jerked the handles on her suitcases so hard, her shoulders popped in their sockets. "Move out of my way."

"No." He planted both feet wide apart in front of the door. "We're not finished."

A hysterical laugh bubbled up. "Oh, we are so finished. We never even got started. You saw to that when you lied to me."

"I didn't lie. I didn't know about the possibility of a link until the morning at my parents'."

"You should have told me then."

"I know. I'm sorry. I didn't know how, especially since more testing needs to be done. And I didn't want you to get mad. Like you are now."

"Mad?" Her cheeks felt inflamed and tears burned her eyes. "I'm so beyond mad. Did you think I would be ecstatic to hear that you only wanted me to be your bitch so you can gain enough control to go bag more babes? Fuck that, fuck you, and get out of my way."

"What?" His jaw dropped. "No. That's not it at all."

"Get out of my way."

"Let me explain better."

Her vision tunneled into a tiny speck, as her mind desperately gathered a protective shell around her heart. Her voice dipped to a guttural level. "I am ten seconds away from ripping your head off and shoving it up your ass. And even then I don't think it would make me feel better. Move."

"Alisia, sweetheart."

"Move!"

"Ready, Alisia?"

Behind Ripley's trembling shoulder Evan Daniels appeared. As a telepath, he and his twin brother promised they would never read anyone on the team's mind unless asked, but by the way her soul was screaming for help, he probably didn't have to work hard to read hers.

Max joined Evan in the hall, and a band of resolve stiffened her spine. Having others witness her humiliation was less than preferable, but she'd endure anything if it got her out of that room.

"I'm more than ready."

Evan held out his hand. "Allow me to help with your bags." The look he leveled at Ripley was both firm and impenetrable. Whatever might have transpired did the job, for Ripley moved enough to allow her to slide out the door.

The last time she left, it was without another glance at what might have been. This time it was much the same. Only now she left her heart behind for good.

✧   ✧   ✧

FANGS BURST THROUGH Ripley's gums as another man reached for his woman.

Easy, buddy, Evan's voice echoed in his mind. *I understand your need, but I'm going to do what the lady wishes. Give her time.*

Blood dripped from his palms where his claws dug into the flesh and his jaws ached, but he fought to do right by his mate.

As she disappeared from sight and her scent began to fade, his animal howled. She might be leaving the mountain, but he refused to leave her on her own. He could still watch over her from a distance.

"Ripley." Max followed hot on his heels as he raced back to his room. "We need to talk. Ripley."

What would be faster, shifting and running after them or driving his truck? Where the hell was his truck?

"Ripley. Goddammit. I'm talking to you."

He tossed the backpack he picked up back into the corner. If he ran, he wouldn't need to waste time packing.

A tight band gripped him around the chest and lifted him in the air. Rough edges of rock bit into his back as Max used his powers to pin him to the wall.

"Son of a bitch," he snarled. "What the fuck, Max?"

"Why didn't you tell me?" Max demanded.

Could Max narrow that down a thousand?

"Tell you what?" Ripley bit out, struggling against the bounds.

"You turned feral. You can't control your shifts."

"I'm not fully feral. I'm handling it."

"Handling it?" His dark brows rose to his hairline. "That's what you call 'handling it'? You deviated from the mission, you tried to kill our suspects, and you attacked *my wife*, endangering our child."

All the fight drained out of Ripley. "Are they all right?"

"So kind of you to ask," he sneered. "They're fine."

"I'm sorry, Max. I never meant for anyone to get hurt."

"Good intentions mean shit when you know you're a danger."

Ripley flinched as the verbal barb nicked him to the quick. "I'm working on it."

"Good. Until you do, you're off the team." Max released him, allowing Ripley to crash to the floor.

"What?" He must have landed on his head. He did not hear that correctly.

"Until you fix whatever this is." He gestured at Ripley. "And make things right, you're no longer part of the team. I want you off the mountain. I will not have you jeopardizing my family."

Ripley struggled to stand on legs that were as supportive as taffy. Off the team? This was his family. His friends. The Evolutioneers gave him a purpose, and now he was being tossed out on his own? Like a freak that fit in nowhere?

"Max, I'm sorry about Crystal. But this is only temporary. Once Alisia becomes my mate it will get better."

"From what I just saw, she'd rather poke her eyes out than be with you right now."

"I will not take her choice from her," he roared. "I want her to *choose* me. Not be forced to choose me. Doc can help me manage until then."

"Yes, Doc." Max rocked back on his heels as he crossed his arms. "She's in her own bit of trouble for her part in your deception."

"What have you done to her?"

"I've reminded her who is in charge, and when it's time to stop being loyal and start being smart. You have fifteen minutes to get what you need and go. I hope things work out for you and Alisia, but I won't risk my family."

He turned on his heel and strode out of the room. The heavy boots on his feet clipped in a short, agitated rhythm down the stone hall.

Ripley sucked in a breath and it lodged in his lungs. For the first time in his life, he was truly on his own.

CHAPTER TWENTY-SIX

"THOSE LOOK GREAT," Alisia reassured her sister, who stood looking into the full-length mirror with a frown.

Mary Beth's world had caved in on her when presented with the full treachery of her father's actions. After a few days of fluctuating between tears and long moments of staring off into nothingness, she began to accept Alisia's presence back in her life. It also helped that Alisia was transparent with every decision and discussion that was going on with the church and her sister's options. The young girl was shy, uncertain, but she was smart, too. Being blind to her surroundings had been what opened her up for heartache with her father. Alisia knew from experience, Mary Beth wasn't going to allow that to happen again. But she was still a young girl with young girl insecurities.

"I don't know." Mary Beth's grimace deepened as she ran her hand over the dark denim covering her backside. "They feel tight."

Alisia smiled and leaned against the opening to her sister's room. "That's because they fit. You're used to wearing clothes that are two sizes too big. Trust me, you look fantastic. I wish my butt looked as cute as yours."

Mary Beth gasped and flushed bright pink. "I—why would I want my rear to look cute?"

"I don't know. But it beats the alternative."

"Which is what?"

"Looking like a frog standing up."

Mary Beth snorted and rubbed the material on her hips.

"Do you—do you think I'll fit in at my new school?" Fear and unease darkened her green eyes. "Or am I going to be the weird religious girl?"

Alisia opened her mouth to answer but hesitated. What did she know about teenagers? She never attended public school and only finished high school by attending night classes and taking the GED.

The "nice" thing to do was to say sure, everything was going to be just fine. But she more than anyone knew how cruel of a place the world could be.

"Maybe. Maybe not. I really can't say. The good thing is that it's only for a few months until you graduate. And if anyone gives you shit, you tell me. I'll take it up with the administration. And if it gets really bad, we'll figure something else out. No matter what, you won't be alone."

"Thank you," her sister murmured and gave her a shy smile before turning back to the mirror. This time the young girl's gaze was more considering than before.

Alisia didn't want to admit it, but the thought of Mary Beth jumping into society scared her witless. Having been cocooned in the false security of the church, the girl knew nothing about the real world. Up until recently her life plan had been to finish school then get married to a man three times her age. It made sense that she'd be overwhelmed with suddenly having options.

A horrible thought struck Alisia, souring her stomach. "Mary Beth, were you looking forward to marrying Deacon Winston?"

Mary Beth bit her lip. With each second she stood with

her gaze narrowed in thought, Alisia's gut twisted more. Then Mary Beth sighed. "I did whatever Father wanted. He wanted me to marry Winston, so I was going to marry Winston." Her brow furrowed and her eyes filled with tears. "Deacon Winston was never unkind to me, but I never felt comfortable around him either. He would look at me in a way that didn't feel appropriate, and there was a darkness to him—I don't know what exactly, it just frightened me at times." She lifted her worried gaze. "I'm going to hell because I wish he'd been killed, aren't I?"

"Oh, Mary Beth, no." Alisia raced to pull her sister into a comforting embrace. "You're not going to hell. He was a bad man and I wish he were dead, too. I'm sorry I brought him up. He was your fiancé. I just didn't know how close you were. Or if you were actually in love with him."

"It's all right. You know, I don't think I even know what love is." She glanced up at her through her lashes. "Are you in love with that beast man?"

Alisia's heart stopped for half a second. "Therian. His name is Therian." Even after everything they went through, she was still protective of his and the rest of the team's identities.

"Therian. What does that mean?"

"It's Latin for…beast man," she answered with a quirk of her lips.

"Really?"

Alisia nodded, and then they both dissolved into giggles that turned into laughter that doubled them over until they fell on the bed. It was the first time in forever that either of them found anything funny enough to have a good laugh about. Her cheeks hurt as she worked muscles that hadn't been used in a long time.

Mary Beth swiped at the tears on her face. "Seriously. Do you love him?"

A sigh hitch in her throat. "I…do."

"Then why aren't you with him now?"

"You need me."

Her smile fell. "I'm keeping you from him?"

"No. No." She waved her hand and patted her sister's thigh. "It's complicated."

"He doesn't love you?"

Depended on what one considered a declaration of love. Actions needed to speak more than words. "I don't know. He says he does, but he's kept things from me. Very important things."

"And it hurt you. And because you love him, it hurt you more."

"I—I…" Damn. Perceptive little thing, wasn't she? Alisia pinched the bridge of her nose. "Maybe."

And maybe because he hadn't tried to reach out once since they separated. Stupid, she knew. She asked the man to stay away. To be mad at him for respecting her wishes was just plain catty.

At some point, and some point soon, they were going to have to talk. Lay it out on the line and say how they really felt about not only each other, but how they saw their place in the world. Could they survive as a couple? What did them as a couple even look like? Too much had happened between them to walk away without any closure. And with so much of her life being spent on the run, just once she'd like to have something settled.

"Can't I join a nunnery?" Mary Beth groaned and wilted against the wall. "I don't think I'll ever understand relationships."

"No one understands relationships. That's why they have marriage counselors, talk shows, and online dating services."

"What's an online dating service?"

Alisia blinked, momentarily forgetting that her sister had next to zero experience with internet. "Nothing you need to worry about yet."

The doorbell rang, ending any further questioning about relationships. She should have been happy for the reprieve from the conversation, but the bell was a signal of potential trouble.

Once their father's indiscretions and crimes became public knowledge, the congregation had exploded in fear and betrayal with his daughters being labeled as saviors and the devil's spawn, sometimes in the same breath.

Several state agencies had stepped in, ranging from the DEA to social services. Children were being taken from their parents, under-age wives from their husbands. The compound was in chaos with many parishioners kept at home, suffering from withdrawals now that their drug supply had been cut off and they were unwilling to seek any kind of medical treatment. A few members who had reached the point of desperation had come to Doc to be healed, or were too weak to protest when she laid a healing hand on them.

For the betterment of all, Alisia had decided to move Mary Beth out of the compound and break all ties with the church. With Max's connections and the money she'd been saving, she was able to rent them a cute little house in the city. Once the announcement had been made, the animosity toward the sisters died down, and the girls had been left in relative peace the last few days as they packed up their father's home.

Which begged the question, who was at the door?

The local sheriff's office had deputies on rotation guarding the house against anyone wanting to retaliate or the media, but no one had come to their door for days. And it was doubtful that a foe would come calling and politely ring the bell, but Alisia trusted in nothing.

She crept near the front door to peer through the slit in the curtain out the window, then drew back with a gasp before opening the door.

"Mr. Jorgensen. What a surprise."

Ripley's father stood on the porch with his hands shoved deep into the pockets of his windbreaker and a nervous smile on his lips. "Hello, Alisia. Or is it Gretchen?"

"Alisia is fine." She stepped to the side. "Please come in."

"Thank you."

A thousand questions sprung to her lips, but she squashed them all down. The man appeared as if he hadn't slept in days with deep lines bracketing his mouth and dividing his brow.

"Mr. Jorgensen, is everything all right? Helene's not sick, is she?"

"No, she's well."

"Oh. Good." Yet a heavy weight continued to sit on her chest. Something was definitely wrong. "This may sound like an odd question, but how did you find me?"

"Asked an old police buddy of mine about where you might be. I've been reading about you in the paper and told him how you were a friend of Ripley's."

"Which paper?" she asked with a wince. There had been some outrageous stories written about her lately. She'd been called every name from Jezebel to Mary Magdalene to others on the cruder side. And that was with the details about her background hidden by Addison.

"All of them." He smiled. "I figure that the truth is somewhere in the middle."

Warmth filled his smile, and no prejudice lurked in his blue eyes. Despite his obvious distress, Georg looked on her in kindness. It was that benevolence that reminded her she was being a terrible hostess. "Please, sit down. Pardon the boxes. My sister and I are moving soon."

She led him through the maze of packing material and sheet-covered furniture and gestured for him to take the chair, waiting for him to sit before taking a seat on the couch. "So, what can I do for you?"

"I'm looking for my son."

The way his voice broke told her that his quest wasn't because Ripley might have missed more than a phone call or two. "I don't understand. When did you last hear from him?"

"The day you two left together." He ran a trembling hand over his hair. "Look, Alisia. I know who my son is. That he's the one called Therian." He held up a hand when she opened her mouth to deny it. "I've been reading the stories about the Evolutioneers from the beginning, and I know that Ripley's been keeping secrets. He used to be so open with his mother and me, until he came back from a research trip a few years ago. He was different, changed. He acted like Ripley, talked like Ripley, but a shadow lived in his smile. At first I was worried that he had fallen into something illegal, or that he was gay and for some reason was afraid to tell us." Alisia bit back a guffaw on that, since the man was most definitely not gay, but that was sweet of him to be concerned about his son. "When the first reports of the Evolutioneers came out, I had a hunch, then your story broke and confirmed it for me. My son can turn into an animal."

Alisia squirmed in her seat, suddenly identifying with how Doc must have felt carrying Ripley's secret about the mating. However, since she also had been on the side of having the truth withheld from her, she understood Georg's point of view as well. He deserved an answer of some kind, and she cared for him enough to at least attempt to ease some of his concern.

"Mr. Jorgensen, Ripley's story is not mine to tell. But I can tell you that he loves you, and he doesn't want you or his mother to worry about him or get caught up in whatever his…abilities might bring. As you've seen, the Evolutioneers aren't getting the most welcoming reception right now. Anyone connected with them is in danger." She paused and rubbed the palms of her hands together. "Also, Ripley and I aren't speaking right now. You weren't the only one he was keeping secrets from."

He waved his giant hand in the air. "He wouldn't let a little lover's spat keep you two apart. My boy has been in love with you forever. He told me so."

She drew back in shock. "He told you he loved me? When?"

"Oh, yeah. Just after he moved back to Washington. He told us the best part of his new job was he got to work with the woman he loved. And I know you care for him, too. I can see it in your eyes."

Ripley told his father he loved her. And that was months ago. She'd never known Ripley to be the most restrained of men. He saw what he wanted and went after it, except when it came to her. He asked, yes. Cajoled, yes. But he was always patient with her. The fact that he waited for her for so long floored her.

Mr. Jorgensen scratched the stubble on his cheeks and got to his feet. "I came here hoping he'd be here with you. He's not answering his phone or returning calls. It wasn't until I tried to find him at his home that I realized I had no idea where he lives. If he's not here, where is he?"

Her feelings for Ripley were ever changing and shifted constantly like sand through an hourglass. She didn't think she was ready to talk to him right yet, but she couldn't ignore a man who was worried for his son. "Let me make a phone call. I'll see what I can find out."

His shoulders sagged as he wilted. "Thank you."

Her smile felt as frail as a thin cookie as she nodded and went into the kitchen to use her cell. The line picked up at the first ring and Addison's cheerful voice answered. "Alisia, sweetie, how are you?"

"Good. There's a lot left to do, but we're all good. Listen, Ripley's parents are looking for him and he hasn't been answering his phone. Is he there?"

"Oh."

Alisia's stomach rolled at the long pause that followed.

"I guess you haven't heard," Addison said.

"Heard what?"

She sighed. "Max kicked Ripley off the team and off the mountain."

"He did what?" she screeched then lowered her voice. "When? Why?"

"The same day you left. Max said he couldn't let Ripley stay if he was a danger, especially with Crystal being pregnant. The way Max acts, you'd think she was the first woman ever to have a baby."

"And Ripley just left? Where did he go?"

"We don't know."

"What about his GPS?"

"He took it off. We don't know where he is. Sorry, Alisia."

"Thanks," she mumbled. "Hey. Will you let me know if you hear from him?"

"Will do."

The team meant everything to Ripley. He was at his happiest when he was chasing down the bad guys and helping right terrible wrongs. If Max kicked him off the team, he must be devastated.

"What's wrong?" Georg asked when she returned. "You look upset."

"No one has seen Ripley for weeks."

"Oh, my word." His knees buckled and he fell to the couch.

She rushed to his side and placed a hand on his shoulder. "I'm sure he's fine. Ripley's a survivor. There's been a lot going on lately but, he's fine, Georg. I know it."

And if he wasn't, she'd do everything in her power to make it right. Her entire adult life had been nothing but uncertainty, but when it came to Ripley, he had gone out of his way to be a constant source of strength and security. She would like to be the same for him.

"I'll find him," she said, hoping she sounded confident. "And everything will be fine. I promise."

Lord help us all.

CHAPTER TWENTY-SEVEN

T O THE NAKED eye this plot of land was nothing special, only a million blades of grass and a few dozen wildflowers. Yet every time she walked across this particular meadow, her life changed forever.

Stepping out into the clearing felt as if she was walking into a bazillion-watt spotlight. Despite the heat of the sun, a shiver rolled across her skin as she stepped deeper into the meadow. She reached out with all her senses, her gaze darting, her nose twitching, ears straining, as she glanced repeatedly in all directions to ensure that no human followed. It would be her luck to have one of the parishioners, or a member of the damn press, stumble upon her. Ah, the headlines that would spawn across the news if she were to get caught, but for Ripley, she would risk it.

Alisia's hands were surprisingly steady as she pulled her T-shirt over her head and reached for the clasp of her bra. Next came the skirt that she folded and set off to the side before lying out on the grass like a human sacrifice.

No one might have known Ripley's location, but she had a hunch. If he did indeed love her as his father said, and his animal was desperate for its mate, he wouldn't have left her on her own. Stories in the local paper about unusual cougar and wolf sightings aroused her suspicion. Ripley was close, she felt it. She only had to draw him out.

Sure, she could have walked the hills, calling his name,

but that didn't mean he would show himself. And if he was lost in the shift, as she feared, the scent of his mate in heat might be the only thing to bring him around. It might also be the only thing that saved him. Huh, and saved her too, if she were honest.

She cupped her breasts in each hand and softly massaged each round mound. Grass pricked her back and a rock dug into her butt, heightening the fact that she was in the middle of the woods in broad daylight. Even after all she had experienced, the girl who grew up as the preacher's daughter rebelled at the notion of being so open, adding tension to her movements.

Pushing past the embarrassment, she slipped her hand over her stomach and between her thighs. The folds of her sex were dry and each pass of her fingertips over her clit chafed.

A frustrated sigh left her lips. This would not do. The point was for Ripley to scent her arousal, not her nervousness.

"Relax. Relax. Relax," she murmured and let her imagination wander.

All of their sexual encounters had been in low light or complete darkness. What would it be like to have all that smooth warm skin under her hands when she could see the fine-fine pelt of tawny hair that covered his body? If she licked his chest, would the flat brown nipples feel satiny against her tongue? Would he taste like salt, or woodsy like the forest he ran in?

She settled deeper into the grass as her fingers began to slip along her now-weeping sex as she remembered the fierce, possessive lust that had glowed in his blue eyes the last time he caught her like this. The strength of his arms as he held her in the night. The smile he reserved just for her whenever she walked into the room. His laugh, oh, his laugh. No one made her laugh like Ripley. Even when she tried her hardest not to find him amusing.

A wave of heat rolled over her skin like a brush fire.

He was near. He had to be.

She licked her lips and opened her eyes. Her gaze instantly spotted the dark shadow that moved among the trees. A golden wolf stepped into the sun, but did not remain a wolf for long. The sharp claws remained on the ends of his fingers as the animal changed into a creature caught between man and beast. He was at least a foot taller than normal and he appeared to have lost weight as every muscle looked to be cut from marble. His skin stretched across his cheeks, lips, and his nose was flat like a lion's. Fangs protruded from between his lips and the pupils of his eyes were thin slits.

Alisia swallowed her gasp as she focused on the meaty cock jutting from his body. So thick and heavy, it bowed under the strain.

Her hand paused as she fought back a brief rush of panic. This claiming was not going to be gentle.

His nostrils flared and his cock pulsed with each beat of his heart. "Run," he growled, as smooth as sandpaper.

She parted her legs wider. "Take me."

"Run." Desperation bled into his plea. His fingers clenched and his shoulders trembled. Even on the edge, he was trying to protect her.

His restraint gave her the courage to spread her legs even wider, exposing all of herself to his hungry gaze. "Ripley. Take me."

She refused to back down, staring him in the eye until

he took one halting step closer, then another. His thighs bunched and flexed, ready to pounce, yet he kept his control on a tight leash. He fell to his knees before her, his nails scraping down her legs as his hands cupped her bottom.

"Alisia," he whispered.

She raised her hand and ran her fingertips over his lips. "Take me."

One growl was her only warning before he dove into her open sex. The rasp of his tongue stroked the bundle of nerves as his mouth sucked her clit between his fangs. She clutched at his shoulders, her body bucking under the onslaught of lips and tongue. Her pussy gushed at the thought of the sinfully decadent display they must be making in the field of green. His soft, golden hair on his head curled around the fingers of her left hand as she held him close while her right cupped her breast and pulled on the straining tip.

His eyes blazed like blue flames as he watched her toy with her nipple and a purr rumbled from his chest against her skin. Her moan matched his when he thrust two blunt fingers into her sheath, preparing her for his possession. The pad of his fingers found the spot inside that tipped her over the edge. Bright sunlight collided with the stars behind her eyelids. All thought, rational and non, were obliterated under the powerful hands and mouth dragging her from one orgasm headlong into another. Blistering heat melted her bones, liquefying her center.

The withdrawal of his hands made her reach out for more of the intoxicating pleasure, but Ripley flipped her over, lifting her hips to nudge his cock into her opening.

"No," she cried and kicked him away.

The animal inside might demand her surrender, but she

wanted the man as well.

"Alisia." The guttural admonition made her passage clench with anticipation.

She rolled away from him and slapped at his hands. Each time she evaded his clutching grasp he gnashed his teeth and snarled.

After another unsuccessful attempt at pinning her down, Ripley sat back on his haunches and bellowed a howl. She leapt at him and wrapped her legs around his waist.

"Look at me. Look at me." He was going to have to look her in the eyes if he wanted to claim her. "Take me like a man, Ripley."

With a wriggle of her hips, the bulbous head of his cock split her in two. His eyes rolled back and his groan vibrated down his torso to the cock twitching inside her.

Her head spun as he bore her back to the ground, his hips thrusting, working deeper and deeper. God, it burned in the most delicious way. The air carried the scent of earth, man, and sex, every molecule humming with vibrancy. The salty tang of his skin burst across her tongue as she licked up his neck and nipped his earlobe.

She barely kept from screaming in his ear as he shoved the last inch home. The muscles of his arms flexed as he held his body above her.

"Mine forever." His pupils flashed from slits to circles.

"Only yours, Ripley..." Her whisper turned into a scream of ecstasy as he pulled all the way out and thrust hard. "Oh fuck, that's good."

All she could do was clutch onto the bulging muscles of his back and hang on as he rode her without mercy. His name became a frantic chant as he carried her higher and higher into the bright sky. His fangs lengthened and his cock swelled, locking them into one heaving, sweating creature.

"Alisia, please," he moaned.

"Do it, Ripley." She tilted her head, baring her neck to the one man she would ever give herself to. There was no one else but Ripley. "I need you, too. Only you."

At the first scrape of his teeth, her sheath convulsed, her release so close she feared her heart would give out before she reached oblivion.

"Mine forever."

The heated brush of his words on her skin was a thousand times louder than the sound of his growl. Then she heard nothing at all as he sank his fangs into her flesh and her world shattered into a million glittering, sunlit pieces.

❖   ❖   ❖

HIS WOMAN. HIS.

These past weeks without his mate had been torture. Ripley had found it easier to allow the animal free to terrorize the local wildlife so the man could mourn the loss of his mate. Not only had his beast flourished, it was as if the animal said fuck you to the man. You had your chance and failed, and refused to give up its control.

Now his woman was here, taking her pleasure and drenched in his scent.

Man and animal merged as Alisia's pussy squeezed his cock in the tightest, silkiest grip imaginable. His tongue lapped at her life's blood, merging their souls into one. Lightning struck the base of his skull, igniting a fiery trail of energy down his spine and up his shaft. The knot swelled larger, locking him into place. His roar of release echoed across the meadow as his cum filled her channel, marking with his seed the womb that would one day birth his young.

Every sinew and fiber of his body was locked in a mighty grip of pleasure while Alisia writhed beneath him, helpless as she fell into another screaming orgasm, milking him of every drop of his release.

Her hands slipped off his sweat-slicked shoulders. "Ripley," she moaned, melting with exhaustion.

Even without the knot locking them together, he couldn't separate from her. He collapsed at her side, drawing her quaking body into his embrace. The last thing he remembered before the crashing darkness descended was the glide of her trembling hand sliding over his pounding heart.

Minutes, days, he couldn't say which, passed as he lay unconscious in the meadow. Above him, the sun cut through the brilliant clear sky, burning against his eyelids and creating spots in his vision. His mouth felt as if he had eaten a truckload of cotton balls, and there wasn't a place on his body that didn't ache.

"Alisia?" he called out quietly, then again, a little louder.

It took two attempts to lift his arm and another three to push up to a sitting position. As his fingertips sank into the soft earth, he stared at his hands in surprise. The claws were gone, a few red welts marked the backsides, but his hands were all human. He reached for his nose. Normal. Human normal. His gums were sore, but the fangs were gone. Running his tongue over the flat surface of his teeth over and over again, he praised the work of his orthodontist.

He glanced to one side, then the other. The wind picked up, setting the blades of grass into motion, rippling like giant green waves across an ocean empty of all but him.

Two finches twittered as they flew across the clearing,

the only sign of life he and his animal could sense.

"Alisia?" Where was she?

He hadn't dreamt her, he was positive he hadn't. Her heat had been real. Her submission had been real. Her screams of pleasure still rang in his ears and her scent was on his skin. She had accepted him as her mate. Where was she?

Ripley collapsed back on the ground and rubbed a weary hand over his stubbly cheek. God, he was such an idiot.

She gave him her body. He hadn't won her heart.

Sadness gripped him around the throat before realization set in and the tears turned into laughter. Oh, that little minx.

Alisia was not prone to whimsy. *She* came to *him*. There was nothing on this earth that would force her to seek him out in the lusty, yet vulnerable, manner she had unless she cared. She loved him, she had to, otherwise she wouldn't have jeopardized her life by facing the beast. This was her challenge. She submitted, but she hadn't yielded.

Message received. To win her heart, he was going to have to work for it. Like a true alpha bitch, she played her hand and now it was up to him to prove he was worthy.

But was he worthy?

Oh, wasn't that the first of a long line of questions without definitive answers. Also on the list was were they mated and his two sides now in harmony, or had the afternoon just been a moment of mind-blowing sex?

He closed his eyes and thought of the wolf who had become his lifeline over the past month. The wolf had kept the body alive while the man worried about their future. He had become Ripley's closest friend, and he would forever be grateful for his strength. But remaining in lupine form for eternity was not how he wanted to live out his life. With each day that passed, the ability to shift had become more difficult. If he and Alisia had truly mated, the struggle with his powers should be over. Shouldn't it?

What if claiming Alisia hadn't grounded him? What if this was just a reprieve, and if he shifted again, he wouldn't be able to change back?

Sweat dotted his lip as he contemplated the change. It was a risky move to call upon the wolf now. Dare he try?

You have to know.

A rolling simmer raced through his veins as the transformation from man to animal was swift and sharp, like popping a dislocated shoulder back into place, but not nearly as painful as it had been in the past. He waited for all of a second before calling on the change, and a heartbeat later, he was back in his own skin. He tried again, this time as the panther, then again as a horse, each time the change coming with ease.

"Yes." A satisfied chuckle burst out and grew into a full belly laugh. "Yes, yes, yes."

He got to his feet with a light heart and an earthy moan as his joints popped and creaked. He had a mate to woo, and the first item on his list was a shower followed by a heaping serving of humility.

CHAPTER TWENTY-EIGHT

T HREE DAYS. THREE days and not a single word from Ripley. Lousy bastard.

Alisia broke down the box that carried Mary Beth's new computer as if it had been the cardboard who had pulled the switchblade. Fibrous particles drifted on the air like snowflakes as she ripped the box into planks.

They still had a lot of baggage to work through in order to embark on a "traditional" relationship, and she thought he would seek her out to resolve the tension between them once he had determined the mating had worked. The least he could say was thank you. Wasn't he appreciative at all that she was willing to forgo all other men? Although, forgoing men forever wasn't going to be that much of a hardship. As if anyone could compare after experiencing Ripley's passion. He had ruined her for all men long before he claimed her, but he didn't have to know that. Still the least he could have done was call, text, or sent a carrier pigeon to make sure she was okay.

The soft step of Mary Beth's sneakers on the carpet reached her ears and Alisia reined in her disappointment. Her sister had enough to worry about with the move, new home, and new life. She didn't need to add to it with her man troubles.

Mary Beth popped her head around the corner. "Are you all right?"

"Yeah. Why?"

"It sounded like you were in a brawl with a box and it was winning."

"Funny." She waved her hands in the direction of the dining table with a grand flourish. "Ta-da!"

Mary Beth gulped and bit her lip, eyeing the laptop as if it would strike like a cobra any second. "Great?"

"Do not stress. You'll be a pro at this in no time."

"If you say so." She shrugged and her lower lip jutted out. "I'm tired of unpacking, and hungry. Can we get takeout?"

Again? Ever since Mary Beth discovered the reality of having delicious, hot and ready food delivered to the front door, the girl had taken to memorizing the menu for every restaurant in a five-mile radius.

"Sounds great," Alisia replied, although after all that takeout, she was starting to long for a salad. "What do you feel like?"

"That teriyaki we had the other day was good, or I really like the pee-ho soup."

Pee-ho? "Oh, you mean phó." Alisia laughed when she realized that Mary Beth meant the soup served at the Vietnamese restaurant three blocks over. "Yeah, give me a minute and I'll go get us some."

"May I go get it? Please?" her sister asked with a hesitant hitch in the soft query.

Alisia sucked in breath of trepidation. A teenager running a quick errand should not be a big deal. The little house she rented in the city was in a quiet neighborhood located near a police station and a fire department. There was a group of little old ladies who walked their dogs every evening and parents who coached their kids on their bicycles out in the street. Running out for takeout was an everyday, no-brainer occurrence for these people.

But Mary Beth wasn't a normal eighteen-year-old. She was an innocent woman-child who only recently learned about debit cards and satellite TV. For her, it wasn't looking both ways before crossing a busy street that was the novelty, it was that the street had traffic at all.

It was on the tip of Alisia's tongue to say no and that she would take care of everything, but coddling her sister would be just as damaging as tossing her into the deep end of the pool.

"Sure." Alisia pulled a twenty from her back pocket. "Here, take this. Get me a bánh mì sandwich."

Mary Beth blinked in surprise. "Really?"

"You're only going down the street. You're not planning on getting into trouble, are you?"

"No," she said with a giggle.

"Then go get me some food. I'm tired. You can feed me."

"Thanks, Gretchen, I mean, Alisia." She pocketed the cash. "I'll be back soon."

Alisia stood by the window and watched her sister glide over the cracked sidewalk as her blonde ponytail bounced with each step. It was difficult not to envy someone with youth and possibility in their favor.

Possibility. Huh. What possibilities were left for Alisia?

Ugh. She gagged. "A pity party for one is unacceptable," she said aloud.

Determined not to think of the future and the what-might-have-beens, she walked into her bedroom and set about exchanging the sleeping bag for bed linen. Her room was sparse, with only a bed, nightstand, and dresser taking up the space.

Max told her she still had her position with the team and her room was there for whenever she was ready to return to the mountain. It was work she loved doing, and she longed to get back to it, but Mary Beth needed her. At least for now. Soon they were going to have to decide if her sister was going to try to go to college or get a job, but priority number one was to heal. Then she would tackle the issue of going back to the place where every corner reminded her of Ripley.

Ripley...

The scent of wood and man hit her senses a second before a blast of heat warmed her back. Either Mary Beth forgot to lock the door behind her or a beast had learned how to pick locks.

"I see you've regained a shape with opposable thumbs," she said, proud that her voice came out strong and unaffected.

"I love you."

Her heart skipped a beat as the rest of her froze. Was that the man or animal talking? Somehow, she found the strength to ignore his declaration and resumed tucking the sheet under the mattress, hyper-aware of his every breath.

"Do you remember the day we met?" he asked. The heat between them grew as he stepped closer, still behind her. "I came to see Doc after that alpha wolf I was studying attacked me when he thought I was trying to take over his pack."

Of course she remembered that day. An argument had broken out at the nurse's station over who got to assist in treating the shirtless Adonis. Every nurse had nattered on and on about jumping his bones, yet no one but her had found it disturbing that he had a history of appearing to be in a knife fight at least every other week. When their comments had become more lewd than the fantasies written on a men's room wall, Doc had put an end to the discussion by sending Alisia in because she had been the only one not to participate in the leering.

And this was the memory he wanted her to recall? A time when every woman in the building was publicly contemplating the size of his cock?

Gah. She snapped the sheet in place. How could she have fallen in love with someone so clueless?

He took another step closer. "You walked into that exam room, so beautiful, so strong. And you hated my ass on sight." There was a smile in his voice. "But your hands were gentle. You touched me like you cared. You didn't want to like me, but somehow I managed to work my way through your defenses. And then I smelled your desire. It was the most alluring scent I have ever encountered, and it made me hunger for you more."

She whirled around in outrage. "You know how much I hate it when you talk about smelling me."

She about swallowed her tongue as she gasped and clutched at her somersaulting stomach.

Good God, he was gorgeous.

Gone was the feral beast man she had left in the meadow and in his place was a Greek deity come to life. Lustrous blond locks, streaked with platinum highlights that women shelled out the big bucks for, fell to his shoulders. Beautiful bronze skin glowed with health and vitality, and his sexual magnetism reached out to punch her right in the libido.

The devilish curl of his smile revealed his perfect white teeth. "I can't help it. Your scent intoxicates me. It always has. That meeting with you was the first time since I had gained my powers that I had felt safe, cared for."

The love and adoration in his eyes stole her ability to think, and when he placed his palm over her pounding heart, she forgot to breathe.

"Alisia, I've been saying all the wrong things to you. Instead of constantly telling you that you belong to me, I should have told you that from that first moment, I've been yours. There's no one else for me but you. All that I am, and wish to be, is because of you. Yes, you calm my beast, but it's the man that needs you to be happy." He slid his hand up to cradle the back of her neck, his thumb angled her quivering chin up. "Alisia, please say you'll be mine?"

All the moisture left her mouth and her vision blurred. This amazing man was giving her his heart and asking for hers in return. The idea scared the crap out of her, but instinct screamed to dig in her claws and never let go.

"I love you, too," she whispered, afraid of bursting the moment like a fragile bubble.

His smile squeezed her heart. "I know. It's just good to hear it from your lips."

Her pout lasted for all of two seconds until he pressed a trail of warm kisses over the firm line, coxing her to open. The feather-soft assault left her dizzy. His passion always excited her, but this gentle exchanged floored her. Nothing was as good or as comforting as Ripley's embrace.

"We're really going to do this, aren't we?" she said. "Holy shit. We're really doing this."

A sensation exploded in her chest of light and heat. It felt as if she stepped off a cliff and was falling, hurtling toward the blue depths of the water below. The feeling was so intense, she swore she could feel the wind in her hair and the sun on her face as she plummeted down, down, and promptly burst into tears.

"Ah, sweetheart," Ripley soothed, hugging her tighter. "I'm here. And I'm not going anywhere."

Caught between tears and hysterical laughter, she clung to his shoulders.

After how many months and years of longing, yearning, now for the first time she believed. She believed him when he said he loved her. She believed him when he said they would be together. No more running. No more hiding from her fears and feelings. She believed, and accepting that belief was terrifying.

She buried her face into his neck and a sharp sweet scent hit her in the back of the throat, igniting a coughing fit.

Ripley ran his hand over her back. "Sweetie, are you okay?"

"Why do you smell like marshmallows?" she gasped.

The soothing motion of his hand stopped. "You can smell that?"

"Yes." The horrified tone in his question frightened her. "What does that mean?"

He pulled back to look into her eyes. His grip on her arms tightened. "Emotions have a scent. Usually only animals can detect them."

"Usually?"

"Baby, I'm a prime example of nature scribbling outside the lines."

"Oh." She stared off over his shoulder, contemplating his words. "That explains a lot."

His eyes widened. "What does *that* mean?"

She licked her lips. "After we mated, I noticed a few

things were different. My senses seemed shaper. My hearing and sense of smell."

"Can you shift?" he asked in alarm.

"No," she said with a laugh. "No. Well, I haven't tried, but no. I haven't felt the urge. At all. I'll leave that to you. I'm still me, just tweaked slightly, I guess. So, what does the scent of marshmallows mean?"

He brushed his nose against hers. "That is the scent of love. Soft and sweet."

"Oh, that sounds lovely."

Sin tipped his grin. "Let's try out your sense of taste."

His lips were going to be her downfall. Hot and fiery like a Bloody Mary, his kiss swept the world out from under her feet. She melted into his heat, letting him hold her in his incredibly strong arms. With her heightened senses, his taste was richer, darker, and more addictive than the finest—

"Chocolate." She sighed and ran her tongue up the side of his neck. "You smell like a melted Cadbury bar spiked with cayenne pepper."

He hummed and skimmed his palms over her hips. "Now you know why I've carried a constant hard-on for you over the last few years."

"Can I make it up to you?" She scored her fingernails over his cotton-covered abdomen.

"Hell yeah."

Her back hit the bed a second before he covered her with more of those scorching kisses. Good thing she hadn't gotten far in the bed-making process.

The front door opened and closed with a bang. "Alisia, I'm back."

"Damn," Ripley groaned. "Living with your sister is

gonna cramp my plans on taking you on every surface in the house."

"Planning on sticking around, are you?"

"Just try to get rid of me." He nipped at his mark on her neck, sending a lick of heat through her body.

She shot him a cheeky grin. "Never. I'm gonna keep you on a short leash, right by my side."

"By your side forever? I can handle that."

Also by Anna Alexander

The Evolutioneers Series

Genesis

Instinct

Men of the Sprawling A Ranch Series

The Cowboy Way

The Marlboro Man

To Have Faith

Sweetest Kisses

Eight Seconds to Forever

Heroes of Saturn Series

Hero Revealed

Hero Unleashed

Hero Unmasked

Hero Rising

Cavern Series

A Night at The Cavern

Only at The Cavern

Elite Metal Series

Bound by Steele

Adamantium's Roar

Thallium's Submission

Vibranium's Truth

About Anna Alexander

Award winning author Anna Alexander is the author of the Heroes of Saturn and the Sprawling A Ranch series. With Hugh Jackman's abs and Christopher Reeve's blue eyes as inspiration, she loves spinning tales of superheroes finding love. Anna also loves to give back and has served on the board for the Greater Seattle Romance Writers of America as chapter president and on the committee for the Emerald City Writers Conference.

Sign up to receive news about Anna's latest releases at
http://eepurl.com/Q0tsz

Anna welcomes comments from readers.

Website
annaalexander.net

Facebook
facebook.com/pages/Anna-Alexander/282170065189471

Twitter
twitter.com/AnnaWriter

Newsletter
http://eepurl.com/Q0tsz